Magic
in the
MIRRORSTONE

Magic
in the
MIRRORSTONE

Tales of Fantasy

Edited by Steve Berman

MIRRORSTONE™

MAGIC IN THE MIRRORSTONE
Tales of Fantasy

Introduction and "Blackwater Baby" ©2008 Wizards
"Princess Bufo marinus, Also Known As Amy" ©2008 by Eugie Foster
"Lights, Camera, Action" ©2008 by Cecil Castellucci
Ten Thousand Waves" ©2008 by Ann Zeddies
"Mauve's Quilt" ©2008 by Craig Laurance Gidney
"Have You Ever Seen a Shoggoth?" ©2008 by Cassandra Clare
"The Amulet of Winter" ©2008 by Lawrence M. Schoen
"Veronica Brown" ©2008 by Sean Manseau
"The Jewel of Abandon" ©2008 by Nina Kiriki Hoffman
"School Spirit" ©2008 by Jim C. Hines
"Old Crimes" ©2008 by J. D. Everyhope
"The Fortunate Dream" ©2008 by Gregory Frost
"Out of Her Element" ©2008 by E. Sedia
"Virgin" ©2008 by Holly Black
"Pig, Crane, Fox: Three Hearts Unfolding" ©2008 by Beth Bernobich

Published by Wizards of the Coast, Inc.
Mirrorstone and its logo are trademarks of Wizards of the Coast, Inc., in the U.S.A. and other countries.

Printed in the U.S.A.

Cover photo © Wes Thompson/ Corbis
Book designed by Kate Irwin and Leon Cortez

First Printing

9 8 7 6 5 4 3 2 1

ISBN: 978-0-7869-4732-4
620-21553720-001-EN

Cataloging in Publication information is on file at the Library of Congress

U.S., CANADA,
ASIA, PACIFIC, & LATIN AMERICA
Wizards of the Coast, Inc.
P.O. Box 707
Renton, WA 98057-0707
+1-800-324-6496

EUROPEAN HEADQUARTERS
Hasbro UK Ltd
Caswell Way
Newport, Gwent NP9 0YH
GREAT BRITAIN
Save this address for your records.

Visit our web site at www.mirrorstonebooks.com

For Jay Paparella, Frank Slattery, and
Jeffery Zauber

You have been more than good friends—
together, we have slain dragons.

Contents

INTRODUCTION

FIFTEEN. WHAT WAS I READING AT FIFTEEN? THAT WAS— cough—many years ago, when I was a sophomore in high school. My backpack always held more dog-eared fantasy paperbacks than schoolbooks. I had grown up on a steady diet of the supernatural and wonder: In third grade I was playing Dungeons & Dragons as if it were a religion. In sixth grade I had exhausted the library's kids' section of any book that had even a whiff of the fantastical. In ninth grade, stories of adventure meant so much to me that I had to start writing my own.

The benefit of being a writer? You have an excuse to read as much as you want—it's all the "tax deductible" or "doing research" lie when the truth is you can't resist a good book. (A side benefit is the chance to meet some wonderful people who also happen to be writers, such as the folks who contributed to this anthology.)

The benefit of being a kid? You have an excuse to read as much as you want—it's the "all education broadens the mind and keeps you out trouble" lie. Or maybe that one's the truth. Maybe you'll throw this book into your bag instead of that algebra tome.

Fifteen. Here are fifteen stories of magic. More than a couple have strange, talking amphibians—or enchanted jewelry. None have any amphibians wearing jewelry, thankfully. Maybe in the sequel. Or the movie version. I'm not sure why some of the authors seemed to share such themes. Writing is a magical endeavor that is quite individual, so personal, yet eager to be shared, after all.

Fantasy offers readers the greatest chance to escape and to explore. We might never have as strange an adventure as the ones the kids in these stories do, but through their deeds (and mis-deeds, because sometimes those *are* the most fun) we can step away from the boring moments of life.

I'm delighted to work with Mirrorstone on this project. The real charm is having a publisher devoted to fantasy for children and teens; whether this is the first such book you pick up this year, or the fifteenth, take a moment to stare at the spine, notice the Mirrorstone logo. You'll be seeing a lot more from them.

Read these tales in order. Editors actually have a reason for arranging stories so, and we all know that spells demand exacting details or else terrible things might happen. Read them out of order. After all, magic is limited only by imagination and anything can happen. My one hope is that you will read each and every one of these fifteen and be as enchanted by them as much as I was.

Steve Berman

Princess Bufo marinus, Also Known As Amy

I REALLY THOUGHT MY LIFE COULDN'T GET ANY WORSE. Of course, after freshman year with Troy Parker and his hobby of bashing on underclassmen named Peter (lucky me), I was dead sure there was no way school could become more of a nightmare. Then I became acquainted with sophomore Social Studies with Mr. Ruis, and football in PE with the very same Troy Parker. The universe couldn't be any crueler.

Apparently, the cosmos had decided to prove me wrong. Coming to grips with the brutality of the Infinite Beyond was the least of my concerns as I sprawled beside a storm drain, fishing for my PDA with a stick. I was late for English—Mrs. Hatton's jurisdiction, a woman who made Mr. Ruis seem downright lovable—and the entirety of my life was in that stupid device: class notes, homework, e-mail addresses, and phone numbers, not to mention the English paper that was due today. I hadn't backed any of it up, and yes, it was raining.

I cursed Troy Parker (for the millionth time in my life) for chucking my PDA down the grate. I also fumed at myself for being foolish enough to ask Rachel Hollander to go to the Spring Fling with me. *Rachel Hollander,* for God's sake! What was I thinking? And worst of all, Troy had witnessed the whole thing from stammering come-on to demoralizing brush-off.

I saw a glint in the darkness. The LCD screen? I fumbled the stick around and succeeded in nudging it . . . farther away. On an up note, I was pretty sure it was indeed my PDA. It seemed to be caught on something. If it weren't raining, I might have written off Mrs. Hatton and the paper, gone home, and come back with a flashlight and the grabber Dad used in the yard when he was too lazy to get out the ladder. But if the rain didn't flush my PDA away, the water would fry it—if it hadn't already.

"Damn it!" I thumped my fist on the curb.

"What's the matter?"

It was a female voice, one low and nasal, as if the speaker had a head cold.

"The matter is my life sucks, Troy Parker is an ass, and Rachel Hollander thinks I'm the world's biggest joke. And I can't think of a way to save my PDA from a watery death." I glanced up to see whom I had railed at but couldn't see anyone else around me in the rain.

"On top of that," I muttered, "I'm hearing disembodied voices."

"Well, I can't do anything about Troy and Rachel, but I think I can get your peeday—assuming it's that gray-tile thing you're poking at."

The inevitable had happened. Troy Parker had finally driven me mental.

"My name is Amaranthia, by the way. Do you want me to fetch your tile or not?"

The universe seemed hell-bent on seeing me unhinged, so I decided to embrace my dementia. "Sure, Amar-Amaranthia. Go for it," I said, even though I was pretty iffy about my subconscious's choice of tongue-tangling name.

"If I do, will you be my friend?"

"Fair enough. Every crazy needs an imaginary friend."

"Will you take me with you, protect me from harm, and feed me at your table?"

"Sure." At that point, I was willing to agree to just about anything if it would get me out of the rain. My jeans were clammy and damp, and they were beginning to chafe in an awkward place.

"Friends are *supposed* to know each other's names." Amaranthia sounded impatient. My auditory hallucination had an attitude.

"I'm Peter. Peter Litton."

I heard a splash and scrabbling, like nails on metal. A huge frog, big as a cantaloupe, crawled out of the drain and hopped onto the curb. It was mottled brown and googly-eyed, and it had my PDA in its mouth.

I wondered if it would bite me if I tried to pry open its mouth. Do frogs even have teeth?

"Nice froggy," I babbled. "Good froggy."

To my relief, the frog spat it out.

I grabbed my PDA and powered it on. Amazingly, being tossed into a storm drain, rained on, and mouthed by a giant frog hadn't wrecked it. The clock display told me I still had time to get to the computer lab, print my paper, and deliver it before class ended.

"Actually, I'm a toad." I recognized Amaranthia's voice. "I'm a *Bufo marinus*, also known as a cane toad."

I backed away. Tonight, I promised myself, I would tell my mom I needed to see a doctor. Maybe if I lied and told her I was doing drugs, she'd line me up with a shrink.

"Hey!" the toad cried. "Where are you going? Pick me up."

I bolted.

Behind me, I heard my delusion calling. "Peter! Peter Litton! Come back! You promised!"

As luck would have it, Mr. Ruis was on hall-monitor duty. He looked pretty focused on going through a stack of homework at the lookout desk, but I knew the man had some kind of sonar or sixth sense when it came to nabbing wayward students. I debated between just walking up and taking the detention—with all the questions and hassles that would mean—or waiting for him to leave so I could try sneaking past.

I had steeled myself for a detention, a dressing-down, and a barrage of questions when Mr. Ruis's head jerked to the side and he sprang from his chair. He rushed off, and I had a full second to marvel at my amazing luck.

I hurried past the monitor desk, doing my best to keep my soggy shoes from squeaking as I made my way to my locker.

Everyone was in class, and the deserted hallways gave me the ominous, guilty feeling I always get when I'm somewhere I'm not supposed to be. I had the urge to tiptoe and skulk past doors. To my credit, I didn't tiptoe, but I did try to open my locker as quietly as I could. Still, when I grabbed the USB cable from my backpack, I felt like a thief even though my name was blazoned in block letters on my locker. Then I had trouble shaking the compulsion to walk-don't-run and ended up speed walking to the computer lab instead of tearing off like I wanted to. Guess this place was really getting to me.

The on-duty monitor, who was used to students coming and going whenever, didn't look up when I hurried in. I logged on to an available workstation, hooked my PDA up, and sent my paper to the print queue. As I hovered at the output tray, I debated whether writing longhand would be faster than printing on the school's antique inkjet.

A hand fell on my shoulder as the last page began inching out.

"There you are, Peter Litton."

I cringed. Even before I turned around, I knew whose hand it was. No one could pour that much irritation and disappointment into five words except Mr. Ruis.

"Hello, Mr. Ruis," I said, resigned.

"Glad you decided to come out of the rain and join us." He wiped the hand he'd grabbed me with on his sports coat as if he'd touched something nasty. I know I was waterlogged and maybe a little muddy from fishing in the storm drain, but c'mon. I wasn't diseased. "Get your things, Peter. Let's go."

"Where are we going?" I yanked the last page free. The printer hadn't been done with it, and the paper tore.

"The principal's office."

The three-word death knell. I tried to act cool and collected as I pocketed my PDA and cable so I could pretend I wasn't terrified. It didn't work.

Mr. Ruis marched me down to the office and turned me over to Joann, the school secretary. She escorted me into Principal Greenlee's office. I'd never been sent to the principal before, hadn't exchanged more than an occasional "good morning" with the woman in passing. With her dour expressions, immaculate wool suits, and iron-gray hair tugged into an austere bun, she had *intimidating* down pat.

When Principal Greenlee glowered at me as I came in, I was prepared for it. But I wasn't expecting to see the toad from the storm drain sitting in a clear plastic box on the principal's desk. From the jumble of erasers, chalk, and rulers strewn around, I guessed the box hadn't been empty before it had been pressed into toad-containment duty.

"Mr. Litton," Principal Greenlee said. "Mr. Ruis found this toad in your locker."

That explained my "amazing" luck from earlier.

"Are you unacquainted with the rule that forbids bringing pets to school?"

"See—"

"Are you also unaware that this species of toad is not indigenous to this state, and is considered a danger to the local ecosystem?"

"Huh?"

"And are you furthermore incapable of comprehending that a school locker is an inappropriate and inadequate enclosure for any animal, amphibian or mammal, especially if you leave it *open?*"

Of her rapid-fire list of crimes, I was guilty only of not shutting my locker—not wanting to slam it, the only reliable method to get it to lock. But I didn't see how pointing that out would help.

"I didn't know cane toads were an environmental hazard," I said. Yes, I was stalling.

"Ignorance is never an excuse," she snapped. *"Bufo marinus* breeds prolifically, has a massive appetite, and preys upon native birds and wildlife. Were this specimen a wild animal and not a pet, I would have it destroyed."

Midlecture, it clicked that if I simply denied my association with the toad, Principal Greenlee couldn't nail me for illicit pet smuggling or putting the school's tenuous ecosystem at risk.

The words "I don't have a pet toad" were sitting in my mouth, ready and eager to come out. Then I glanced at the toad. She looked terrified and pitiful—as much as a toad can. Her eyes were wide and her mouth was trembling, like people get when they're about to cry. Then again, toads don't have eyelids, and for all I knew, a mouth tremor was equivalent to a belly laugh in toad-speak.

Still, I couldn't do it. She reminded me of how raw and panicky I felt when Troy worked me over, how I wished someone would help me stand up to him. At least I could be that someone for Amaranthia. Plus, it wasn't her fault I was gearing up for a straitjacket and a padded cell.

"I'm sorry, Principal Greenlee," I said. "I wanted to show Amy to a couple friends who've been asking about her."

"And you thought your locker was a humane place to confine"—Principal Greenlee raised an eyebrow—"Amy?"

Hey, I was already taking one for the toad; I wasn't about to own up to the name *Amaranthia* too.

"You're right. It's inexcusable," I said. "But please believe that normally, Amy's comfort and well-being are my topmost priorities. She's got a really nice terrarium at home with clean water and live plants and . . . and a, uh, sunlamp. But my friends were so excited about seeing her—"

I clamped my lips shut, cutting off my spill of gibberish before I got myself into more trouble. I'm a bad liar.

"It won't happen again," I finished.

"It certainly will not. You are suspended for the remainder of the day." The bell rang, signaling the beginning of lunch.

It also meant my English paper was officially late. "You will take your animal to the science room and transfer it to a suitable container for transport while I call your mother to pick you up."

Glum pictures of Mom stringing me up by my ears danced through my head as I retrieved the toad box from Principal Greenlee's desk. Maybe if I sprang the "I'm hearing voices" card, she'd be lenient. I doubted it.

My stomach gurgled. It *was* lunchtime, after all. I detoured to my (wide-open) locker so I could take some food with me into exile. In hindsight, I should have toughed it out and double-timed it to the science room. The halls were filled with students hanging by their lockers, getting ready to go out, and milling with their friends. A herd of freshmen girls saw me—or rather, saw Amaranthia—and screeched as if I were a boogey monster with the plague, then stampeded away.

Alerted by their noisy exit, everyone rubbernecked to check out the fuss. No doubt by tomorrow, I would be known throughout school as "Toad Boy." I found myself having to press through a mob of sightseers throwing out questions I wasn't in the mood to answer.

"Where'd you get the frog?"

"Dude, what're you feeding that thing? Steroids?"

"Is it yours?"

My humiliation became complete when I saw Rachel Hollander, surrounded by a gaggle of her friends, pointing at me. An eruption of giggles confirmed that I was the official laughingstock of the school.

My face burning, I put my head down and forged ahead.

"Is that your lunch, Petey?"

I knew that voice. Since the first day of freshman year,

hearing it gave me icy sweats and made my stomach clench. I looked up to see Troy Parker leaning against my locker. I had again underestimated the universe's ability to ream me. My humiliation was just beginning.

"Is fresh frog like sushi? You chop it up and slurp it down?"

I decided starvation was an acceptable alternative to confrontation and about-faced. Unfortunately, Troy had anticipated my move. Brett Ludlow, Troy's crony and thug-in-training, flanked me.

"Where you going, Petey?" Troy asked. "Hey, I'm talking to you."

"Leave me alone."

"Or what? You'll beat me up?" Troy shoved me and I staggered back into Brett.

Brett, predictably, shoved me back at Troy.

"Watch it, freak." Troy sidestepped my ricochet, and I staggered off balance. He yanked the box out of my hands and kicked my legs out from under me. I sprawled flat on my face.

By the time I scrambled to my feet, Troy had wrenched off the box's lid and seized Amaranthia. He dangled her by her hind legs as the box clattered to the floor.

"Stop it!" I shouted. "You'll hurt her!" I grabbed for her, but Troy swung her out of reach.

"Her? Your frog's a girl?" he jeered. "That's pretty sick. You couldn't get a date so you put moves on a frog? They've got places for sickos like you."

"Shut up!" I lunged again, wishing he didn't have nearly a foot of height on me.

For my efforts, he jammed his hand into my face and knocked me on my butt.

"Dumbass," Troy said. He hoisted Amaranthia to eye level and studied her. "Your girlfriend's gross. Slimy too. Listen up, Petey. This is for your own good. You're not supposed to eat frogs, and you sure as hell don't screw them. What are you supposed to do with frogs, Brett?"

Brett smirked. "Dissect 'em."

"See? Brett's with the program. Frogs are for dissecting. You open them up and pull out their insides. Then you pitch them in the trash." Troy clutched Amaranthia in both hands, as if she were a basketball, and mimed aiming for the garbage can down the hall. I surged to my feet. All my pent-up resentment from Troy's taunts and degradations, his harassment and abuse, concentrated into a white-hot kernel of fury. I cocked my fist, putting shoulder and body behind it, and plowed it into Troy's gut. At the same time, I saw a splatter of white goo shoot from Amaranthia and hit Troy right in the face.

Troy screamed and doubled over. Amaranthia spilled out of his hands. I dived, arms outstretched to catch her, and she flopped squarely into my arms, unhurt.

Troy writhed and thrashed on the floor, one hand over his belly, and the other scrubbing at his face. "The frog squirted me in the eye!" he yelled. "I can't see!"

"Good toad," I whispered, gripping Amaranthia to my chest.

Brett was at Troy's side, hauling him to his feet. "Man, we gotta get you to the nurse."

As they staggered away, I retrieved the plastic box. Troy's howls faded into mewling whimpers. I put Amaranthia inside and closed the lid.

The crowd scrambled back, giving us plenty of space, as I got my lunch.

A senior surprised me with a thumbs-up as I passed him. "Hey, dude. Cool attack frog."

"Actually," I said, "she's a toad. She's a *Bufo marinus*, also known as a cane toad."

No one followed me, and the science room was empty, thankfully. I collapsed into my usual spot at the back of the room, next to the line of microscopes, and set the box on the desk. I couldn't believe I'd slugged Troy Parker. More than that, I'd been outnumbered and still sent him running. I grimaced. And I'd talked back to a senior. OK, that wasn't so cool, but still, Troy Parker, flat out on the floor, was a memory I'd be telling my grandkids about.

I unpacked my lunch as I savored my triumph.

On my desk, Amaranthia regarded me through the plastic.

I took a bite of peanut butter sandwich. "I didn't know you could shoot poison. Pretty sweet."

Her eyes fixed on my sandwich.

"Are you hungry? I've got peanut butter on wheat and a pudding cup. The pudding is probably a bad idea, but maybe you'd like some peanut butter?" I tore a corner off my sandwich, popped off the box's lid, and dropped it in.

Amaranthia lunged for the morsel and snapped it down in one convulsive swallow. Before I could get the lid back on, she leaped out. I scrambled after her as she bounded across the floor and hopped out the door. When I saw where she was heading, I shouted and waved my arms, but that had zero effect. She hurtled straight into the girls' bathroom.

"Crap!"

I floundered to a stop and peeped around the corner, trying not to look like a pervert. "Hello?" I called. "Is there anyone in there?"

Silence.

"My toad jumped into the bathroom," I shouted. "If there's someone in there, can you, uh, shoo her out?"

My voice echoed, bouncing off ceramic and tile.

"Hello?" I felt stupid helloing into an empty room, but I was paralyzed by the girls' room taboo. There was only one thing worse than a guy going into the girls' bathroom, and that was a guy going into the girls' bathroom while it was occupied.

"If there's no one in there," I called, "I'm coming in."

I waited.

"Last chance to tell me to get lost."

More moments passed.

"OK, here I come!"

"Geez, give a person half a minute, why don't you?"

To my total and utter mortification, a girl stepped out. Her huge, hazel eyes squinted at me from behind a pair of retro glasses. A sprinkling of freckles powdered her cheeks, and cinnamon hair tumbled to her hips. The chestnut-brown dress she wore, with its flared sleeves and high waist, was unlike any of the clothes I'd seen at school. But then, what did I know about fashion?

"S-sorry," I stammered. "My toad—" I felt my face flush. "Y'see, I need to, uh—"

"Yes, I heard. She hopped in, and you want to get her. You needn't bother. There's no toad in there."

"But I saw her go in. Are you sure?"

The girl studied me, her hands on her hips. "Peter Litton, I assure you, there is no toad."

I blinked. "How come you know my name? Have we met?"

She rolled her eyes. "Do a guy a favor, fight at his side, and still he forgets you." She winked. "Friends are supposed to know each other's names, silly."

"Amaranthia?" I blurted.

"You do remember!" She laced her arm through mine. "But you can call me Amy."

"B-but, how?"

"It's a long story, hero, and a downer for most of it. In a nutshell, there was a witch and a curse with some conditions." She rested her head on my shoulder. "Don't worry about it. You did good. Thank you." She kissed my cheek, and I discovered I was happy to believe anything she said.

"Hey," she continued, "when I was looking for your locker, I saw a sign about some dance. The Spring Fling? You want to go with me?"

It took a second for her words to sink in—a cute girl asking *me* out?—but as soon as they did, I tripped over my own tongue trying to say "yes" fast enough.

"Yeah!" I said. "Yeah a lot. I mean definitely. Yes."

She grinned. "Super. It's a date. By the way, I'm a princess."

Call it a hunch, but I bet the universe was done picking on me.

Lights, Camera, Action

A T THE FILM PREMIERE OF THE EPIC MOVIE *THALEN'S QUEST*, I stop and pose. The cameras flash as I walk the red carpet.

Pop.

Pop.

Pop.

I walk the line and the paparazzi keep yelling my name. I love it when they yell my name.

"Holly!"

"Over here!"

"Holly!"

"HOLLY!!"

"Over here!"

"HOLLY!!!"

Makes me feel a bit dizzy. Makes me feel like a star. Glad to get inside and be in the dark. Warm popcorn with M&M's

and butter mix and melt together. My two best friends, my mini entourage, Violet and Dre, sit next to me, holding my hands as the title sequence starts.

This is it, I think to myself. The day my career changes. No more child parts for me!

When I read the script my agent sent me for *Thalen's Quest*, I was keen on playing the part of Seemie because I knew she'd be a character that would wear a lot of special-effects makeup to make her look like a monster and a teeny little barely there bikini. After playing the part of little goody-two-shoes Alice Macklebee on *The Macklebee Show*, I was ready for something different. I didn't want high-school parts anymore. I wanted to play a part with edge and a lot of makeup because I'd heard in an acting class that playing bad was how you got people to notice that you were good.

That is exactly what I liked about the prospect of playing Seemie. She betrays everyone in the movie and the audience would hate her and love me.

OK, I thought. Great! Some elf ears. A big battle scene. A really skimpy outfit. Working with Gavin LeRoy, only the hottest guy working in film ever and a chance to do something totally different. Maybe I'll even get to play a college girl in my next film instead of being stuck in high school forever. Maybe I'll finally be a star! Sign. Me. Up.

Everybody says they like the nice girl, but really, it's no better than being a wallflower. I wanted to stand out.

I knew I had the real goods to be a great actress. It was just that no one had ever given me a chance to show it. I looked at *Thalen's Quest* as my opportunity to show everyone that I had the chops to go all the way and be more than just a Goody Two-shoes on a C-list TV show.

When I showed up on set, I swore I was not going to freak out that I was playing opposite Gavin LeRoy, only a dream of mine since I was eleven. I also tried to ignore that my makeup included big sideburns and whiskers that looked like a walrus moustache. I really wanted to be friends with Gavin LeRoy, but there was no way he was even going to notice me, Holly Webber, the only kid on the set. He was twenty-two and way out of my league. Besides, I didn't party like the other seventeen-year-olds in Hollywood. I never acted older than my age.

The truth is, I *was* as good as Alice Macklebee, the part I used to play, which is why I needed a character that was bad to give me some edge.

"Will you go as far as you need to go?" the director asked me.

"Yes." I said. "I'm going to give you my guts."

And I meant it.

I was going to be evil. I was going to cut out my own heart.

Gavin LeRoy was playing a centaur named Moran, so he'd wear these really green tights on set, and no shirt. Green tights. But his face was untouched. Just simply gorgeous. And his eyes. Oh, his eyes. Those eyes had such charm in them as to be enchanting.

I saw him sometimes at craft food services, but I was never invited to sit with the adults. They thought I was younger than I was because for a seventeen-year-old, I looked twelve. I just kept my head down at lunch, studied my lines, did my homework, stayed in character. I tried to convince myself that I didn't want to get to know those actors or Gavin LeRoy anyway since my character betrays them all in the movie. It was better that I just watched him from afar.

My character, Seemie, is a little coward. That's kind of cool, I think. You know, a part you can really sink your teeth into. I didn't want to blow it. I didn't want to be just like other kid actors whose careers end once they turn eighteen. This was going to be my chance to take my career to the next level. I told myself that it was my method acting kicking in. But the truth is, I didn't think I had it in me to play a bad character if I liked my costars. I had to work extra hard at being evil because I'm a nice girl.

So here I am, at the premiere. I'm finally watching the movie and even though it's usually hard to watch yourself on-screen, I forget that it's me, or that we're acting because the movie is so good. I am frightened by how real I seem. *I'm* so evil. I'm scary.

No one is going to like me.

I don't like me.

I can hardly remember the day we shot the scene. I have to force myself to remember that the armor I was wearing was backbreaking and the horseflies were eating me alive. I was so focused on being terrible that I am terrible. And everything looks so *real.* The world feels like I've been there, like I actually lived it, or you could go there and visit. It doesn't look like I am acting. And so I'm watching the other people in the movie and I care about them.

Me, Holly, sitting in my seat, really cares about them.

Not Seemie. I know she doesn't care about anything because I created her. A monster.

I'm watching myself do my skanky, cowardly thing on screen. And I hate me. I just hate me on-screen. I look like the weaselly little snitch that I am.

And I know what's going to happen.

I'm such a wuss.

I'm sitting in the movie theater, crying and shaking.

My character is going to duck and because I don't hold the line, those people I care about now are going to die.

Seemie's not careless. She told the Ketchek that she'd stand in front, where the most important warriors were, so the Ketchek could aim right for them.

Why does Seemie have to duck? I wonder. She's already shown the Ketchek where they are. If she doesn't duck, then she would be a better person. Sort of.

I want her to be a better person. I don't like how evil I've played her. I'm so frustrated that I want to smack her like she's a real person.

No. I want to smack me.

My character is so horrible. She's a terrible person. And she never gets better. And it's all my doing. And it's an awful performance. If only I had not played her to be so one-note.

I don't want to be known for being so evil.

I think up a million ways in which Seemie could grow a heart. If only I had let her have soft parts. If I had it would have been a million times better. If I had, people could love to hate me.

I wonder how many others in the audience are watching, wishing, just wishing that my character would *do* something so that people don't have to die. And then there's Moran. I can't bear the thought of him saying and thinking those terrible things about Seemie. Because they would be true and he would be right. I don't want to see the look of hate in his eyes at the end of the movie when they discover that I've been betraying them all along.

I'm cringing as I watch Moran gallop across the battlefield, raising his sword as the Ketchek advance because Seemie—no, me, I'm the one—has maneuvered him into position.

And then the screen goes white.

It's like the film had burnt and I start to groan, because I just do, because I just want this battle scene to be over with so I don't have to feel any worse about what my character does to Moran and Thalen and all those other people for one second longer and I know it's going to take them at least fifteen minutes to fix the film.

Then I remember *Thalen's Quest* is a digital projection—no film to burn.

I stand up. I stand up in the middle of the movie theater and I know my two BFFs are supposed to be sitting in the seats beside me. Only there is nothing but black, empty space and no sound. I'm cold. Shivering. My heart is beating really fast. I'm scared. The blackness finally lightens up until there is this harsh white light and a slight wind. I put my arm up in front of my eyes because the light is so bright and then I'm amazed, because it's the sun I'm shielding my eyes from.

I blink.

I'm standing outside.

My armor is weighing me down.

A horsefly lands on my lips.

Everything goes slow and quiet for a moment.

Wait, I think. How did I get outside?

Then in a rush, everything speeds up again.

There are people screaming and bleeding next to me., And it smells like sweat and blood and death. It's awful. I gag. And that's when I hear it—the whistle. I'd heard it before, when I was Seemie. And like Seemie, I know that the Ketchek are just over the hill and that the sound was a signal for me to get out of harm's way because the Ketchek are ready to attack and know exactly where Moran's battalion is.

I know what is going to happen next. Moran is going to get shot in the shoulder with that bolt. It is going to pierce his shoulder and he is going to bleed and he is not going to be at the final confrontation at the White Cliffs. And all of his men are going to die. Right now. It's really happening. I know exactly where I am.

I hear it again, that whistle.

In the movie, I am told to count to three and then bend and crouch like the coward I am, digging in amongst the wounded and dead.

It's funny how both the enemy and the stunt coordinator say the same thing.

"When you hear the whistle, get into position, count to three," the Ketchek say.

"Count to three when you hear the whistle and pretend to react to the bolt whizzing over your head. The special-effects people in postproduction will put the bolt in later."

The stunt coordinator made it very clear to me. There is no bolt. There is only a sound.

I want the outcome to be different. It can be, if I stay standing up. It can be, if I do everything a nice person would do.

"Get down! Get down!" I know that voice. It is the sweetest, most beautiful voice I know. It's Moran. Not Gavin LeRoy the actor, but Moran the centaur, trying to save me. I hold my body in position and turn my face to look at him.

He is looking right at me, like he sees me for the first time, or rather, I know he's seeing Seemie for the first time, and as the girl who plays Seemie, that feels so good.

I smile.

And then the bolt hits me.

Hard.

And it hurts.

And I am bleeding.

Bleeding hard.

And I feel wobbly and everything seems kind of yellow.

And I am falling.

Falling right onto the ground.

And it's muddy.

And horrible.

There is a dead Ketchek next to me.

I want to vomit.

And I have to pee.

So I do both.

There are things happening around me, things I don't remember filming. There are horses and people and centaurs running and galloping and screaming. More whistles. I start to feel warm. And buzzy. I add my voice to the screaming.

I am in pain and I am screaming until everything goes black again and when I come to someone is poking me with a stick.

"Alive!" someone screams. I hear trotting. I look up and there is Moran, beautiful Moran, looking down at me. Only

I know it can't be him, it must be Gavin LeRoy. I lift my head up but there are no green tights, just horse legs. I vomit, again, as gracefully as I can. His eyes are on me—there's concern in them. It's a stunning sight. I never thought a look could make me feel so full.

"Easy there," Moran says, and then calls for water. Someone comes over and Moran lifts a cup to my mouth and I drink. Water tastes good. I cough. I'm in pain.

I try to talk, but I can't. I have no voice.

"You were brave out there, Seemie. I never knew you to do anything so bold," Moran says. "You saved my life, and by doing that, the lives of many others."

I feel ashamed because I never once thought that Moran knew that my character was so lame. I had made the adjustment in my mind that Moran, like the actor who played him, had just never noticed me. I didn't even think that they knew my name.

Moran calls out to someone else to come and care for me. He squeezes my uninjured shoulder tenderly and then moves on. Hands come and transfer me onto a stretcher and I overhear that the troops are moving on.

I know where they were going. They are going to the White Cliffs. Moran is going to the White Cliffs and I am not. Everything is going to be OK. I'm still a nice girl. Moran and everyone will live happily ever after. I am not important anymore.

Only. . . . Wait.

Seemie isn't going to be at the White Cliffs.

If I'm not there, then the battle would go according to the Ketchek's plan. A slaughter. Evil would win. Moran would die.

I tried to get up. I had to go with them to the White Cliffs.

And suddenly I knew why Seemie, my character, has to betray everyone. And Moran's battalion has to find out I do so that they change their plan and go through the Biddle Pass at the last minute.

I softened myself too much!

If it weren't for my awful character, evil would win. I couldn't turn good or grow a heart. Not now. Not ever.

And now, by being be good, I'd ruined everything.

A cup was placed in front of me and I could smell a sleeping draught. It smells like licorice. I hate the taste of licorice.

"No," I tried to say. I tried to push the cup away. "I have to go."

But the caretakers are stronger than me and they force the sickly sweet liquid down my throat. Despite my best efforts, I fall into a deep sleep.

"Ew, you were totally drooling," my friend Violet says, elbowing me.

"This movie blows chunks," my friend Dre whispers back.

And now I am very awake and back in the movie theater at the premiere. I'm watching the screen and Thalen and Moran and the others are at the White Cliffs and I'm not. They are not going to the Biddle Pass. They are all going to die and it's all because of me. I watch in horror as the Ketchek win. They are winning. That's it. It's over. They won. Evil takes over the world. Darkness falls over everything. Credits roll.

But the story doesn't go this way! I want to yell it. But I feel kind of faint.

"Why did they call this *Thalen's Quest?* They should call it *Thalen's Slaughter,*" Violet says.

"Also, hello! Hot outfit!" Dre says. "Your bod is slammin'

even if you have sideburns and whiskers!"

"At one point, in the beginning of the film, I thought you were going to go totally evil," Violet says. "And I was like, ew. I don't want to be her friend anymore. I'm glad you straightened out and went over to the good side."

"But the story doesn't go this way," I say out loud. "Moran should get shot. I should die!"

"Now that would have been a good story," Dre says.

"But then I wouldn't like you," Violet says.

We walk into the after party and head for the plates of food and I am running on autopilot. No one seems as stunned as I am that the movie is just all . . . *wrong.*

At the sushi station, I run into Gavin LeRoy.

"Holly."

I can't breathe. I'm looking into those eyes. It's those same eyes.

"Yeah," I say.

"It would have been nice to have had lunch once on set," Gavin says. "We should have done that."

"I guess I was a kid then," I say. "And evil."

"You look all grown up," he says.

"Yeah," I say.

"And I never thought you were evil," Gavin says.

He smiles at me, like the way that Moran smiles at me when he's giving me a cup of water after I take the bolt for him. And I melt a little.

Don't panic. Don't panic. He's just talking to you and well, while it's the same eyes as Moran's, it's not Moran. This guy has two legs. This guy is just an actor.

"Well, we should fix that. How about lunch sometime?" Gavin asks.

I say yes. Gavin seems happy I agreed.

People write reviews so horrible that *Thalen's Quest* becomes synonymous with cinematic failure. The collectible action figures go straight to the dollar store, and they sell for a penny. I bought one hundred of them and decorate my bathroom with my own likeness. I like to look at Seemie and think about where I went wrong with her by making her turn good. People make lists where *Thalen's Quest* is cited as one of the biggest Hollywood blunders of all time. People actually laugh at my performance.

Gavin's career goes into the toilet. So does mine.

I'm almost relieved. I don't have any auditions. I can't get any parts. My agent lets me go. But as some kind of weird consolation prize, Gavin and I have been going out for five months. It's my first grown-up relationship.

Yet, when I think about that other ending, the one only I know about and how *Thalen's Quest* might have been huge, I'm miserable.

I wonder what would have happened if maybe Seemie always knew what she was doing all along. That was a character choice I had never thought of. Maybe she thought that by betraying everyone, she had a line into what the Ketchek were up to. She could keep tabs on them.

I know one thing: I should not be dating Gavin LeRoy. He shouldn't even know my name. Neither should his character, Moran. Seemie was meant to betray everyone.

Redemption?

Not for Seemie. If I had stuck to the script when I had that choice, in that world, in that moment, then Moran and Thalen and the others would live and see victory. And in this world, Gavin would still be a big star. And so would I. And I wouldn't have this hole inside of me because I know the truth. I just didn't have the guts to play Seemie the way she should have been played—messed up, weak, flawed.

Evil.

On my nineteenth birthday, Gavin and I are in the car driving down Hollywood Boulevard and I see the marquee.

"Hey," I say. "Look! *Thalen's Quest* is playing at the $2 theater!"

"So?" Gavin musses up my hair like I'm a kid. Which, I guess to him, I still kind of am.

"*Thalen's Quest,*" I say. "I haven't seen it since the premiere."

"I haven't either and I don't want to," Gavin says.

"Come on, it's my birthday," I say.

He rolls his eyes at me, but smiles. He smiles in that way that slays me. In the way that makes me think I would do anything for him, because it really was his heart that made the character of Moran so alive.

He turns off Hollywood Boulevard and we find a parking spot and go buy tickets. I am nervous.

No.

I'm hopeful.

The music comes up, oh what a beautiful score, and the movie starts exactly the same. I start sweating and I'm watching the movie more closely than I ever have before. I can see that Seemie is still cold and cruel and not learning anything. I see how unimportant she seems and how important she really is to the plot of the movie. Gavin is sitting next to me and I'm holding his hand and I'm wishing.

I'm wishing that I hadn't chosen to make my character

find her heart on that battlefield. I wish that she found it at the White Cliffs, and sees how what she's done has been so wrong, that she can only betray them to save them, that she lets herself be found out. I want that world on the silver screen to stand a chance at being saved, because to me it seems like a real place. I'm wishing that I do it—that I betray them all. I'm wishing that they find me out, and that I get pushed off the White Cliffs and killed, just like I do in the script. I'm wishing that I do it because I know how to do it right this time.

I squeeze my eyes shut and wish.

And all of a sudden, I am there again.

I'm standing outside.

I blink.

There are people screaming and bleeding next to me. And it smells like sweat and blood and death. It's awful. And that's when I hear it —the whistle.

This time, I get into position. I count to three. I don't step in front of the bolt. I do what Seemie would do.

I lie down and watch as Moran gets shot in the shoulder. I laugh, because I'm so nervous. I can't believe I'm getting a second chance. I watch as Moran's men and women die and each one I see die makes me feel resolved. My blood is pumping, it feels so right.

I look back when I ride off with the others to the White Cliffs, at the place where the dead fell , and I'm smiling because I know I did good. And because I am smiling, everyone thinks that it is because I am coldhearted. But when I look at Thalen and the others I am filled with love for them. I am determined to betray them all so that they can win. I know that what I do will help them, not harm them.

When I secretly meet with the Ketchek, I am almost

filled with joy. My friends, the ones in the film, they'll never know what I did. They'll just think I was bad all along and could have never been redeemed. They'll think this so much that they will push me off the White Cliffs as a traitor without batting an eye. They will think this so much that my character will die.

But me, I will be smiling as Moran says his hateful words about me to my face, spitting at me as he exposes all of my character flaws, because I will know I did the right thing. They will live happily ever after.

The lights come up.

I'm sitting at the movie premiere. Violet and Dre are sitting next to me. I know everything is back to the way it should be.

"God, you could win an Oscar for that," Violet says.

"You are so good in this movie, it's scary," Dre says.

"I want to see it again," Violet says. "Let's go Friday when it actually opens."

A girl comes up to me and asks me for my autograph. While I finish signing, she tells me that she hates me.

"Doesn't that bug you?" Violet asks.

"She thinks you're that awful," Dre points out.

I smile.

They say that Los Angeles is full of magic—movie magic, not real magic.

They say that in Hollywood you can walk down a street that looks like New York, or the old West, and it looks so real that you think you are really there. But if you look closely, if you open up the doors, you see that you're nowhere. It's just a set, a façade, a place held up by two-by-fours.

I should know that there's no magic here that isn't makeup or special effects or postproduction tricks.

Except for the magic you make yourself, of course.

ANN ZEDDIES

Ten Thousand Waves

THE SMELL OF KIMCHI IS OVERPOWERING ON A HOT MAY day in Kansas. It assaults Jun Ho's nose as he enters the kitchen for dinner. His mother stands at the stove, apron lashed about her short, solid frame. She doesn't just cook the food, she subdues it. She slaps it down with her plastic spoon. The fan on the windowsill whines softly to itself like a small animal in distress. It can't keep up with the powerful alien scents rising from the stove in an irresistible force to meet the immovable, thick, hot, Kansas air.

Jun Ho gazes at the food in despair. He has to eat it. He has no choice. He tries to tell his mother he wants American food like other boys, but she brushes the words aside as she brushes crumbs from the table with the side of her hand. Foolishness, she says. It is foolishness.

He craves the food on TV—it's bigger than life, shinier, brighter, more delicious. But when he tastes it, it's like the food in a dream. It's like cheap magic, spun from a few grains of salt or sand.

He picks up the chopsticks and stuffs a redolent wad of pickled cabbage into his mouth. Sweat pops out on his face. Kimchi ignites a fire inside that is stronger than Kansas and will protect him.

Fumes from the last fat slice of onion still sting in his nose when he hears the Uncle's steps on the creaky stairs. The Uncle mops his face with a large hankie as he hobbles through the door. Propped on his cane, he complains of the heat, the long stairs, an old man's bones.

"Jun Ho! Get your Uncle a cold drink!" his mother orders.

Reluctantly, Jun Ho brings a Dr Pepper from the refrigerator. As always, he tries to dodge the Uncle's sudden pinch on his ear. As always, he fails. The old man's hands are nimble as parrot claws, and their grasp is surprisingly powerful.

"Heh heh heh," the Uncle chuckles.

Heh heh heh, Jun Ho echoes silently without moving a muscle of his face. *How are your studies, young man? All A's? Eh?*

"How are your studies, young man? All A's? Eh?" the Uncle says.

"Not quite," Jun Ho mumbles.

The Uncle tilts his head and slurps the Dr Pepper. Jun Ho counts the swallows as they go down the old man's throat. *Glug. Glug. Glug.* Jun Ho's mother won't buy Coke for him. She says it is a waste of money, he will rot his teeth, and that he does not need to be spoiled with sugary drinks. She believes the voices on TV that say milk is good for growing boys. Jun Ho hates milk.

But she buys Dr Pepper for the Uncle, who thinks it's a

medicinal beverage because of the name. Jun Ho hates Dr Pepper, so he won't even sneak a drink of the old man's pop.

Why can't they be normal? he thinks for the thousandth time.

The Uncle lowers himself into a plastic chair, and Jun Ho's mother sets bowls on the table before him. *Click, click, clack*—three, four, five, six bowls, each with its own color, texture, and spicy cloud of steam. Then she puts down the noodles and the rice with millet.

"Sit down, Jun Ho," the Uncle says. "Eat with me!"

"Thank you, Uncle, I ate already," Jun Ho says. "I have homework to do."

He's relieved when his mother nods dismissal, and he retreats to his room. As he goes, he hears the Uncle slurping noodles, his mother clattering the pots and pans into the sink, eating dinner off the kitchen counter as the Uncle calls out a stream of gossip from his place at the table. The Uncle likes conversation with his meal.

Jun Ho escapes into his math. He doesn't understand why other kids resent his ability to complete the problems. Math is a puzzle to be solved. It just takes concentration, like scrubbing the big white stove to his mother's satisfaction. It's nothing he's proud of.

Then comes the textbook called *Kansas Land.* It's not hard, because all the worksheet answers are in the book. But he doesn't enjoy it. The book shows pictures of tallgrass prairie and shortgrass prairie. Both are flat and yellow. Tall spindly trees hold up crowns of brownish leaves beside a flat brown river. They're cottonwoods, and even in May, the leaves have a tough, shiny skin that makes a metallic rattling in the hot wind.

The construction of large dams and reservoirs has greatly reduced the likelihood of another flood on the Kansas River, the book says. Jun Ho wipes the sweat off his face. A drop falls, leaving a smudge across the river photo. He dreams of a cold wind sighing through pine branches while his pen slyly doodles eyes and claws around the blotch on the photograph.

Then he sees what his own treacherous hand has done. He'll be charged money at the end of the year for the marks on the book. His mother will yell at him. He scrubs with the eraser, but ghost lines of the doodled dragon face still show.

"Jun Ho!" His mother's voice makes him slam the betraying book shut and leap to his feet.

"You will walk Uncle home. He has things to carry," she grumbles. "You will come straight back! No hanging around!"

The Uncle has a big bag of laundry, washed for him by Jun Ho's mother at Mrs. Kim's laundromat downstairs, where she works. Bending under the bulging bag, Jun Ho shuffles along with the Uncle. His parents will never buy a car. *Foolishness! Too much money!* he imagines his mother's voice explaining. When his father is in town, he rides the bicycle every day, sitting up straight in his dark suit, pedaling across the bridge to the university. Jun Ho has seen neighborhood kids laughing at his father. People with cars fly to distant places. People without cars are like beetles, always with their noses to the dirt.

Jun Ho and the Uncle descend the steps by the overpass to cross the highway, then climb to the levee on the other side. The Uncle taps the undergirders of the railroad bridge next to the levee with his cane and says something in Korean. At Jun Ho's blank look, he translates: "Always tap before crossing, even if the bridge is stone."

"Why?"

"Things not always how they appear," the Uncle says. "No matter how solid a thing appear, someday that gonna change."

Jun Ho hefts the laundry again and follows, thinking that some things are definitely permanent. He will always be treated like a child, always be stuck in a place he hates. There will always be something heavy on his back and a drop of sweat trickling down his nose. Stone bridges will fall before his life will change.

Halfway to the trailer park, the Uncle pauses to rest. Jun Ho sets down the bag and ambles to the edge of the levee to peer down into the turbid waters. It's been a dry spring, and the low water exposes tangles of roots, shoals of pebbles, and streaks of black sand. Jun Ho sees a darkness that might be a cave under the bank, or maybe it's only a shadow under the ledge. He crouches at the edge, trying to see.

"What you looking for?" the Uncle asks.

Jun Ho scrambles back, sending sand crumbling and breaking away under his feet.

"Nothing, Uncle. I thought there was a hole down there. Maybe an animal."

"Water dragons sometimes find welcome in caves by water," the Uncle announces. "Did you know King Munmu of Silla became a dragon after his death?"

I'm not a little kid any more, Jun Ho says, but only in his own mind. *I don't need your stupid stories.*

The Uncle is full of stories. Jun Ho used to like some of them—the ones with magic in them, not the ones about Buddhist monks, and certainly not the stories of good young men who let mosquitoes bite their bare flesh so their parents can sleep, or who study for five years without food or rest. The moral is: Boys should work hard to please their parents. Jun Ho is sick of these tales.

"Yes, he became a guardian dragon," the Uncle said, taking Jun Ho's silence for respectful interest. "His body was buried under a big rock in the Eastern Sea, and the next king built a golden temple on the rock. Underneath is a cave that opens to the sea so the dragon can come in and rest."

"Wait, how can he become a dragon if he's buried under a big rock?"

"His mortal bones are buried there, but he himself became a dragon," the Uncle says, just as if it makes some kind of sense. "Dragons are immortal. Understand?"

Not really, Jun Ho thinks, but he doesn't say anything.

"Anyway," the Uncle continues. "One day the next king saw a floating mountain coming through the ocean toward his kingdom. The top of the mountain looked like a turtle's head, and a bamboo with a split stem grew on top. When the king sailed out to see the floating island, there was thunder and the earth shook, and the split bamboo united into one. The storm and darkness lasted seven days. When the wind died down and the waves calmed, the king finally reached the island.

"He was met by a huge dragon.

" 'Why have you come here?' the dragon rumbled.

" 'Lord Dragon,' the king said, 'I want to know the meaning of this split bamboo.'

" 'My king,' the dragon answered, 'one hand makes no sound, but when two hands strike each other, they make music. Likewise, the split bamboo makes a good sound when its halves unite. If you make a flute from this bamboo, its music will bring peace and happiness to your kingdom. This is a gift from your father, who is now king of all the dragons.'

"So the king cut a piece of the bamboo. As soon as he got into his boat with it, the dragon and the floating mountain vanished into the mist."

"So then what happened?" Jun Ho asks. He has become interested enough to forget the sun beating down on the flat, treeless levee.

"Oh, that's another story."

Now it appears to be another story with no point. Jun Ho hurries along the dusty path. He just wants this trip to be over.

"The king did make a flute from the bamboo," the Uncle says, forcing Jun Ho to slow down to hear the rest of it.

"It is said in the *Samguk Yusa,* the book of history stories, 'When this flute was played, attacking enemies fled, spreading plagues receded, sweet rains came after drought, the bright sun shone in the downpour, the wind was mild, and the water was calm.' It was called the Flute to Calm Ten Thousand Waves. It is one of the great treasures of Korea."

At last they come down off the levee into the trailer park that huddles nearby and find the little box that is the Uncle's. It's not like the apartment, all shiny and bright inside. There's one chair, with plastic tape concealing the torn seat. There's a sagging sofa that doubles as a bed. A mountain of stacked cardboard boxes, plastic milk crates, parts of packing cases, all piled atop each other and crammed with books fills the remaining space.

The books are paperbound, lined with thorny, jagged symbols. One lies open on the table. A picture circles in a barricade of characters, painted in bold black ink: sinuous body, fierce head with moon-round eyes, fantastic claws, and whiskers. A dragon? Jun Ho can puzzle out the boxy logic of Korean *hangul* writing, but he has never learned Chinese characters.

The Uncle sweeps up the book and deposits it in one of the boxes.

"No books like these in all Korea," he says. "Treasure of knowledge, right here in this trailer. Older than all this new American country, if people here only knew. Too bad you can't read."

"I can read. I read American books."

But the Uncle seldom hears what he doesn't want to hear. He pulls a Coke out of the cold cave of the refrigerator and offers it. Jun Ho turns away a little, politely, though American boys don't do that, and pours a long draft down his dusty throat. The taste is extreme and intense. It's more than pop. It's a dark, ice-cold syrup that sparkles inside him. He puts the can down to absorb the shock of it.

"Hungry?" The Uncle offers a cellophane package of steamed buns. It's a six-pack, one of them already eaten. Jun Ho has tasted them before—a dense egg of dough with a center of sweet beany paste. They make him sick. He shakes his head.

"You sure?" the Uncle asks.

Jun Ho rubs his fingers, cooled by the Coke can, across his sweat-stung eyes. When he opens his eyes, the package is still on the table, but it contains chocolate cupcakes with a smooth shell of brown frosting. He takes one and bites in. He's almost afraid it will taste like beans, but it's chocolate—frosting that melts against his tongue, spongy, fragrant cake, and a puff of pale cream in the center. The cakes taste the way he always hopes the food on TV would taste if he could reach in and grab it: bigger, sweeter, brighter than life.

"Why does it taste better at your house?" He moves his tongue through carbonated chocolate ghosts.

"Your mother, she doesn't want you to get so used to foreign food."

When Jun Ho talks to his mother and the Uncle, he senses invisible things of great size moving past. The words are only their traces. His father is different. His father's words contain their own meaning and nothing else.

"I'd better go, she told me not to hang around."

"Bring your flute and play for me next time," the Uncle calls after him. Jun Ho pretends not to hear.

The levee is the shortcut, but it's hot and dry up there. Jun Ho takes the long way around, through the streets and past the school. On the playground, a few boys are still playing basketball. The court is uneven asphalt in a field of coarse grass, bounded by jangling, rusty fence. But the slap and scrape of rubber soles against the paving draws Jun Ho like music. This game promises him something sparkling and intense, a long cool taste of freedom.

"Hey, Junie!"

He hates the name, but it's the voice of a friend—Two Bears Parker. Two Bears' sister, Wynonna, looks up at him under the shadow of her long dark hair. She looks away, but he has seen her smile.

Two Bears talks about the blonde cheerleaders, and Jun Ho pretends to like them too. But Wynonna is the one he can't erase from the margins in his head. Her hair is thick and shining. Her eyes are dark. She's like him and not like him. She smiles but runs away. She wears white tank tops and strawberry frosted lipstick. She haunts him, but he can't talk to her.

He can hear his mother's voice in his head: *You don't hang around with American girl! You grow up, marry good girl, good wife!* It's followed by *chop, chop, chop* as her busy cleaver dices an innocent weeping onion.

His heart leaps as the ball thuds against his chest to be safely cradled in his hands, and he's flying. The dark, fizzing energy is still strong inside him. He spurns the ground with his feet and slaps its resounding surface with the ball. He lives for the rattle of the dingy backboard when his shots slam against it. And then *swoosh, swoosh, swoosh!* Nothing but net.

And then, as the sun sinks lower, the shadow boys appear around the fence. Jun Ho calls them the shadow boys, though they come in all shades, some cordovan dark, others bleach white. They're all spectral in the dusk, their long legs doubled by trailing the shadows trailing them. The boys stake out the court, possessing it, pegging it down with their feet. Jun Ho's friends melt into the darker corners, leaving him alone in the forest of tall, tough arms and legs.

"Hey, Jun Ho," one of the shadow boys calls. It's a soft voice, but with a mean emphasis. "Hey, give us the ball, Ho-boy."

He's not about to give up the ball, not after his friends trusted him with it. Not with Wynonna watching.

The tall boys grab him and rattle him as if he were a vending machine. He kicks, throws elbows, but can't let go of the ball. A slap to the back of his head sends his face crashing into the chain-link fence. He falls to the pebbled asphalt, which rubs the skin off his knee like a grater crushing a garlic clove.

"Give them the ball, Junie," someone calls out of the darkness. "It's not worth it."

He has no choice. They twist it out of his hands and leap over him.

"Ho Ho, son of Ding Dong," one of them calls, and the fence rattles like laughter.

The scolding sizzles around him like a boiling pot.

"If you obey your mother this never happen! Instead you are hanging around! Fighting! Hanging around like a bum! What you going to grow up to be—a bum like them?"

When she has cleaned him up, scolded herself out of breath, she sticks her face suspiciously close to his.

"What did you eat at the Uncle's? Some kind of junk?"

Always she asks him this question, and he can never fool her.

"You better drink this."

She puts a scalding cup in his hand. It has a tongue-twisting flavor that seems to put hooks into him like the smells of her spices. She hardly gives him time to drink it before she pushes him into his room.

"Finish your homework. I have to talk to your father."

He can't follow her rapid-fire Korean, but he knows it's all about him, and long distance too. His father has been away on business for a long time.

On the shelf there's a baseball glove his father bought him.

"The American soldiers taught me to play ball," his father told him. "I want you to study hard, but I know a boy has to play too." His father doesn't understand that basketball is the game now, that you have to be there to play. Jun Ho tries screwing the eraser end of his pencil into his ear, but he can still hear the expensive story of his badness flowing on. Other kids have cell phones. He can't call anyone.

There's change in his desk drawer. He slides the coins out silently and slips through the door, down the stairs. With luck, he can get to the vending machines without being caught by Mrs. Kim. The machine has one package of cupcakes left. He stuffs them down the front of his shirt and sidles back up the stairs. His mother is still arguing vigorously into the telephone.

He haggles the wrapping open with his teeth and bites into the cake. Sawdust. Cardboard. The cream filling is a faintly chemical paste. The flavor is gone. All he can taste is his mother's tea.

His father must have told her to leave him alone, or she'd be bustling into his room to tell him his punishment. Instead, the smell of incense creeps under the door, and the sound of peremptory hand claps that call the attention of gods to her problem resonate. Soon he hears her turn on the TV. Jun Ho can't stand waiting any longer to be told his fate.

Looking over her shoulder, he sees that the program is one of her favorite game shows. When Jun Ho watches TV, she calls it "wasting your time on trash." But she insists that her programs contain valuable information. Her eyes gleam when she gets the right answer before the Americans on the show. She keeps track of how much money she would win if they would let her compete.

She has a paperbound book filled with charts and notations in Chinese characters on her lap. This is her manual for calculating lucky numbers and fortunate moments for action. Occasionally she wins a small prize in the lottery. Jun Ho's father doesn't like her gambling, but she tells him someday she will find the right numbers for luck in this strange place, and then they will win big. He tells her that when he finishes his degree they will not need to win big. Then they begin to argue, and Jun Ho quietly closes his door.

"Ama, I'm sorry." He steps up beside her chair.

"Look." Her eyes remain on the screen. "The matching card is behind that door—there."

"How do you always know?" he asks humbly.

"I know plenty. I know you will spend afternoons with your Uncle for a couple of weeks. I got to work for Mrs. Kim downstairs. I can't watch lazy boy all day. Your father says you can do your homework at the Uncle's. And no hanging around on the way there. I will know if you do."

"Yes, Ama."

He tries to sleep, but a hot wind rattles the leaves of the cottonwoods. It turns and coils in the branches like something trying to pull free. In his dream, Jun Ho keeps erasing the marks from his book, but the more he scrubs at them the clearer they become, till the page has tattered away and only the dragon face remains.

School is not a bad place. Jun Ho doesn't mind it as long as he can stay invisible. He's marching with the band, on the edge of the playing field. He's wondering if his parents set him up to play the flute somehow. He wanted bright, loud brass. The teacher handed out trumpets to Travis, Antwon, and Tranh Loc. Two Bears got the drums. But when the teacher reached Jun Ho, there was a silver flute in his hand. Jun Ho wanted to change instruments.

"If your teacher chose the flute, he must have had a good reason," his father said. "You should try to learn."

The Uncle had been visiting.

"Trumpet too loud for Mrs. Kim downstairs." He stabbed

toward the floor with a sweating can of pop. "You should play flute."

One good thing is that most of the flutes are girls, and Wynonna marches in front of Jun Ho, where he can watch as her pleated skirt flicks back and forth across her tanned legs.

He's counting her steps when a shadow boy from last night drifts toward him from the track where runners practice. The boy trails a wake of whispered insults. Jun Ho squints at the bobbing music on his rack. Sweat tickles in his eyelashes. Two boys pace him, then three, all of them tall and knotty like cottonwood saplings.

Be kind to your web-footed friends, the music trills. *For the duck may be somebody's mother . . .*

"Your mama . . . your mama," the boys hiss.

Someone sticks a foot between Jun Ho's ankles to trip him. He misses a step and jolts into the player beside him.

His tongue stutters against the music as if the notes were something hard and real trying to muscle their way out of the flute. He imagines wielding the instrument like a sword, slashing through the long-legged shadows, and the music soars into a hard, bright descant that isn't in the score. He gasps and burbles as he tries to find his place again—a sound like a fart. The girls ahead of him giggle.

The boy who tripped him slips and curses.

Jun Ho passes him, back straight, eyes facing forward. He catches a glimpse of hundred-dollar basketball shoes sliding through a coil of smelly dog crap.

"That was very nice, Jun Ho," the teacher says when they reach the end of the field. "Very musical. But next time, ask me before you improvise."

At the end of the school day, all the classroom windows

stand open, but no cooling breeze comes in. Jun Ho tries to stay awake, his fingers tracing the twisting grain of the wooden desk. He blinks his eyes open and sees the pen in his hand. He has inked the dragon's fierce mask and sinuous body deep into the knotted wood. He covers the pattern with his hand, but it's too late to erase it.

He runs past the basketball court and arrives at the Uncle's house damp with sweat, yellow dust clinging to his shoes. The Uncle isn't in the trailer. Jun Ho opens the refrigerator. He plans just to snatch a Coke, but he stares at the array of strange roots and jars of many colors inside. The refrigerator hums in a deep voice, exhaling scents that even Jun Ho's mother doesn't know. He lifts the Coke out carefully, without touching anything else. He sips it cautiously, but it tastes as wonderful as the last one, and he ends up squeezing his eyes shut, pouring that dark river down his throat.

The tiny yard is empty. He scrunches up over rocks and gravel to the top of the levee and sees the Uncle far off, beyond the levee on a sandbank.

"You brought your flute? Go back and get it," the Uncle orders as soon as he sees Jun Ho. "And bring me a Coke."

The Uncle comes up the side of the levee with a big chunk of limestone in his hands. Next to the levee, in a bend in the river, there's a hump of earth that stands out from the sandy bluff. Its crest is crowned with strange structures, built of sharp-edged rock fragments broken from the bluff. The rock piles look like small towers with animal ears. The Uncle positions the new rock on top, rocks it gently to settle it, and pauses to rub his back and complain.

He reaches for the Coke. "Now play your flute."

The flute feels hot as Jun Ho lifts it to his lips.

Be kind to your web-footed friends, the flute tootles. It sounds weak and shrill in this vast golden room enclosed by the yellow earth and the blue sky.

"Play with feeling. Play from your heart."

The Uncle takes the flute and blows. It's a long, vibrating note that lasts longer than any breath Jun Ho has ever taken. It makes the air shimmer and the ground hum. Jun Ho feels something struggle out from inside him, and he wraps his arms around his middle to hold onto himself.

"Play like that when you practice."

Jun Ho puts the flute away. It feels the same, but he wonders if the Uncle has changed it in some way.

The Uncle goes back to his rock-picking.

"What are you doing?" Jun Ho asks.

The Uncle rubs the sparse gray hairs on his chin.

"Every place has its own forces. It's lucky to be on the right side of them, but to approach them wrong is dangerous. This town was built by ignorant people. They built it unlucky. These stones may deflect the energy of the water dragon."

He points, but Jun Ho sees only ripples in the water.

"Living here is dangerous till we make peace with the spirits of this place."

He hums as he works, low notes that vibrate in his chest.

Jun Ho fidgets. "Aren't we Methodists?" he asks.

The Uncle stops humming. "Didn't we all go to church last Sunday?"

"Yes, but last night Amani burned incense and I don't think it was for the Methodist god. She has her book of numbers for lucky times, and now you with these stones for the earth spirits. Which one is real?"

The Uncle returns to his humming and sorting rocks.

"Many kinds of people come and go across Korea," he says finally. "Buddhist kings, Confucian kings. Chinese with their books, fierce Manchus, Japanese invaders, and the Westerners with their one God who has a Methodist face and a Catholic face, and so many others. All of them walk around like conquerors, but all of them pass. Something from each of them makes roots and grows. The oldest, strongest power is in the earth, and that doesn't pass. Real is what lasts. Have to wait and see.

"Methodist is your father's choice. Your mother and I come from a different way of thinking. But we all get along."

"You don't."

"What are you saying?"

"You—and Amani." Jun Ho is shocked at the words that pop out of his mouth. "Whenever I come over here, she says don't do this, do that, don't eat his food, listen to his songs. On the outside, respect, respect, respect. On the inside, nothing but arguing. You don't agree on one thing."

The Uncle fishes a squashy candy bar from his pocket, peels back the paper, and hands it to Jun Ho. The chocolate outer coat has melted to perfection, and the caramel inside is soft and rich.

"Don't tell your mother I spoke of this to you. You know how your father and mother met?"

"Yes, I know." Jun Ho tries to focus as his senses melt in dark chocolate. His mother has told him the story several times: children of successful families introduced by parents to marry and bring happiness to their relatives by joining the families together. The lesson is that children should be trustful of parents and let wiser heads choose for them.

"Yes, yes, happiness and good business. But reason for success is understanding the old powers. Building lucky, knowing the times and places.

"Your father's father, my dear brother—he was a great man. Many important people came to hear his wisdom. He could tell them when to marry, where to build, what is written for them in the lines of the hands and the shape of the face. Important people were grateful to him, and in this way, he became great. Your mother's people were the same way, but always there is jealousy between the families. Your grandfather hoped his son would follow in his steps, and if the two families start to get along, then everybody benefits."

Jun Ho's fingers melt tiny craters into the stub of the candy bar as he holds it without eating, trying to understand.

"Your father was nice boy, like you, but stubborn. Very stubborn. They always told him, study, study, study. He studied too much. Came home not believing in the old powers any more. Told his parents modern way of success was *in-ter-national business law*."

The Uncle rolls the words on his tongue like candy.

"So he came here to study and brought your mother— and me, to look after them for my dear older brother. But your father is still very stubborn. The family doesn't approve. They scold him, yell at him. So he won't take money from them, even though they are a little bit sorry now. That's why your mother is so mad all the time. At home in Korea, she has plenty of money, nice big house and everything. Here she works for Mrs. Kim at the laundromat. All because of your father and his stubborn pride."

"If the power comes from the earth, why don't the Americans know about it? This is their country, not ours."

"No, it is not. They are new people. They know nothing. Your friend with the bear's eyes—if you bring his grandfather here, *he* will know."

"But we're new people here too."

"Yes, but old people at home. We bring old knowledge with us. Americans think like conquerors. We do not conquer the powers. To think like that is dangerous. We learn harmony with them."

Stories, lessons. Jun Ho is bored now.

"Where is my father? When is he coming home?"

"Some kind of big deal. Grain futures. Wants to bring big money to prove he's right. If he wins, he will come home and graduate."

Jun Ho knows what grain futures are. It's like putting a bet on how big the crop will be.

"Which way did he bet?"

"There's no future if the sun burns up the grain before it grows."

The Uncle adjusts a flake of slate atop the nearest cairn. "Go to the trailer and do your homework. I am going to sing now, and your mother does not want me to teach you any songs. Do your homework. Practice the flute. Play with harmony, you understand? Play from the heart. Then the dragons will listen to you."

Jun Ho walks back on the sandy soil marked with cracks and ruts. He thinks of the ink dragon graven into his desk. He sees the dragon twisting and turning, pulling the knots out of the wood. *Go back, be invisible,* he orders the dragon, but it isn't listening.

Night comes to turn off the light, but the sullen heat doesn't take the hint and go. It sprawls heavily across the land.

Through his wide-open window, Jun Ho feels the evening air settle wearily over trailer park, town, and the raw sandy clay of the riverbank. He lifts the flute to his lips and blows softly, not a tune for marching, just a lonely silver sound that steals out into the hot night. He tries again and again, calling into the darkness, but the earth won't hum for him as it did for the Uncle.

His mother raps sharply on his door.

"You are not practicing! That is just fooling around!"

Faint wisps of cloud curl around the bubble of the moon, like a coiling dragon trying to seize a floating pearl. He turns from the window and punches deep into his pillow, but all night long he turns and twists. In the morning, his sheets are tangled into a dragon coil. He leaps out of bed and smooths the cover tight, banishing the shape.

He pushes through the crowd coming out of school at the end of the day, sticking one hand in his pocket to make sure he has the list of small items for the Uncle. His mother has given him an envelope with money to buy the groceries and a lottery ticket. She chose the numbers from her lucky book. He hurries toward the Northside Market, on the corner near the overpass. Wynonna goes there sometimes. He could meet her there, buy her a lemon-lime Slurpee and a cinnamon sugar pretzel instead of a lottery ticket for his mother. He would tell his mother there was not enough money and face the consequences.

He sees her, walking slowly up the street, laughing with her friends. He can catch up if he hurries. He doesn't see the shadow boys until they've closed in like hunting dogs.

"Hi there, gook boy." They shove his shoulders in mock

fellowship so he bumps from one side to the other. "Hey, gook boy, watch where you're going. Who are you pushing?"

Someone yanks at his hand and the envelope falls.

"Look, little Ho-baby dropped something."

"It's mine, give it back." But he knows there is no power behind the fierce words. They can take what they want.

"Oh, look, it's money! Thanks, Ho-boy. But you still owe me for ruining my shoes," one of them says.

"I didn't touch your shoes!"

"You tripped me. Made me step in something. Eww, I can smell it now—stinky and yellow."

Jun Ho grabs for the money, but they push him against the dumpster by the side wall, so hard his head thumps the dented green metal. When his vision clears, they're laughing, running up the steps of a house three doors down. He's left sitting with empty boxes, cut strings—trash that didn't quite make it into the can. He can't see Wynonna and doesn't want to.

He walks slowly up the levee, alone. He can't go straight to the Uncle. He slides down the bluff and explores the sandbanks exposed by the low water. Even this low, the river makes an ominous rushing sound as it hurries toward the dam. Sometimes his feet sink too far into the yielding sand, scaring him. There's quicksand, they say. He's been told never to go here. The banks are treacherous and could spill him into the current that rushes over the dam. Drunks and homeless people go walking here and turn up weeks later, pinned beneath the dam by the churning green water.

He picks up a stick and pokes among bottles and rusted cans. Without a metal detector, he can't even pretend to be looking for treasure. He crouches at the edge, where water curls

over the toes of his shoes, and looks up and sees something coming—a tangle of branches sailing down the river. Clumps of earth are caught in the twisted limbs. Green things still grow in the torn turf: grass, garden flowers, ferns, and the sword-shaped leaves of bamboo. As the clump nears him, it catches in an eddy and twirls closer to the bank. He hooks his stick into the tangle and pulls.

It looks light, floating on the water, but once he hooks it, it's massive and heavy. Something moves in the leaves. Eyes are looking out at him, and a wide toothless mouth opens silently. It's a huge turtle with a domed shell the size of a scaly green basketball. He jabs his stick toward it, but he's afraid to get too close. Snapping turtles can bite your fingers off like Twix.

The turtle blinks its streaky yellow eyes, then slides off the floating island and disappears. The island bobbles with the removal of the turtle's weight, bringing the tip of the bamboo clump just within his reach. He grabs, but the island of debris slides past, leaving one dry stalk in his grasp.

He watches for the turtle awhile, but finally climbs back up with the bamboo stalk. It's hardened and dry, maybe four feet long. Sure he's alone, he whirls it through the air to strike sand and brush, listening to the whistle and smack. He could break some heads with that.

He doesn't tell the Uncle about the money, hoping he'll forget. But the Uncle has sharp eyes.

"Where did this come from?" The Uncle touches the lump on the back of Jun Ho's head. "I see no grocery bag. Is this what you traded my money for?"

The Uncle's fingers look crooked and old but feel like steel tongs, boring into the soft points of Jun Ho's skull.

"There are lines in your body, just like lines on the earth—meridians. Press correct points, the energy moves over. Pain moves away. Same thing, placing stones on riverbank. Move the energy."

When the Uncle stops pressing, some of the ache has gone. Jun Ho is never sure if the Uncle's pressure treatments really work, or if they just hurt so much that he forgets the original pain.

"Don't tell my mother I was fighting. Don't tell about the money. I'll get it back some way."

But the Uncle is not listening. "What's this?" He seizes the bamboo stalk. "Long time since I saw this. Bamboo doesn't grow in Kansas."

"It came down the river. Maybe from somebody's garden."

The Uncle gets a rusty file and lays it across the stove burner till the pointed tip glows red hot. Then he wraps the other end in a rag, picks up the file, and begins boring holes in Jun Ho's bamboo.

"This is the kind of flute you need," the Uncle says with satisfaction.

Jun Ho doesn't think he needs a flute at all. Nothing has been said about the money. He will have to wait in fear until he finds out what the Uncle will tell his mother.

He walks slowly on the way home too. He wonders if the Uncle will call his mother, wonders if they even need a phone, if they have some way to talk about him when he isn't there. When he comes to the place where he'd caught a glimpse of the cave beneath the bank, he slides down the bluff again. He can't see the cave, though. He sees the river surging along like a live creature, its green and brown body rolling to and fro. *It's powerful*, he thinks, *but it's not free. It must follow the lines laid out for it by the powers the Uncle studies.*

Jun Ho turns the flute over, shaking out a thin trickle of sand. He puts it to his lips, and tastes the burnt bamboo. He rubs the mouth hole vigorously with his sleeve before trying again.

A low, plaintive note swells from the wood. It vibrates with his breath and dies away like the call of a strange animal in a twilight forest. The intervals aren't precisely spaced like the keys on his band flute. The tune he makes surprises him. It wavers and ripples like water. It's all his own. No one has ever played it marching 'round and 'round the field.

He plays for the river, plays its curves and its frothing feelers, always probing the sand for a way out of its narrow prison. He feels the breath of the flute vibrate through him, as if it played him and not the other way around. He feels the sandbank hum beneath him.

He's forgotten the time till the setting sun hangs just above the opposite bank. He jumps up and runs. He'll have to hurry to get home before dark. He's making good time till he comes to the overpass.

A police car blocks the walkway over the bridge. There's no more dry pavement next to the levee. There's a dark pool of water. Car roofs spot the surface like turtle shells. A huge red machine squats in the middle of the street. Its thick gray hose snakes down into the water.

"Hey, Junie!" Two Bears catches up with him. "Junie, where'd you go? You missed everything. There was a cop and a guy from the fire department, even someone from the city council. The news van was here interviewing. They said the river ate a hole under the street, or maybe an old water tunnel collapsed. You have to watch the news—I think maybe I'm in it. You should have been here."

Striped wooden barricades surround the hole. The pavement is tilted. Broken metal rods stick out above the dark opening. Jun Ho darts around the red pump and crawls under the barricades. Cold, dank air breathes out from the hole in the earth. The fading light gleams on something moving under the street. He hears it rustling and chuckling as it turns and twists. It has a jade green body like the river, and whiskers of white foam.

"No—go back," he whispers, but it isn't listening. Or maybe his whisper has no heart in it.

"Hey, you! Get away from there!" It's the cop on the bridge. Jun Ho scrambles out of the street and runs, leaving Two Bears behind. He doesn't stop till he reaches the laundromat. For once, the hot, steamy air inside is welcome. It feels safe.

His mother is watching the news with her numbers book on her lap. The room smells like incense. She has left his dinner on the table.

Finally, this night, Jun Ho can't swallow his mother's food. He chews a few bites of rice, but his stomach knots at the sight of the chopped meats, the pickled and spiced vegetables. His mother thinks he must be getting sick.

"What kind of junk does the Uncle feed you?" She makes him swallow a dose that twists his lips, and sends him to his room early. He can't sleep. The hot air is no longer dry. It's swollen and ominous with invisible rain that is not yet ready to fall. He lies awake until the TV falls silent. Then he finds the jar where his mother keeps spare change, fishes out quarters without clinking, slides the door open, and creeps downstairs.

Faint light from a street lamp glows on the glass front of the vending machine. Next to it, in the corner, there's a pay phone. Jun Ho feeds it quarters, punches numbers. He knows Two Bears' number. He hopes Two Bears is at a soccer game and won't answer the phone.

"Hello?" Wynonna's voice answers.

"Hi, it's Jun Ho."

"Oh, Junie. Did you want to talk to Bears? He isn't here right now."

"I know. I wanted to talk to you."

"Okay . . . ." She laughs nervously. He hopes that's not bad.

"Did you watch the news? That big hole?"

"Yeah . . ."

"I think I know how that happened. I think it's something I did."

"Junie, that's crazy."

"I can show you. Can you come over now? Can you come to the laundromat?"

"Junie . . . does your mom know about this?"

"No! It's a secret. You'll be the only one who knows what really happened. Please come. It's really important." He worries that she'll say no, or worse, laugh again and hang up.

"If you're punking me, I'll kill you. This isn't some kind of a set-up, is it? You and Bears'?"

"No, I swear. Just me and you. I just want to talk to you."

"Okay then, but just for a minute."

Jun Ho runs his hands through his brush cut, pulls

out his shirt tails. He feeds quarters to the machine until a cascade of treasures thumps down: Cokes and Mello Yello, button-sized cream-filled cookies, rolls of jewel-colored hard candy, bars of chocolate studded with nuts, rolls of golden cake enclosing white puffs of sugary cream. He piles his loot on an empty table like a temple offering.

Finally, he sees her through the plate-glass windows.

The doors to the street are locked, but he knows where Mrs. Kim keeps the spare key. He grabs his flute and lets himself out.

"So . . . what is this important thing you were going to show me?"

"I—" He can't say it. The story sounds too crazy. He looks up at the sky. Mist wreathes the moon. Beyond the city lights, clouds writhe and churn, pleading for something to set them free. It's so hot and damp he's already sweating. Wynonna shakes her hair back from her neck.

"It's so hot. I wish it would rain," she says. She rubs the back of her neck.

"It's this." He holds out the flute. "My Uncle made this for me. I played it today and . . . well, things happened."

"You're crazy."

But she is smiling and he wants to show her everything, as long as she keeps smiling at him.

"Watch," he says.

This time, notes stab the air, sharp and insistent. The sky darkens and shudders. A cold breath hisses through the cotton-woods, and the street is pelted with raindrops as big and cold as marbles. Thunder rolls.

She isn't smiling now, but staring at him with wide eyes. His chest swells with a powerful breath, and he plays louder.

Wynonna shields her face with a raised arm. "Junie, stop! That's enough!"

The rain comes down like a wall. Its roar is deafening. Jun Ho lowers the flute. He doesn't have to explain it to her. She believes. He'll take her inside and they'll watch the rain fall through the big windows. He'll offer a towel to dry the rain from her bare, wet shoulders. He puts his hand on her arm. Her hair flaps in the wind and slaps against his cheek. Is this when he could kiss her? But she's not looking at him. She's gazing at the storm with her mouth open. She looks scared. It's not how he imagined.

His mother descends like a crack of thunder, unexpected.

"What are you doing out here? You take my money, you take the key, you hang out on the street—"

She glares at Wynonna. "You better go home! And you"—she turns on Jun Ho—"go inside! Clean up all that mess! Throw out that stuff! Go to your room!"

Wynonna dashes away through the rain.

Jun Ho retreats inside and leaves tracks of rain on the laundromat floor. The wind slams the door behind him with a shattering crash. His mother has run upstairs and he can hear her talking out loud in Korean as she slams all the windows shut against the onslaught of rain. No matter how he twists and turns, the lines of his destiny keep him moving in a direction he can't choose.

He tucks his T-shirt in and stuffs the crackling packages of the forgotten feast down his shirt, one arm across his body to hold them there, the other hand free to carry the flute. He shoulders his way out the door.

He runs to the levee through the blinding rain. He pulls

the contraband packages from his shirt front and hurls them into the river.

"Dragon! Dragon! Dragon!" he screams into the storm. He raises the flute, and it shrills and wails. He is playing from his heart. Clouds rumble and the earth shudders as the flute pulls the breath from his lungs. Lightning rips the sky, traced by a dragon's claw, and the river spills over its banks.

He lowers the flute when he's so drenched that only a drowned gurgle sputters from the holes. He sees the river climb the bank, its true form no longer a sketch in clouds and ripples, but a power pulling itself free of concealment, breaking all boundaries.

"Dragon."

The river won't stop. It slides over the levee and into the sleeping streets. A gush of jade-dark water splashes his feet. He runs for home, the earth rocking around him in the crackle and thunder of the freed storm's laughter.

His mother doesn't even speak to him. She's mopping rainwater off the floor. Alone in his room, he plays the flute with low wailing sounds as the storm roars outside.

In the morning, he expects her to scold him more, but the tornado siren sounds. They hurry to Mrs. Kim's cellar and find a foot of murky water. The tornado dissolves back into the swirling clouds without touching down, but more water keeps pouring in. Jun Ho and his mother work for hours to drag Mrs. Kim's possessions and their own from the basement storage area to higher ground. Thunder roams the sky, and the rain is still falling. Jun Ho's mother sends him upstairs to fix a cold lunch while she helps Mrs. Kim clean up the laundromat.

Jun Ho thinks his father will have to come home. He'll

see it on the news—floods in Kansas. River bursts its banks. Water is everywhere. His father will say they have to leave this place. Go somewhere always bright, without dust and shadows. California, maybe.

Jun Ho is about to turn on the TV and see how bad it looks, but he sees his mother's lucky book laid out to dry on the table. The careful diagrams of numbers are crinkled and blurred on the damp pages.

Jun Ho remembers the Uncle and his books, right next to the levee.

This time he goes out the kitchen window and down the rickety fire escape. He holds the flute close to his chest as he jumps from the last rung. The rain falls heavily, constantly. His shoes are full of water before he has run a block. As he comes to the overpass, he can hear the pumps thrumming, but the water has risen in the night, not fallen.

Men pile sandbags around the Northside Market. The shadow boys are out, loading sandbags in front of their houses. Two Bears and Wynonna carry boxes out of their house and pile them into the back of their father's camper truck.

"Junie! Come and help us!"

Jun Ho doesn't stop.

The iron bridge that seemed so strong vibrates to the rush of the current. The river gnaws at sand and concrete, growing hungrier the more it eats. Jun Ho can't follow the levee. He swerves through puddles and roadblocks till he reaches the Uncle's house.

Water pools around the skirts of the trailer. Jun Ho finds a book that has been blown out into the storm. The lines and characters have faded into ghosts. The river has dissolved them and swallowed their power.

Where is the Uncle? Jun Ho looks into the darkened trailer and sees him stacking his books in an unsteady tower, all his rickety furniture piled up beneath. "You're here," the Uncle says. "Come—to the river! Bring the flute."

Jun Ho follows through mud that sticks to his sneakers like butterscotch frosting. At the top of the levee, the Uncle is already dancing, beating his hand-held drum, singing in a harsh, quavering voice that turns each syllable to an invocation. Beneath his eyelids, the rolled-up eyes show white.

"Play! Hold the dragon on this line!" he says.

The flute feels heavy as a crowbar. Jun Ho tries to play a note called "stop," called "take it back," but only a sigh emerges. *Go back*, he trills, but his lips feel stiff.

The Uncle's feet now slip in mud that quickens with branching rivulets, like a quick brood of little vipers that go before the great brown serpent. Brown water rises around the Uncle's calves. The water will tear his roots out of the earth.

Jun Ho sees his mother ascending the mountain of boxes. He sees the water swallowing the street, licking greedily at the market, running into Two Bears' house.

He closes his eyes and tries to find notes for what he wants to see: his mother smiling, golden waves of grain, money in his father's pocket, his father coming home in a big, black, shiny truck.

Go back now, his music tells the river. *Go back! Stop!*

He hears the water chuckle and growl. His feet are sinking in the sand. The Uncle's singing stops. The Uncle opens his eyes.

"What kind of a song is that?" He's mocking, like the water. "Eh? I can guess. Wish song—mother is happy, father comes back, boy gets all what he wants? That is little boy song. Little boy can't ride the dragon."

Jun Ho sees the water spilling over, dancing into the trailer park. He sees the books, their pages bursting with syllables like thickets full of thorns, words that have been growing for thousands of years, as old as the river itself. The river wants to rush through them, uproot them, and carry them away. He has to call it back.

"Dragon," he whispers. He blows an ascending rush of cool dry notes to carry the books above the mud. He feels the rain pause and soften. Jun Ho plays the hustle and stutter of feet flying on the dusty basketball court. He feels the rush of energy that he felt then, darker and stronger than the rain.

Dragon. He calls it with his flute. He feels the humming in the earth now, the humming in his chest. He draws a strong breath and plays the shine of long dark hair and the flash of a smile in sunlight. He plays the ache in the sound of footsteps running away. The dragon knows hunger. It knows anger. It can hear that song.

He feels a dragon calling inside him. The dragon outside rushes toward him, away from the town. He feels its smooth, jade-cool back surge up beneath his feet and carry him. He sees above the flood. He is the eagle on the shattered cottonwood, he is the turtle on the floating branch, he is riding on the dragon's back. He plays from the heart of the dragon.

The dragon's mighty head, whiskered and fanged with shiny pearl, bends back toward him. For a breath, Jun Ho looks into its moon-colored eye and sees himself reflected there. The dragon bows its head, turns from the shore, and plunges back into the brown depths of the subsiding river.

Jun Ho feels solid ground again. He's stamping the earth in step with the Uncle, and the clay firms beneath their pounding feet. A last tongue of water disappears into the drying sand.

Brilliant sunlight has already erased the last traces of cloud from the sky. Soon the warm, mild breeze will sweep away its tracks from the earth.

They cross the bridge together, the Uncle's fingers clutching Jun Ho's shoulder for support. The pump sits in a drying puddle by the overpass. People stand on the corner, watching in wonder as the flooding water stills and ebbs away.

The words leap out. "Lines in the book," Jun Ho says. "Lines in the earth. I need to know. You have to teach me. Teach me to read."

Jun Ho waits for the pinch on the ear to punish him for rudeness, but the Uncle's hand stays on his shoulder. The Uncle nods.

"Your mother boasts you know your math. She'll say yes this time," he says.

Ama says nothing when they reach the laundromat. She doesn't scold or push. She clutches Jun Ho like a lottery ticket. He thinks that she might cry, but she doesn't. She pats his damp T-shirt. "You must change this! Clean clothes on laundry table!"

She sniffs and stands up straight. "Your father will come home soon to graduate. We must clean this house."

The next day, Jun Ho stands on the levee again, flute in one hand, money in the other. His mother has sent him to the store for cleaning supplies, rice, and a lottery ticket. They need something lucky, but her book is still too damp to read.

"You pick the number. You are good at math. Pick something lucky."

Looking toward the town, Jun Ho sees houses with doors

and windows open, rugs hung out to dry. Maybe Wynonna will be at the market. Maybe she'll say, "Junie, you're crazy." Maybe she'll run away.

Jun Ho crinkles the money in his hand. He could win big. He could lose it all.

On the other side of the levee, the river spreads out into the fields, sleepy and calm. From up here, Jun Ho still sees ten thousand ripples come and go, ten thousand waves.

He takes a deep breath and heads for the market. He can almost see the lucky numbers in his head. He feels the lines moving in the earth as he moves his feet toward a lucky path. He'll give Wynonna a flower in a plastic tube, and he'll speak to her. He doesn't know yet what he'll say—something that will make her smile.

He taps on the bridge as he passes. Dragons wake up. Rivers change their course. Things can change.

CRAIG LAURANCE GIDNEY

Mauve's Quilt

THE SKY WAS COMING UNDONE. MAUVE COULD SEE A PATCH where the fabric had frayed. One of the stars was about to fall, its rhinestone glitter askew. She found that she didn't really care all that much. There was a time when she would have jumped up with her needle and repaired any imperfection immediately. Now, the tear in space caused only the briefest flicker of concern.

She wasn't bored, exactly. Even now, the sheer beauty of the field where she lay, with its lilacs, irises, and hydrangeas took her breath away. It was just that she was so alone here. And she would always be alone, until the world she made ended. How would it end? With a slow unraveling, as time, moths, and dust dimmed her colors and her life. Her life would end in silence.

She knew it was wrong, what she was feeling. It had the texture of sin.

She stood and climbed up into the broken sky.

The attic was the color of a secret, a vague and shadowy tone. Quentin searched through in the dim light, picking out patterns. He saw a skeletal hat rack, a broken rocking chair, a shelf full of mangled toys. Bears without eyes and dolls with cracked skulls watched him as he moved through the room, ducking beams. There was a bookcase full of dusty volumes with old-style typography .

He found an old hope chest wedged against the far wall. Opening it released a scent of cedar mingled with potpourri and mothballs. It was like opening a coffin. A quilt was folded at the bottom of the chest, nested in dried petals that crumbled as he lifted it out. It was soft and cool to the touch.

His father called his name. He took the sweet-smelling quilt down the ladder with him.

Quentin unfolded the quilt on his bed. A few withered petals drifted to the floor. The quilt was floral, six square panels against a deeply purple background of interlocking violets. The two bottom panels had flowers of different hues of purple: lavender, mauve, and plum. The two panels above had appliquéd moths of gray and silver, one with folded wings praying over the throat of a flower, the other with its wings open. The final two squares showed a sky of dark blue. Most of the sequins that dotted the sky had fallen away. He flipped the quilt over and saw a wild explosion of bright purple blossoms. Their cups were black as eyes, and they stared at him.

Where did you get that ugly thing? That's what Mom would have said. She'd hated crafty things. This was too afghanlike for her taste.

"Hey." Quentin turned and saw Dad in the doorway. He was disheveled and sweating. One of his fingers had a cut on it that was still bleeding—he was a mess; Mom would have had a adhesive bandage on it, at the very least.

"Hey."

"What did you find in the attic?" Dad stepped into the room, then stepped back as if he wasn't sure if he was invited in.

Quentin turned back to the quilt. "Nothing. Just a bunch of junk."

Dad lingered in the doorway for a couple of uncomfortable seconds. "Well," he said finally. "When you're finished, maybe you can help me in the kitchen?"

The heat wrapped itself around Quentin like a wet towel in spite of the air conditioning. There was a fan in his room set to full blast, and he was lying naked on top of the quilt.

What I am doing here? he wondered. Summer in Chicago wasn't as brutal as it was here in Azalea. Everything here sucked. There was nothing to do, everything was at least forty minutes away by car, and even the people moved slowly, as if they were drugged. Quentin thought his dad was crazy. Mom was the one who held them both together. In his own way, Dad was as lost as Quentin was.

The quilt is cool.

It was true. On a whim, Quentin went under the covers. Miraculously, it was cooler underneath the covers than it was above. His face was warmer than the part of his body that was submerged beneath. He dipped his head under.

He fell into a fractal. He felt the petals of African violets brush his body. The world kept getting bigger and bigger, until the pixels were the size of windows. He ended up straddling a thread the size of a suspension bridge that hung over endless, frozen folds of water that were bright purple. Gauze fell over his face, enfolded him, and tickled his face as if they were spiderwebs. Through the tinted mesh, he saw his room—except that it was different. Next to a canopy bed, a black woman sat in a rocking chair. An unfinished quilt was folded on her lap. She was working on it intently.

The quilt grew slowly beneath her fingers. Her skin was dark, the color of coffee, and her short hair was styled in some old-fashioned way that he'd seen in black and white movies. She wore a black dress with purple flowers on it. He watched her for a long time, placing pieces of fabric together and cutting thread with scissors. A silver needle pierced fabric.

When he woke up, African violets stained the air around him with their color.

"Come on, baby, it will be all right." Momma held her hand and gave it a squeeze. Mauve smiled in response.

"OK," she said.

The path to the house wasn't so long after all. It was just a little overgrown. The two-story house did have a certain masculine charm about it. Two saplings with infant magnolias grew in the yard, and there were flowering bushes, forsythia and, of course, azaleas. Beds of phlox hemmed in these bushes. The house still had a decrepit feel to it, but the cold feeling in the pit of Mauve's stomach would change with time, wouldn't it? The lack of color made her feel queasy. But she didn't want to upset her mother, who had worked so long and hard for the two of them. And now, she was getting sicker. Her joints ached with arthritis, and she had a touch of gout. This *had* to work out.

"It's not so scary,"

"That's right, baby," said Momma. "You'll do fine here. I know you will."

They walked up the stairs and onto the wide porch. It was cool and shaded there. Mauve shivered in spite of herself. She wished she'd worn her shawl. Momma rang the doorbell. A deep sound echoed through the depth of the house. Professor Foxworth opened the door. He was tall, thin, and pale like a birch tree. His bald head was egg-shaped and fringed with wispy white hair. Bushy tufts of sideburns framed his bespectacled face, and his eyes were a watery shade of blue. His eyes were so washed out they were almost colorless.

"Hello, Doreen. You must be Mauve." Mauve saw that he didn't look at either her or her mother. She took his hand, which was limp and cool. It was a disinterested grip. He didn't smile.

Both women followed the professor into the house. The ceilings were high, the woodwork ornate. Mauve felt as if she were being swallowed by some beast. The professor's thin shadow on the wall was skeletal.

Mauve and her mother were led to a study outfitted with a large desk. Thousands of books lined the shelves; the spines were in dull, uninteresting colors. The professor sat in a high-backed chair behind the desk. Mauve noticed that her mother didn't sit down on the green velvet couch that faced the desk. The professor didn't seem to notice this, and did not give any permission. The couch looks uncomfortable anyway. Mauve looked around the dark room while her mother and the professor spoke.

"I can't offer your daughter much in the way of compensation, Doreen. But she will have her own room and use of the kitchen."

"You are too kind." Momma looked down at her feet. Mauve followed her gaze and became hypnotized by the faded pattern in the rug. There was a repeating circular arrangement of birds and vines. If you stared long enough, the amber birds moved slightly.

". . . can cook a few dishes well. Nothing too complicated, sir," Momma was saying.

"I hardly expect gourmet fare. I am sure what she can provide will be sufficient."

"Sir, I was wondering, though. In addition to Sunday, could she have Saturday evening off as well? So she could spend the night? That way, I would have more time with her . . ."

The professor paused. "I see no reason why not. Though, occasionally, I do entertain on Saturday evenings. In which case, I would be in need of her help."

"Of course, of course, sir."

"Yes, well, Mauve, do you have any questions about your duties?"

She looked up from the birds and vines. Both the professor and her mother were looking at her expectantly.

"I would like to see the room where I'll be sleeping—if that is okay."

He stood up from the desk, all his long limbs straightening themselves out with audible cracks. "Please follow me."

They walked up a staircase and down a hall full of sepia photographs of severe-faced men and women. They all frowned at Mauve. She felt out of place in her purple dress—it was too bright. It felt like the house, with its browns, grays and blacks, wanted to devour her. The professor opened a door at the end of the hall. The room was bare, with a twin bed and single dresser. The floor had no rugs. Sunlight illuminated the room at an oblique angle. At once, she saw the walls were painted pale purple, and there was a rug in the same shade. She could buy new curtains. This would never be like at her room at home, but she could try her best to bring something of home in this cold place.

"It's not much," the professor said, "but it should be sufficient. You may, of course, decorate the room anyway you see fit."

"Can I paint it, sir?" she said before she thought of it.

Momma touched her shoulder, signaling her disapproval.

The white-haired man paused thoughtfully, still not looking at them. "I don't see why not."

Her purple dress burned in the room.

The professor left the room. "A quick tour of the house is in order, don't you agree, Doreen?"

"Yes, sir," she answered, following him.

Mauve gave one last look at the pale room before leaving.

Life in Azalea limped along, crippled by the ever-present heat. Quentin tried to make the best of it by biking through sedate neighborhoods filled with old mansions and seemingly older residents. He felt out of place here. But then, he felt out of place everywhere. Blue-haired ladies with huge hats waved at him as he glided by. He biked to another section of town and saw diners and boutique shops that were never crowded. Farther on, he saw neighborhoods full of more recent housing with dull beige aluminum siding and matchbox-sized yards. The people who stood outside of these places were mostly darker, black and Hispanic.

The twenty-first century was in evidence here. He heard

rap music booming from car speakers. The neighborhood where he lived was trapped in a snow globe. It seemed like the 1950s, stagnant and fossilized. Quentin felt odd whenever he switched on his computer. It was sleek and modern, white and liquid crystal. It was out of place.

The doorbell was so seldom used that Quentin didn't know what the sound was. He set the computer in sleep mode. A screensaver of floating African violets spun on a darkened screen. He moved through the house quickly, expertly avoiding the points were the floor creaked.

He opened the door and saw a large black woman in pale green suit. Her fat legs were encased in white stockings. She carried a bakery box in front of her.

"Welcome to the neighborhood," she said. She held out the box to him. "I'm Eula Banks. I live at the end of the block, in the yellow Tudor on the corner. Are your parents home?"

It took Quentin a moment to remember how to speak. "No," he said as he took the box. "Dad's at work. Mom's . . . I don't have a mother. I mean, she's passed."

Eula Banks's face fell. "I'm sorry to hear that."

"It's okay."

"Was it recent?"

"Yes. I mean, in March."

The silence after that lasted forever. He couldn't take the look she gave him. He saw his mom, pale and hairless, with blue veins like trees underneath her waxen skin. He saw the shadows on her coffin, purplish black, like the shadows in the attic above.

He said, "What's in the box?"

"My lemon chess pie." She stepped into the foyer and

looked around. *Quentin, where are you manners?* he heard his mom's voice ask in his head.

"Come on in," he said. "I think there's leftover coffee."

"There was a girl who worked here in this house," Eula said, while sipping microwaved coffee, "a girl I knew from church. Mauve Willoughby. After her mother died, we'd take turns visiting her. She had no one, you know—no husband or brothers or sisters. Plus, she was a little slow, if you know what I mean."

"She took over her mother's job as a housekeeper for the professor who lived here. Mauve was a sweet girl. I remember going up to her room one time. I was maybe thirteen or so. Her room was the brightest one in the house, full of flowers and bold colors—all purples and magentas.

"One day, she didn't come to church, and no one saw her again. Her employer, the professor, only told the police that she was missing when he became annoyed by the church folk who were asking about her.

"Most people thought she'd run away, though to where, who knows? Some us think that she might have, you know, died by her own hand somewhere . . ."

Eula's voice trailed off. Quentin knew that she saw Mauve in the distance, in her flowers and fabrics. She shook her head.

The quilt was growing in her hands, stitch by stitch. Flowers and moths of purple bloomed and flew against a white background. Mauve became the silver needle, piercing the skin of quilt, tattooing it with images. Soft music from the radio played in the background. The light from the lamp next to her bed guided her patient movements. During moments like these, she could forget the last few months.

The feel of a satin petal reminded her of the satin lining the coffin in which her mother lay. They had filled in the cracks of her face with powder, hiding age marks. Momma wore bright red lipstick, something she would have never done in life. Smudged red circles were painted over her sunken cheeks. She had been laid out against the pristine white satin, surrounded by flower bouquets and flickering candles. She still looked out of place—a shriveled-up dead thing, no different from the day when Mauve had found her sitting on the living room.

In went the needle, joining fabric together with a thin thread.

The professor had given Mauve a week off to attend to the funeral and her mother's estate. He hadn't come to the funeral, even though his mother had worked for him for more than ten years. His absence was glaring, but not unwelcome. He was a strange, distant man, she found in the months she lived with him.

It was a week of planning, of numbers and papers and signatures. It was a week of days that wouldn't end, and of tons of food that went untouched. It was a week of people from the church giving her sad looks, strangers stroking her shoulders, prayers, and sleepless nights.

Honestly, it was somewhat a relief to get back to work. Then she didn't have to think about it. There was just a silent house of dust devils and ancient furniture—a house her mother had cleaned for ten years. There, in a patch of sunlight, beneath the magnolia tree, in the pupils of the professor's distracted eyes, she could see her momma.

Out went the needle, emerging with an umbilical chord trailing behind. It had been three months since Momma's passing. Church ladies still visited Mauve, coming to the back of the house, laden with cakes, pies, and other treats.

Poor Mauve, their eyes said. Each bite of the treats whispered, *It's so sad.* Each reassuring pat on her back said, *You know she's a little slow, but Doreen looked out for her.*

Mauve snapped the thread between her teeth.

Quentin dreamed of African violets. Their heavy cups swayed in the breeze, their open throats tasting the air. They grew out of an earth rich and smooth as skin, and reached for a sky that was cobalt and black at the same time. When he woke from these dreams, the images burned in the air. It was like the light itself was bleeding.

He woke up, surrounded by a field of wild flowers on fire. The woman was always there. She never seemed to notice him. She was so involved with her sewing, and what she made was so beautiful and intricate that he didn't feel slighted in the least.

She was child-sized, with a gentle swelling bosom and curving hips. Her face was kind of gaunt, her cheeks sunken, as if she had lost her natural plumpness during a long illness. Her dark brown eyes—the color of maple syrup—were sad and downcast. But she smiled as she worked, making petals, earth, and sky.

He wanted to touch her. It was odd. He didn't like touching people. He twitched involuntarily whenever his mother had touched him or his father had patted his back. His space was his own; he didn't like it to be invaded. But he wanted to touch her, to feel her skin and the blood pulsing in her veins. He could take her sadness away, maybe.

Once, she looked up and saw him. She was far away, in a wrinkle of hill. He waved at her.

Mauve laid down the batting for her quilt. It was mounds of white cotton. She felt it with her hands, running them over the clouds. But this batch wasn't soft enough. It didn't float. It wasn't buoyant. She wanted a quilt so soft and light that it would send her to the place in her dreams, the hills where there were millions of wild flowers that swayed in the breeze. Surely, it was heaven: The swirl of lavender and green, the sky of robin's egg blue was a place where God lived. Over one of the hills, her mother would come striding in her vibrant best any moment now, with swan wings sprouting from her Sunday-best dress of black and blue fabric. Mauve had visited the sanctuary of silk flowers last night. She knew that it was dream. But it wasn't a normal dream. This was a vision, one like Sister Vivian had in church when God touched her soul and she spoke in the divine tongue of angels. The vision was a glimpse, a promise of a golden future in the afterlife. During the dream, she saw an angel on one of the hills in the distance. His skin had been as pale as cream, his hair white gold. She had smiled at him warmly. Was he her Guardian?

"Mauve."

The professor's voice broke into her reverie. She put the clouds back into their bag and went to attend to him.

In his study, a pipe smoldered next to scatted sheets of yellow legal paper marked with his cryptic scrawl.

"Yes, sir."

She curtsied.

He didn't look up.

Wreathed in smoke like a Hollywood gangster, he gave his instruction: "A cup of Earl Grey tea and some crackers."

In the kitchen, Mauve set the kettle to boil and rummaged through the shelf where the tea was kept. She found three canisters. Two of them had the letter E on them. It took a short while for the sequence of letters to reveal their meaning to her. Mauve thought that letters where magic. They changed their places and shifted their shapes before her eyes. This didn't happen to other people. She understood that. She found it sad that others couldn't see the hidden movement of things.

When she set the tea and crackers down on the professor's desk, he didn't acknowledge her. She noticed that a few books written by him were on the table. *A Study of the Feeble-Minded*, one of the titles read.

"Mauve?" He looked up at her, his spectacle lenses flashing with late afternoon light. "Was there something else?"

She realized that she'd been staring at the book for a while, and she must have slipped into one of her "states," as her mother called them.

"No, sir," she said. She curtsied and left the room.

She worked on her quilt that evening, slowly shifting through fabrics of her favorite color. She cut the fabric into isosceles triangles and listened to the radio until she dozed off.

She woke a while later, disturbed by the crick in her neck. The lamp on her nightstand was still on, and she'd dropped her scissors. As she stretched her neck to the left, she saw that the door to her room was slightly ajar. She saw a shadow rushing away.

Mauve jumped. She listened for footsteps and checked the hallway as she closed the door. He was long gone.

Quentin was wrapped in a cocoon of purple fibers. The field where she worked bloomed before his eyes, hill after hill of lavender, plum, and mauve, spreading out as far as the eye can see. She floated in the air, stitching glittering, jewel-encrusted fabric to the cobalt drape of the sky. Her needle flashed. The star shapes flamed and glowed after she placed them. Her feet hovered over blossom heads.

Hill after hill passed, a blur of green, farmhouses, and cows. His dad was trying to talk to him.

"I'm guessing that you're pretty mad at me. I don't blame you. It must seem like I'm crazy. I've uprooted you from the only life that you know, away from your friends, just when you might need familiar things the most . . ."

Heat mirages danced on the horizon, and static from the radio bled songs in shards. The world was full of ghosts, ghosts of sound, ghosts of the road.

" . . . I had to get away, Quentin. Chicago was full of her. She was everywhere. And when this job offer came, I . . ."

Quentin saw plowed fields, as neat as squares on a quilt. He passed an ostrich farm. The tall, skinny birds looked out of place in this world.

"It's not so bad, you know. I grew up here. Small-town life has its own pace, and it's much more relaxing . . ."

He passed by a field of flowers. Miles upon miles of purple blossoms spilled out over the edge of the world. They nodded their heads in the breeze from the passing traffic.

"It's OK," Quentin said to shut his dad up.

Afterwards, things went back to normal. She cooked his meals, cleaned the house, and went to church on Sundays. Her days and weeks were routine, and they slipped into months and seasons. Sunny mornings and gray, rain-filled ones were the same to her. The day was divided into tasks and chores, and the nights were filled with dreamless slumber.

The times she had to speak to the professor weren't difficult at all. She could look straight at him and not see his face or his body. He was an indistinct shape, an absence given form. He was nothing. She didn't hear his voice. The instructions he gave just appeared in her mind somehow. She didn't examine why too closely.

She would take her dinner in her room, but she wouldn't eat much. Food made her feel nauseated. At first, she thought that maybe something lived inside her belly. But it was clear after a while that nothing lived there. She still bled. She didn't eat because food was connected to living.

Her evenings were special, the time of day she always looked forward to. There was a ritual to it all: First, Mauve lit a few candles, mostly for effect. She would turn on the radio and then work on the quilt. As the silver needle sparkled through the fabric, she would go to the place where flowers covered the hillside and the stars spangled the sky. She sewed herself inside the world of thread, stitch, and fabric. The pattern of the quilt became clear then, in this space. She made an endless field of flowers, a world where angels watched her and love was just over the horizon. It was a small bit of time, as small as thimble, but it was hers. Petals were bright here, and they never withered.

Once, she caught him looking at her afterwards. This was before he became the absence.

She recalled it was a terrifying moment, and truly thought it couldn't happen again. She'd bitten his finger and peed on him. But that hadn't stopped him, not even throwing the unfinished quilt over her body. It was a childish thing to do, the sort of thing a feebleminded fool might do. Of course, he would rip the quilt off her body, and rip her clothes, like he did before. And he would burn her insides.

It was cool beneath the quilt. And she dived into it, the sea of flowers—cool irises and furry African violets, hydrangeas, and bluebells. Tulips covered her face. The flowers grew out of her brown earth body and hid her female form. The professor blinked, not seeing her, and moved on.

Now, he could never see her properly, just as she could never see him. She was earth and fabric. Both her earth body and her real body were protected by flowers.

"I'm going to catch a movie, Quentin. Why don't you come with me?"

"No, I'm okay." Quentin stared at the computer screen and watched the slow dance of equalization bars. Sound waves were like threads, he thought. Strands that could be stretched across a loom and turned into a tapestry.

"Son?" His father still stood in the doorway. "You sure? I mean, we don't have to go to a movie. We can eat out. I heard that there's a great place about twenty minutes away that makes excellent Italian food. It's been there forever."

Quentin glanced at his father. He saw nothing. His face, the arrangement of his features, was a mystery to him. Was he sad? Was Quentin supposed to react somehow?

He tried, "Maybe some other time."

Even when he was awake, Quentin saw Mauve everywhere, both the color and the woman. It's there, on a woman's scarf. He saw it in the hair dye of a young punk woman, or on a gazebo with a roof covered in bougainvillea. She would like that, he thought.

Quentin waited for the night, when he could curl up beneath Mauve's quilt. He doesn't always see her quiet, woven world. But she was always there. Satiny soft, he sometimes felt her swimming within the quilt. Something brushed against him in the thin mesh between them.

Quentin saw her in the field of purple flowers. He was closer to her than ever before. He watched for a while as she repaired the wing of a moth. The creature patiently hovered over a tulip as Mauve's needle healed the wing. She worked with such precision and concentration, she hardly noticed when he walked up behind her. When she finished, the silver moth fluttered away.

"Mauve," he said to her softly.

She faced him. Mauve was shorter than he was, and her eyes were a lovely shade of clear brown somewhere between honey and amber. Her dress of violets moved with the breeze, with the rest of the flowers of the field that she'd made. She held the needle in front of her like a knife.

"I didn't make you," she said after a while. "I didn't think anyone could find me, ever. How did you find me?"

Quentin shrugged. "How did you make this?" His gesture took in the woven world.

She lowered the needle, perhaps conceding the point. They both sat down on the soft earth and watched the unchanging sky above them.

"It's coming apart, you know," she said.

Quentin saw a section of the sky that was threadbare. In the distance, a few hills had faded. A few stars dangled, threatening to fall.

"I guess you can't stay here forever." He glanced at her. Mauve stared out into space, maybe remembering why she'd come here in the first place. "He's gone. Long gone."

When she turned back to him, there were tears in her eyes. Her eyes glistened like stars. She wiped them away, stood up, and picked up a frayed violet. Mauve tore off a damaged petal and let it fall to ground.

Quentin woke up covered in dried petals. He sat up and found that the quilt was destroyed, spread in pieces around the room. Petals, bright and withered, filled his bed and spilled out onto the floor. Some were soft as new skin while others were blackened and curled. A few dead moths were strewn about, their wings full of holes, their filigree bodies forever frozen.

"Mauve!" The word escaped his lips. In the corner of the room, he saw an unmolested swath of fabric on the floor. It was the fallen sky, pierced with stars. As he moved toward it, his bare foot stepped on a still-cooling chip of heaven. It burned him, so he jumped back, landing on his rear.

The piece of sky moved. There was something underneath it—or within it, struggling to get out.

Time unknotted and unraveled as the fragment rose above the floor. It floated, becoming an upside down V, the skirt of a dress. Mauve formed out of fabric—a torso and two arms of cinnamon burst through thread and ether.

Mauve stood in a puddle of thread, dead petals, and moths, wearing a dress of purple flowers that glowed. She looked at Quentin. He couldn't really say what emotion played across her face, but he knew that it wasn't fear.

"Welcome back, Mauve," he said, because it sounded like the right thing to say.

CASSANDRA CLARE

Have You Ever Seen a Shoggoth?

WHEN I CAME INTO THE THIRD-FLOOR BATHROOM TUESDAY morning, *they* were beating Wendell James up for approximately the one zillionth time this school year.

Wendell James is the weirdest kid in Wilton High's ninth-grade class and *they* are Troy Garroway, Jesse Wegman, and Billy Pritchard, the biggest, meanest kids in the whole school. They were standing over Wen like prison guards in an exploitation flick, their sweatshirt sleeves pushed up to their elbows. Wendell was lying on the floor, hands at his sides, blood pooling under his nose. He never even tried to fight them off. He wasn't that type.

I'm not that type either. If you think this is one of those stories where I save unpopular, picked-on Wen from the bullies by appealing to their humanity—reminding them of their moms, telling them we're all the same underneath, and making them cry tears of bitter remorse—well, think again. This isn't that story and I'm not that kind of guy. High school is a war zone and I get by on not being noticed. So when I saw them whaling on Wen in the bathroom, I scrunched my head down, washed my hands real quick at the sink, and left.

I thought I saw Wendell watching me as I went. He was lying hunched against the bathroom wall just under some smeared graffiti—some kind of nonsense word like *ryleh*, repeated over and over. Behind his glasses his yellowy eyes were big and staring. I pulled my hood up and scuttled out.

I didn't think about Wen again for a while, until we both ended up in detention together. There was no one else in the room but us so I didn't see the harm in replying when he asked me what I was in there for. "Downloading porn on the library computers," I told him. It was the truth.

"I wrote graffiti on the bathroom wall," he said.

That didn't seem like Wen. It was hard to put a finger on what was so weird about him. He was little, so little he looked like he should still be in sixth grade. He had pale skin, almost translucent, with blue veins showing through at the temples. His hair was long, lank, and greasy, and he wore black every day, nothing but black.

"You mean Jesse and Troy graffitied the bathroom wall and pinned it on you," I said.

He just smiled vaguely. His smile was creepy too. "No, it was me," he said. "I did it."

I wondered if maybe he was developing Stockholm syndrome, where you get attached to people who torture you. Or maybe he was just hoping that if he did something normal, like scrawling graffiti on the bathroom wall, he would fit in more.

Everyone fits into some kind of slot in high school. It's

how you stay safe. You might be sporty, in band, a drama geek, a brainiac, a hipster, dedicated to saving the earth, or whatever. You would have thought Wen, with all that black, would have hung out with the Goth kids and their silver skull rings and artfully ripped fishnets. But it seemed like he creeped them out too. It was something about his eyes. They bulged sort of fishy—like a frog's eyes—and they followed you wherever you went.

"If you say so," I said, but I didn't believe him, not till I walked into the third-floor bathroom again a few weeks later and found Wen in there, scrawling words on the wall with a big piece of black grease paint. He turned around when I came in, but when he saw it was me he just smiled that creepy smile.

"What are you writing?" I asked. He didn't answer me, but he moved aside so I could see. I was disappointed. It was just a bunch of made-up words with exclamation points after them: *Ia-R'lyeh Cthulu fhtagn flgagnl id Ia! Shub-Niggurath!*

"Is that English?" I asked.

His creepy smile flickered. "Sort of," he said. "Listen, have you ever seen a *shoggoth?*"

"Uh, no," I said, thinking that Wen clearly was pretty crazy, though whether he'd started out crazy or had been driven crazy by Troy and his gang was anyone's guess. "Do I want to?"

The smile came back. "Probably not."

I didn't say anything. I didn't have to, because the bathroom door banged open and Billy, Jesse, and Troy came in swaggering. Their cold eyes slid right over me as if I weren't even there and fixed right on Wen. "I thought I told you to stop scribbling your crazy garbage all over the walls, freak," said Troy, getting right up in Wen's face. Billy and Jesse were

circling the two of them like sharks. That's when I did something totally uncharacteristic for me, something I knew I'd
live to regret.

"Come on, Wen," I said. "Let's just get out of here."

Wen rolled his big, froggy eyes around to look at me. He
almost looked surprised, but since his eyes always bulged it was
hard to tell. Troy and the others looked at me too. "You know
this freak?" Troy fisted the front of Wen's shirt. Jesse came up
to Wen then and kicked him in the back of the knees. Wen
went right down like a sack of rocks. My feet sort of took off
without me and I realized I was backed up to the bathroom
door. Troy looked over at me, smirking. "That's right," he said.
"Get out of here."

I got out of there, but I looked back once as the door
closed behind me. I saw Wen curled up on the ground as the
others kicked him. He wasn't moving, but something else was.
The words he'd scrawled on the walls looked like they were
moving, sort of crawling. That's when I ran.

When I got home that night I got on the Internet and
looked online for *Shub-Niggurath* and *shoggoth*. It turns out they
weren't nonsense words after all. Shub-Niggurath was an
Outer God, a powerful deity who was locked up in some sort
of prison with a bunch of other dark gods like him—except
the prisons weren't really prisons, they were dimensions close
to our own. Shub-Niggurath and the other gods were always
trying to break through and get into our dimension, though it
didn't say why. The other gods had names like Yog-Sothoth,
the Dweller on the Threshold; Azathoth, Lord of All Things;
and Nyarlathotep, the Crawling Chaos.

I didn't find out what a shoggoth was, though. In the end
I bought the *Necronomicon* a book that was supposed to explain

all this stuff, off Amazon.com. Then I went to sleep, or tried to. All night, things with black tentacles flapped and screamed in my dreams.

The next day at school I went straight to the third-floor bathroom, but all the words on the wall were gone. When I left, I found Wen standing in the hallway, even though first-period classes had already started and he should have been downstairs in World History. He had a bruised cheek and a split lip, and his left arm was wrapped up in bandages. I guess Troy and the rest of them had worked him over pretty good after I'd run off. He was staring into space but he sort of snapped to attention when he saw me.

"You," he said mildly. "How come you're always up here?"

I thought about it for a second. "Nobody uses the bathroom up here," I said. "I avoid people when I can. I guess I'm afraid of them."

"Really?" He seemed sort of interested. "I just hate them. People, I mean."

I was going to say that considering the way Troy and his gang were always beating up on him, he might want to start being afraid of people, but when I opened my mouth to say it, something else came out instead. "I know what Shub-Niggurath is," I told him. "I bought the *Necronomicon* too. Online. Amazon had it 'Better Together' with a book called *Nameless Cults,* so I got them both for $33.95 plus shipping."

He seemed to shake himself then, and looked at me thoughtfully with his big yellow eyes. "Really? The Outer Gods interest you?"

I could have told him that it was his complete craziness that interested me, but I didn't. "Sure. I like horror stuff."

His eyes gleamed. "I've got something I'm sure you'd like to see," he said. "Meet me out in front of school by the mascot statue in ten minutes and I'll show you."

I said something about first-period history class, but I knew I sounded unconvincing. Class had already started and it's generally better to miss one totally than show up twenty minutes late. Besides, I don't mind hanging around outside school when there's nobody else there. It's quiet. I left Wen and headed outside, where I sat in front of the mascot statue, listened to tunes, and read a copy of *Naruto* that I'd been carrying around in my bag. After a while I heard a noise that sounded like a wave crashing. I pulled my earbuds out and looked back at the school.

It looked mostly the same—a big brick and cement square with metal guards over all the windows—except that now there were huge black tentacles like the fronds of a giant sea plant waving all around it. I can't explain how huge the tentacles were. Each one of them was covered with suckers that were bigger than the biggest satellite dish. My iPod fell on the ground and cracked but I didn't notice. The tentacles stopped waving because they were gripping the school in a hug so tight that cracks were running up and down the concrete, and bricks were falling and smashing to the ground, sending up puffs of red powder. I thought I saw white faces pressed to the glass of one of the first-floor classroom windows—it might have been World History—before the whole structure gave a huge groaning scream and was yanked down through the earth and out of sight. For a moment nothing remained on the surface but a boiling mass of tentacles, and then those were gone too, and there was nothing but a flat and featureless plain, bare as a parking lot, where the school had stood.

I walked home after that. There didn't seem to be much else to do.

There have been some reporters hanging around my house for the past few days, wanting to know what it was like to be the only survivor of what they're calling a "seismic event." In other words, they think it was an earthquake. I haven't told them anything different.

Sometimes I think about Wen and how he didn't come out of the school that day, even though he told me to get outside. I guess he saved me, but I wonder why he didn't save himself when he called the Outer Gods through. That's who it was, of course. The Outer Gods came through where the walls were thin and yanked the whole school back to their own hellish dimension. But as for Wen . . . I wonder. There were all sorts of stories online about people bringing the Outer Gods through to this world, but there were other stories too. Stories about people *becoming* the Outer Gods. Especially people with big, staring, froglike eyes . . .

My mind keeps going back to that day and what I saw. Those tentacles were huge. Bigger than anything I could have imagined. Then something heaved itself up over the school—a shapeless, faceless thing. Actually, it wasn't shapeless. It had a shape, just a shape that was all wrong, with thin slits all over it that might have been mouths and might have been something else. The only recognizable feature of the face was a pair of big, yellowish, staring eyes—they stared at *me* as the school frothed and vanished . . .

But I try not to think about that stuff. My parents said they're sending me to private school next year. They come in to check on me all the time, like they're scared of what I might be doing in my room with the door shut and the music playing low. That's rich, isn't it? My parents scared of me? I wonder if Wen's parents were scared of him. No one knows. No one's seen them since what happened to the high school.

One day, the package from Amazon with the books in it showed up at my house. I threw it away at first. Then I fished it out of the trash later. The books are under my bed now. Sometimes I think I can hear them whispering to me at night. They tell me how hard it is to start over at another school, how I'll never fit in. They tell me how everyone will stare at me, the only survivor of the Wilton Disaster, how they'll call me a freak and a monster. They tell me how it all starts with charcoal scrawling on a bathroom wall or under some stairs, in the dark where nobody goes. They tell me that even though high school is hell, there are other hells, maybe even some where I might find that I belong. I try to suppress the whispers, say I'll never use the books, that I don't need those words. But they're there, waiting for me—in case I ever need to find them.

LAWRENCE M. SCHOEN

The Amulet of Winter

M OST ALLEY-BORN CUTPURSES HAVE LOST THREE OR MORE fingers to local justice before they hit puberty, but not Aleks. At fifteen he not only had all his digits intact, but had developed an impressive repertoire of burglary skills and acrobatic prowess. His instincts were solid and he'd never been caught. If this combination of circumstances made him cocky, it had also brought him a patron. Aleks worked for a mage.

An older thief would have run from such employment. Aleks saw it as a challenge and an opportunity to learn the kind of things the alleys could never teach him. For example, wizards tend to create magical artifacts with specific intentions, even though the things themselves often end up being used for other purposes. So it was with the Amulet of Winter, a fabled trinket Aleks had never heard of until the day Collin sent him to the Calentine's city to steal it.

Aleks didn't anticipate any problems. True, this was his

first trip to a real city, and a far cry from the village marketplace where he had perfected the ways of snatch and grab before Collin took him on. But Aleks was young and full of himself. Before leaving he'd equipped with everything he might need, from a coil of rope to his lock-picking tools to a spare knife blade hidden behind the obvious knife in his boot. He also carried a few nonstandard tricks the mage had provided to back him up. Though the Keep of the Calentine still lay days' travel away, on the morning he set off, Aleks counted the amulet as already his.

The city only existed because of the Amulet of Winter. Centuries ago the first Calentine had created a fertile valley amidst the surrounding desert, and his successors used the amulet to renew the enchantment with a ritual every seven years. Nonetheless, Collin insisted the artifact had another purpose, something involving gateways into ancient times when the world had been covered with ice. Aleks hadn't followed the explanation—he didn't need to. That was mage business. He just had to steal the thing.

He headed south and after several days encountered a brandy-woman on her way to offer her wares to the Calentine. Though small for his age, Aleks was strong, and after some haggling entered into her service for an eight bit per day, to be paid after the brandywoman completed her sale. Aleks didn't care that he'd never collect his wages. For the next few days he walked alongside the second of two wagons and, under the watchful gaze of her apprentice, he traveled with them across the desert, down into the cool valley, and eventually through the gates of the Keep of the Calentine.

More than a dozen wagons were scattered about,

each with one or two of the Calentine's household dressed in overshirts of burgundy and blue, shouting instructions and directions. The more garishly painted wagons belonged to traders from across the eastern sea, bearish looking men offering lenses and tubes of unfamiliar wood. Closer at hand, Aleks noted a troupe of traveling acrobats and another of actors dressed in outlandish costumes full of dyed feathers and tassels. Beyond these, four of the Calentine's people argued with ten green-cloaked scholars from the College in the Wood, far to the south. Farther along, a trio of monks under a vow of silence gazed stonily at a young woman in burgundy and blue who kept yelling at them as if they were deaf rather than mute. And just past them a small, dark-skinned boy rode on the head of a gray beast larger than a house, with tusks like a wild boar's but bigger, and a snout that quested about, long and sinuous, moving as if possessed of a life of its own.

Aleks soaked it all in, reveling in the glorious chaos. The vibrancy and excitement here exceeded market day back in his simple village a hundredfold, filling him with such joy that he momentarily forgot what he had come to do. But then his purpose reasserted itself and Aleks remembered to behave like a professional. He became, if not jaded, then at least inured. He climbed down from the second wagon as a stableboy arrived. He and the apprentice unhitched the horses and let the boy lead them to feed and fresh water. Wonderment filled the air, and endless distraction lay all about. Aleks smiled. It would make his own work that much easier.

As the last light faded, servants ran through,

lighting torches. Guards in the Calentine's colors directed the traders, along with the scholars and monks, to the feasting hall to present themselves, their merchandise, and petitions, to the Calentine himself amidst entertainment, food, and wine. This was mere formality, a noble's perverse sense of amusement, or so the brandywoman had told Aleks on the way to the city. The Calentine's steward would visit each trader in the morning to negotiate on his lord's behalf. The lot of them would be on their way before midday, making room for the next wave of travelers, merchants, and petitioners.

The entertainers had a different fate. Aleks watched as they followed somewhat behind the others, each troupe biding its time until called to perform. If the Calentine enjoyed the show they might stay another night; if not, they, too, would leave in the morning.

Aleks, along with the rest, was left behind in the courtyard. Servants and apprentices, assistants and acolytes, were beneath the Calentine's notice. They busied themselves with a myriad tasks, from taking final inventories to making last-minute repairs, from serving the needs of their horses and other livestock to laying out their masters' best garments for the morning's negotiations. Aleks did his share of work alongside the brandywoman's apprentice, biding his time.

Near enough to two hours had passed when a servant in burgundy and blue stepped into the courtyard and clapped her hands above her head for attention. To Aleks's surprise, she invited everyone into the hall and then nimbly stepped out of the way to avoid being trampled. Like a hungry tide they rushed the entrance, Aleks among them. They scattered once inside, eager to claim a share of whatever was left.

Plenty remained. Aleks noted the carnage of a respectable meal laid out across more than a dozen tables. The feast had defeated the men and women who had attacked it. Though much of the table was bare, more than a few wooden platters were still piled high with slabs of wild boar meat, coarse-grained loaves, blue- and purple-veined cheeses, and candied turnips. The guests had eaten and drunk while the players and jugglers entertained. Aleks caught a brief glimpse of the Calentine, tall and lanky with dark hair and a trim beard. Like his servants, he was dressed all in burgundy and blue, but of rich fabrics that gleamed in the torchlight. As Aleks watched, the noble and several of his court departed through a door that opened onto a colonnade, half laughing to themselves at some jape of a puppeteer's show. No one seemed to take notice.

A friendly pandemonium had already descended as traders and scholars, players and petitioners, broke off into small groups to share lies and tales and drunken camaraderie. They appeared content to drink still more of the Calentine's wine and ale, and claim some spot of floor before the wide hearth and bed down for the night. The servants and apprentices followed their masters' example once they ate. They had to settle for sleeping spots at the other end of the hall, but comfortable enough with the heat of so many bodies.

Aleks hung back as the others laid claim to one space or another and set out their bedrolls. He waited to ensure himself a spot in a shadowed nook beneath an open window. He wouldn't have enough room to be comfortable, but it would allow a convenient and unnoticed escape. Cold air flowed down on him, and the stone beneath his back felt damp. He fidgeted, hoping the combination wouldn't cause him to cramp up before he could slip away without notice. Without warning, a monk squeezed in alongside him, determined to claim half of Aleks's meager floor space. Aleks scowled at the crowding, and though the monk gave him a sympathetic look he didn't offer to move. Aleks regarded the intruder, spared a glance to the window above their heads, and decided on a solution to the problem of an unwanted witness. He had prepared to deal with a chance encounter with one of the Calentine's guards, and the plan would serve here as well. From within his shirt, Aleks withdrew a small flask he had liberated from the brandywoman's wagon. He offered it to the monk.

"Care for a swallow?" he whispered, passing the container. The silent monk nodded, and took a hesitant sip. He smiled and took a larger gulp and then returned the flask. Aleks raised it to his own lips, feigned a drink, and then put it away. He folded his hands over his chest, closed his eyes, and waited.

The brandy was, of course, tainted. Aleks had used the sleeping powder on two previous jobs he'd done for Collin, usually mixing it with cheap wine. A few grains of it combined with the potent alcohol created an effective sleep aid. A few minutes later, the monk was snoring like a fat bear in winter. Aleks wondered if snoring violated the monk's vow of silence.

He bided his time until both the torches and hearth burned low. The room swirled in shadows and Aleks's nook lay in full darkness. He eased himself out from alongside the monk, and with unnecessary stealth, pulled himself up onto the window ledge and slipped silently from the feast hall. He landed back in the courtyard and darted around to the same colonnade the Calentine had taken earlier, followed that to an open door, and down a narrow corridor. Most keeps shared many common elements of construction, layout, and design. He had managed a good look at the general shape of the outer buildings while stabling the horses and had a fair idea where he would find the amulet that had drawn him here.

Magic and mages liked altitude and solitude. Nine of every ten of the enchanted rings, talismans, and wards that he had pilfered, both before and since entering Collin's service, had been taken from the top of towers rising in isolation above the other floors of a building. Why should the Calentine be any different? Aleks continued down the hallway, pausing to look along both directions of a connecting passage. He took the route that led deeper into the keep. If his mental map held, it would lead him to the tallest of the Calentine's three towers.

Even at this late hour the keep remained active. Torches burned at intervals along the hallway, creating brief pools of light throughout the longer lengths of darkness. Aleks clung to the dark, avoiding the notice of the servants hurrying past on errands, and the liveried guards walking their patrols. By starts and stops he made his way to the end of the hall and the winding stair that was the third tower's only access. Mindful of shadows that might cover treacherous steps, Aleks ascended two full turns of the stair. He ignored the second-floor landing, assuming it held only apartments for the Calentine and his guests. Higher still was where the magic would be.

The third-floor landing contained a single door with torches set on either side. Five locks stood above the door's handle, each of them gleaming with a distinctive blue metal. Collin had described such locks to him. At a time of dire need a simple word could either seal or unseal them all in an instant—it was single-use magic. For daily use the locks responded to a set of five traditional keys. Aleks pulled his set of less traditional picks from their hiding spot in his boot and set to work, making a wager with himself that he could pop each lock more quickly than the one before it. Minutes later, he pulled the door open and stepped into the room.

His first thought was that Collin would have loved the place. It seemed larger than could exist at the top of the tower, a good-sized room, with every bit of every wall shelved full of books, floor to high ceiling. A massive pale globe, larger than a man could wrap his arms around, hung from above and somehow provided unshadowed and constant illumination. A long table of blond, local wood occupied the center of the room, surrounded by a complement of eight heavy chairs. Several bookstands with tiny brass wheels stood just away from the walls, holding volumes, some open, and some closed. At the opposite end of the room, two wide windows provided the sole relief from the sea of books. Mounted in a case on the sliver of wall between the windows lay the object of Aleks's desire: the Amulet of Winter.

It called to him, an ornate bauble of platinum and sapphire, an elegant broach no larger than a peach pit. It lay pinned in its wooden case by a slender pane of crystal, nestled securely to curling layers of cream-colored silk. It would be so simple to open the case and take it, or snatch the case itself; it wasn't large. Aleks knew better. Magic always protected magic. He knelt just inside the doorway and searched the room for trip wires. He found none. He studied the pattern of wear on the broad flagstones that

made up the floor, seeking signs of interrupted strolls or avoided stones. Nothing was amiss. He closed his eyes and sought the stillness inside himself as Collin had taught him, and felt for the tingle of magic that would indicate potential traps. The result made him gasp. Magic lay all around him. It filled the room itself, creeping into every corner and crevice, hanging in the very air. The entire library was a trap.

He opened his eyes and stared as something began to form at the far end of the room by the base of the windows. Fog frothed and congealed into vapors. The vapors swirled, thickened, and rose to a shoulder-height mist. The mist coalesced and solidified into the figure of a young woman with silvery hair and dark eyes. The eyes stared into his. She raised one hand, stretched it out to him, and abruptly closed the fingers in a fist. The door at his back shut with a soundless rush, bumping Aleks forward into the room. She lowered her hand and began to walk around the table towards him.

"You are not supposed to be here," she said. "But now that you're here, understand that I cannot let you leave."

Aleks took a step into the room, of his own volition this time. One did not need to be a master thief to realize that a girl manifesting out of vapor called for caution and outright deception. "Excuse me, I must be lost. I was supposed to meet someone, and I guess I got the directions wrong. I'm sorry if I've caused you any trouble, I'll just be on my way." He placed one hand on the door handle but it wouldn't move.

As she came closer, Aleks realized she was just a girl, younger than he'd first thought, probably no more than his own age.

She wore a simple burgundy dress with a blue sash just below her breasts. Solid now, she walked with an easy grace. A blur of grays and white gave her hair a metallic look as it cascaded over her shoulders. Her skin was pale and unattractive, but the eerie darkness of her eyes made the strongest impression. There was a secret hidden in those eyes.

"You lie very smoothly, I will grant you," she said, her hand still closed in a fist. "When my master comes, if it proves you are telling the truth, I will beg your forgiveness for not believing you. But in either case, we'll wait until he comes."

"Do you expect him soon?" asked Aleks, trying to remain casual and glancing around the room. "My friend is probably looking for me, and I'd hate to miss him. We have so much to talk about."

"I'm sure it will seem very soon to you." She frowned. "Although, if you really are telling the truth I fear your friend will have given up seeking you before you leave."

"Why is that? You just said your master would arrive shortly."

She shook her head and tendrils of silvery gray flew about her face. "No, I said it would *seem* soon to you. This is the library of the Calentine, and time is different here."

"The library? Now I know I'm in the wrong place." Aleks turned to the door and tried the handle again. "Would you mind helping me with the door here? It seems to be stuck. Poor Ollie, he must be worrying where I am."

"The door isn't stuck. I'm holding it closed. And I don't believe you came here by accident. If you had, why didn't you just step in? You stood at the door and looked around. You *crouched* and looked around."

He shrugged. He didn't much care for lying anyway. "Well,

you have me there. But be fair now, I didn't know I was being watched."

"I am Seyn," the girl said, as if that explained everything. "I keep the library. In many ways I *am* the library. I know everything in here—every book upon the shelves, every person who has ever entered."

Aleks nodded. It wouldn't hurt to be polite even though he doubted her words. How could this girl be the library? An enchanted guardian, perhaps, though even that seemed absurd given her youth. There was more magic involved in this place than just the amulet he had come for.

"I have a friend who can read. I wonder if he's read any of these books?" Aleks began walking away from Seyn, keeping the table between them. He made a show of looking all around. He tapped a finger against his chin as he studied the shelves.

"That's not very likely. Nothing that belongs to the library can leave here except by my permission or the Calentine's own hand. Only a few books have ever left this room. Most have been here since the Calentine's arrival."

"Arrival? You mean the first Calentine? How would you know a thing like that?" asked Aleks.

She shrugged. "My mother was one of his lady wife's servants. When he built this library, I was chosen to tend it. I've cataloged each book as it was brought in."

Aleks held his breath and felt himself pale. More than three hundred years had passed since the first Calentine built his keep in the valley.

"Really? You don't look old enough to have seen sixteen summers, let alone served the first Calentine."

Seyn frowned at him again. "You don't listen carefully.

I told you, time is different here. It barely moves at all unless someone comes to use the library and opens the door. When the Calentine needs my assistance, or if he has allowed another to make use of the books, time inside is much as it is outside. But since you don't belong here I've begun slowing it. Eventually, the Calentine will come again, though it might not be until the next festival, years away."

"Years?"

"Less than a day for us, though. The library doesn't follow the same stream of time as the rest of the world."

"But you said you were causing it," said Aleks.

She shrugged again. "I am the library. I keep this place. Nothing leaves that belongs to it, and visitors remain until I permit them to leave. You should have learned this before you tried to steal one of my books."

"I'm not here to steal any of your precious books," said Aleks as he continued moving around the table, turning when he reached the back of the room with its pair of windows. The table stood between them. The small case with the Amulet of Winter lay within reach behind him.

"Not a book? Then what?" she asked.

"This!" cried Aleks as he plucked the case from the wall. His free hand pulled a small pouch from around his neck, another of Collin's preparations. He spilled its contents onto the table—a round bit of gray glass—and shielded his eyes. The sun pearl flared. Its brilliance turned the enclosed room to purest white. Aleks used the diversion to move to the right-hand window. He braced his back against the adjacent wall of books and drove his foot into the frame. Behind him Seyn flinched but nothing else happened. The glass didn't break. The frame didn't shatter. The window didn't move.

"Stop that," she said as the sun pearl's light died away. "Why won't you listen to anything I say? I told you, nothing leaves the library. How much of a demonstration do you need?" Blinking, she joined him at the back of the library and placed her hand upon the other window. It opened outward at her touch. "There, that's what you wanted, isn't it? Take a look. You would have fallen to your death."

"I brought rope," Aleks said somewhat sheepishly.

She stepped back. "Fine. Secure your rope then. Use a table leg. See how well your plan would work. Go on."

Aleks flinched at her orders. She didn't sound like any of the girls he knew, not that he knew very many. Perfecting his craft as a thief hadn't left much time for more traditional activities. Still, other than her pallor, the girl looked pretty enough. Aleks found himself wondering what her hair smelled like. He shook the thought from his head. All the time issues confused him. Was she hundreds of years old or not? It didn't matter. He lifted his shirt and began uncoiling the rope he had hidden there, securing one end around the table's nearest stout leg. He flung the rest of the rope out the open window. It didn't fall. The rope hung in the air, just outside the window's frame, suspended. He stared at it, his hands clutching the case with the amulet.

"Nothing leaves," repeated Seyn. "Even if I had let you open the window you wouldn't have gotten out. Not if I didn't want it. Go on. Try again. Throw the case out the window. Maybe you have an accomplice waiting on the ground below to catch it. Maybe that will work."

Aleks stepped closer to the open window, trusting his back to the girl. He raised the case in front of him, deftly slipped two fingers inside to grasp and palm the amulet, then hurled the case with all his strength. It traveled about as far as the rope had, then stopped.

"Nothing leaves," he murmured.

"Good, maybe you *can* learn." She reached past him, retrieved the case from midair and returned it to its space on the wall. All on its own the window snapped back into place, carrying Aleks's rope back into the room, where it fell to the floor. "It takes a few hours to slow the library all the way down, so unless someone saw you come in or discovers you're not where you're supposed to be, you have a bit of a wait. Have a seat; you might as well be comfortable. You're welcome to read if you want to. You won't get another chance."

"I can't read," said Aleks. He stalked away from her, back to the door, and tried the handle again. It still wouldn't move.

"Would you like me to read to you? There are several books that you might like. I could read you tales of other thieves if you want. It might help you pass the time."

Aleks smirked. "Dashing fellows of remarkable skill and daring, no doubt?"

Seyn returned the smile. "Certainly they all thought so. Curiously, all of them were significantly taller than you."

Aleks ignored the jibe. "Have you read every book in here?"

"You really don't listen, do you? I told you, I am the library. The library is me. I know every word on every page of every book in this room."

"I'm sorry. It just sounds so unreal. This is strange for me. I'm not used to having the people I steal from offer to entertain me while I'm trying to make off with their stuff."

She smiled again. "That's because you can't. You

don't think you're the first person to try to steal from the Calentine's library? I've been through this many times, and it's simpler, easier, to be courteous and polite. You can't escape, so you might as well wait comfortably."

"What exactly are we waiting for?"

Seyn bit her lip and Aleks wondered at her suddenly sad expression. "No one's tried to steal the amulet during the current Calentine's reign, but it's happened several times since the creation of the library. Historically, the ruling Calentine makes an example of the would-be thief. It has occasioned the addition of several treatises on torture to my shelves."

The color drained from Aleks's face as the realities of being captured sunk in. "I'm going to be tortured?"

The girl nodded. "Quite slowly, according to the books. You'll die eventually, and your body will be kept to be displayed at the next festival day, when the Calentine uses the amulet to renew the valley's enchantment."

"I'd rather not be tortured, or killed, or turned into some festival ornament."

"I can't imagine anyone who would," said Seyn, "but it's out of my hands. I'm sorry."

"How is it out of your hands? Why not just let me go? I promise I'll never bother you or your library again."

Seyn shook her head. "I can't do that. We both know you're a liar and a thief. You'd just try again. Or word would get out that a thief had escaped, and others would come that much sooner. Sorry."

Aleks stepped away from the door, trying to figure a way out of this trap. He pulled a chair back from the table and settled into it. "Fine, I understand about the rope and the case not being able to go out the window, but why didn't the other window shatter when I kicked it?"

"It's part of the enchantment, from when the first Calentine built this. As archivist, as long as I am in the library, I cannot be harmed."

"What does that have to with the window?"

She rolled her eyes. "The window is part of the library. And I am the library—"

Aleks nodded, "—which makes the window a part of you. And you cannot be harmed. That's some enchantment."

"The first Calentine was a very powerful mage, and a great man. Should I read you a story about him? There are seventeen separate biographies of the different Calentines that have ruled, and he is mentioned in each of them."

"Why not?" Aleks shrugged, reaching a hand into his shirt and coming out with the small brandy flask. He offered it to her. "As you say, I've got plenty of time. Here, you're going out of your way to be so civil, more or less. The least I can do is share with you."

"What is that?"

"Brandy. It's quite good."

"I've never had brandy, only wine." She smiled and Aleks had to admit that she looked lovely when she did so. "You're the first thief to offer me anything in return. That's very nice of you. Thank you."

"Just take a sip or two at first. It's very strong. It tastes a bit foul the first time you drink it, but it makes a nice, warm burning feeling down your throat if you take a good sized swallow."

She took the flask from him, raising it to her lips with hesitation. Her nose crinkled a bit in disgust at the initial taste, then relaxed as she swallowed. She took another sip and returned the flask. Aleks brought it to his own lips and pretended to drink deeply while keeping the mouth of the flask sealed with his tongue. He made a great show of swallowing, wiped his lips with the back of his hand in satisfaction, and passed the flask back. She drank again, a larger gulp and began coughing. Aleks took the flask from her, faked another swig, and sealed it.

"There, now despite whatever happens, we've shared a drink." Aleks gestured at a nearby chair. "Why don't you sit down and tell me about the first Calentine. I bet he was a fascinating man."

"He was a visionary, really." She sat across from Aleks and began to tell him tales from the first of the seventeen biographies. She was midway through her second story, having reached the part where the Calentine first used the Amulet of Winter to create the lush valley in the midst of a barren land, when she slumped over. Her head fell across her outstretched arms upon the table, her silvery hair pooling all around her.

Aleks chuckled. "No harm, just a deep sleep." He hurried to the door, but the handle still wouldn't budge. He stepped back to the table, lifted the archivist into his arms, and carried her over. She hiccoughed once in her sleep but otherwise didn't stir. Aleks propped her against the door's frame, laid her hand upon the handle and his own hand on top of hers. He pressed down. The handle turned and the door swung open. He caught her before she could fall, pressed her back against the jamb of the open door and then eased her to the floor.

He leaned out, looked around, and saw no one on the

landing. Aleks started to move forward and almost fell. Something was holding him back, like a hand gripping him at the waist. He stepped back into the room and drew out the small belt pouch in which he had slipped the Amulet of Winter. The pouch, or more accurately, the amulet, wouldn't leave the room.

He opened the pouch and set the amulet on the floor. Then he stepped out. No problem. He could leave. He went back in and grabbed a book at random from a shelf and tossed it at the open door. It stopped in midair, just like the rope and case had at the window.

"Nothing that belongs to the library can leave here," Aleks muttered. He stepped back out, turned and faced the doorway. Placing his hands around the book he pushed it back into the library. It came unstuck and he caught it before it could fall to the ground. He glanced at the Amulet of Winter on the floor and then over to Seyn where she slept against the threshold. And he smiled.

"Every chicken was once an egg waiting to be a chicken waiting to lay an egg," he said as he bent down, picked up the amulet, and placed it on the table. Next Aleks crouched by the doorway and lifted the girl into his arms again. He carried her back into the room, over to the table, and set her down in a chair. He again picked up the amulet.

"Just don't swallow it," he said and pressed the sides of her jaw to open her mouth. He popped the amulet onto her tongue and eased her mouth closed. He lifted her again, turned, and walked toward the door. They passed through without incident.

Once outside, Aleks took the amulet from her mouth, wiped it on his shirt, and let it drop to the floor. Then he

carried her back across the threshold one last time, and set her in her chair again. "Maybe you'll get a new book," he said to her. "One about the thief who got away." He made her as comfortable as he could and left, closing the door behind him. With luck, time in the library would begin to slow again, and she would sleep until the Calentine happened to come by.

Aleks stooped and plucked the amulet from the floor, hiding it away again. He smirked. "Nothing belonging to the library can leave it," he repeated. "And she is the library. The library contains the library. I wonder if all mages are so literal?"

Mindful once more of guards and servants, he crept back down the stairs and out of the tower. Late morning light and a confusion of voices met him. It was a moment's effort to slip in among the throng of traders and wagons slowly exiting the courtyard. He recognized none of them and wondered just how much time had passed while he had been trapped in the library. No matter. He had completed another burglary, and if this one had cut a bit closer than most, he had nonetheless come away unscathed. Or had he?

As he walked up and out of the peaceful and fertile valley the first Calentine had created, he realized he lacked the elation he normally felt after finishing a job. Instead, Aleks couldn't help thinking about the next festival, when the Amulet of Winter was not on hand to renew the enchantment. What would happen to the valley, to its people? What would happen to the archivist in her library? Always before, when Collin had sent him for one artifact or another, he'd let the mage worry about the consequences. Something had changed, maybe several

things. He had stolen the Amulet of Winter from Seyn, but she in turn had managed to steal his peace of mind. He wondered at the cost of it, and how he might ransom it back.

SEAN MANSEAU

Veronica Brown

LET ME TELL YOU ABOUT A GIRL NAMED VERONICA BROWN, an average girl with average parents, and the subject of this story only by dint of bad vacation planning.

Every year her family summered on the shore of Vermont's Lake Champlain. "How is *that* bad?" you're probably asking yourself. "It actually sounds quite nice." And you're right— Lake Champlain is lovely. The beaches are clean, there are lots of fir trees to sit under when you need a break from the sun, and the mosquitoes mostly leave you alone. When I said bad, I meant bad for *Veronica*. Locals liked to tell tourists that a monster haunted the lake's bottomless depths, and everyone, especially the tourists, considered the stories good for a laugh. Everyone but Veronica, that is. Through no fault of her own, she and the monster were bitter, bitter enemies.

His name was not Champ, as was commonly held. It was Don Diego Luis Al-Montans Cornelius. The only offspring of a Spanish count and a Moorish princess, he'd been born

into his unfortunate condition due to a fright his mother took while pleasure boating on Loch Ness. The tale of how he came to be living in exile in a Vermont lake, and how he made Veronica's acquaintance, are best saved for some other time. Suffice it to say that our young friend knew him well enough to address him as Don Cornelius (as he preferred), or when she was feeling saucy, Big Daddy C. She also knew him well enough never to venture into the frigid deep waters of Lake Champlain, because Don Cornelius had promised the moment she did, he'd take her the way a snake takes a mouse. He never threatened anyone else (in fact never spoke to anyone else), and why she was his special enemy he never deigned to explain, except to say, "Honor can only be avenged with blood, even if it takes lifetimes."

Veronica's sister Ashley teased her about her fear of the water with all the cruelty a sixteen-year-old girl can muster, which is quite a lot. Veronica, who was thirteen, did her best to weather such sobriquets as "kiddie pool" and "water wings" without crying, but when Ashley started teasing her about her weight, Veronica always started blubbering like a little kid and hated herself for it.

"Mom says I'm big-boned!" she'd say.

"Oh sure," Ashley would sneer. "That's what they tell all the fat kids."

Was Veronica fat? Until a year or so ago the thought would never have crossed her mind. She was strong, that was for sure. She'd won a blue President's Physical Fitness Council badge two years in a row, and when she'd played catcher in Little League, she could sit in a squat longer than anyone without getting tired.

But lately she'd seen the look on her mother's face when

she had second helpings of meatloaf, and she'd found herself yelling at her dad when he called her "dumpling" or "Pikachu." The last straw was the day she and Ashley watched *Laguna Beach* together. Ashley kept making little comments about the girls on the show, sometimes snide ("She could use some remedial Stairmaster"), sometimes envious ("God, she's, like, a size negative one"). Veronica felt a little sick after those comments. When the commercial break came, she locked herself in the bathroom, stood in front of the full-length mirror mounted on the inside of the door, and pulled her T-shirt and jeans off. Her arms were thick and her legs were short. Her belly stretched the elastic waistband of her underpants, making the tiny white cups of her training bra seem even smaller by comparison. She turned her head to examine her profile, holding up the flesh under her chin, and then faced the mirror again and sucked in her cheeks. It was no use. Those girls on TV were beautiful, in the same way Ashley was beautiful, and Veronica realized that she was never going to look like that, no matter what she did.

It bothered Veronica enough that she never appeared on the beach in anything other than surfer shorts and a big T-shirt, even though underneath she wore a swimsuit—always blue, which was her favorite color. Ashley, tall and slender and already filling out the bikini she'd insisted their mother buy for her, would eye Veronica's outfit and snicker.

It was lonely staying on shore while everyone else was splashing about and having water fights and diving contests, but it was better than getting dragged away by a vengeful old monster with terrible breath. And she knew better than to try to tell anyone about Don Cornelius. The one time Veronica tried to explain the truth of the situation to her sister, Ashley had given her a look of such cockeyed disbelief that Veronica stopped trying almost before she'd begun.

Every year on the best day of the summer—July 14th—people from miles around would gather in Burlington to frolic on the shores of the great lake. They'd have cookouts and play badminton and cheer the little parade that marched proudly through the center of town, with the high-school band trumpeting red-faced out in front of a great inflatable plesiosaur that everyone thought was a perfect likeness of the lake's most famous denizen. Only Veronica knew that they'd gotten it all wrong. Don Cornelius was actually more of a giant eel with the head of a dog and the eyes of a cross old man. But would anyone listen to her? They would not, so she kept her own counsel on the matter.

The highlight of the day was a swim race out to a platform floating one hundred yards offshore. One hundred yards was where the truly deep water began. How deep, you ask? Well, in 1974 a geologist from the University of Vermont decided to find out. He rowed a boat out to the middle of the lake and began to play out fishing line attached to a plumb weight. When the weight stopped sinking, he would measure the line and at last have a definitive answer.

That was thirty-three years ago. The weight is still sinking.

The winner of the race (which was open to all children sixteen and under) was crowned the Champ of Lake Champlain, and all summer long was allowed to eat as much free Ben & Jerry's ice cream as he or she wanted. And who had been the winner the last three years running?

Ashley. Oh, her bragging! The exaggerated smacking

sounds of delight she made as she ate her fourth ice cream cone of the day! And no matter how much she ate, she never got fat. That probably had something to do with Ashley's elaborate and grueling exercise formulas (two minutes on the Stairmaster for every potato chip, five for every spoonful of ice cream, twenty-five for a slice of pizza). Still, what Veronica wouldn't give to put her in her place just once! Ashley was skinny, but Veronica was athletic, even if she didn't look it. She was sure she could beat her sister if there wasn't a monster with an old grudge waiting out there for her. But each year, she was left standing on the beach with all the broken-down old people and the diaper-swaddled babies, shading her eyes with her hand, watching her sister humiliate all of her rivals. The worst thing was, after this summer, Ashley would be too old to be Champ of Lake Champlain. She'd retire, and Veronica would never have a chance to beat her. Ashley would brag forever, and there'd be no shutting her up.

So Veronica decided that this year, she would race. She *had* to race. But if she went into the deep water, Don Cornelius would surely get her! What was the point of winning if you didn't live long enough to enjoy it? She thought and thought and thought about it, and eventually, a plan began to form.

Her mother, when informed of Veronica's intention to race, was so pleased that she brought Veronica into Burlington to shop for a new swimsuit. It didn't take long, because Veronica knew exactly which swimsuit she wanted. She'd found it in one of Ashley's catalogs, circled many times with a marker and decorated with stars and little notes that said, "I WANT THIS!"

When she came out of the dressing room, her mother smiled apprehensively and said, "Are you sure that's really the

one you want? It's a little . . . revealing, isn't it?"

Veronica could see it in her mother's face: She looked fat, and her mother was afraid the other kids would tease her. Veronica was afraid of that too, but she screwed up her courage and simply said, "I think it looks good."

It was a red one-piece cut high up the hips, with stripes up the side and a logo on the front that resembled something you'd see in a superhero comic. It really was quite a swimsuit. When Ashley saw it, she went wild with jealousy.

"But why does *Ver* get a new swimsuit this year and I *don't?*" she whined.

"You're just growing into last year's now," her mother reminded her. "We're not made of money, you know."

But Ashley carried on and on until their mother finally gave in. Unfortunately, the shop had that particular swimsuit only in one color, so Ashley was forced to wear the exact same suit as her sister.

"But that's okay," she told Veronica, "because I've got the body for it, whereas you look like you should be dipped in oil and fried up for dim sum."

That night, when everyone was asleep, Veronica climbed out of bed and pulled off her pajamas. She changed into her new red swimsuit and padded out of their vacation house and down to the beach. As the sand crunched between her toes, she could see Don Cornelius was already there, a few dozen yards offshore, his dog's head silhouetted in the moonlight.

"Veronica, my old enemy," he said with his wheezy voice and Castilian accent. "Come clother, tho I can thee you better."

"You know, I really think you need glasses," said Veronica. "If I got you some, would you leave me alone?"

"I thee well enough to determine that your thwimsuit ith the color of all the blood you'll bleed thould you ever be foolish enough to enter the deep water!"

"Well," said Veronica, "that's what I wanted to talk to you about. Tomorrow is Champ Day—"

"Idiot villagerth! How I dethpithe them. I'm no damned dinothaur!"

"—and I'm going to take part in the race to the platform," Veronica finished. "If you're smart, you'll stay away. I told everyone about you, and there'll be men on shore with sniper rifles just waiting for you to make your move. One word from me, and no more Big Daddy C."

"You know I hate it when you call me that," Don Cornelius sniffed. "Truly, you are my greateth enemy. But even if you did manage to convinth thomeone of my exithenth—which I doubt—I am not worried about men with gunth. One hundred yardth ith a long way to try to pick out an underwater target. If you come clothe enough to touch the platform, your life will be over."

"We'll just see about that. I've been practicing at the YMCA pool all winter. I'm way too quick for the likes of you." That was true. While her mother did water aerobics and Ashley flirted with the college-boy lifeguards, Veronica swam lap after lap. It had seemed horribly unfair that after all that strenuous effort she still looked more like a fire hydrant than a fashion model, but maybe now all that work might pay off.

"You *think* tho!" The water churned to white foam around his little flippers as Don Cornelius went into a perfect rage. "I've marked you, my foe. My eyeth may be bad, but your thwimthuit is red—red like the color of your blood, which I'll taste tomorrow! You'll make a fine mouthful, my plump little rabbit!"

"Oh, up yours, you Snoopy-faced sea snake," Veronica said.

But she was shaking like a leaf as she turned on her heel without another word and stomped back to her house. Through her sister's bedroom window she could see Ashley was up late doing Tae Bo with the TV volume turned down.

"Ash," Veronica whispered through the open window. "What are you doing? Shouldn't you be resting for the race?"

Ashley turned to face her, but didn't stop pumping her knees or punching the air. "What does it *look* like I'm doing, lard ass? If I'm going to eat tons of ice cream tomorrow, I need to burn the extra calories *now.*"

"But Ash—"

"*Some* of us, Ver, understand that wearing Lycra in public is a privilege, not a right." Ashley used her wristband to wipe her glistening cheeks. "And privileges are paid for . . . in *sweat.* You might want to think about that when you see the looks you get in that new swimsuit." And with that she turned back to Billy Blanks and started kicking even higher.

Back in her room, Veronica climbed into bed, but her thoughts wouldn't quiet. Even Don Cornelius, a horrible monster of the deep, felt like he could tease her about her weight. Well, she'd show him. She'd show *everybody.* When the birds began to announce the dawn of July 14th, she'd hardly slept at all.

It really was the most perfect day of summer. Eighty-three degrees, with the lightest of cooling breezes coming down from Canada, and the sky so clear that errant helium balloons were still visible even as they entered the stratosphere. It seemed all of Vermont had come to Burlington that day to enjoy the cookouts and the badminton and the parade, and most especially the race. Ben and Jerry themselves were standing by with a truck packed with ice cream in flavors that no one had even tried yet. That privilege was reserved for the Champ of Lake Champlain.

Down on the beach, Veronica found Ashley milling about with a hundred other youngsters, flirting with the older boys who sat up in the lifeguard chairs and pointedly ignoring those her age and younger.

"Hah!" Ashley cried when she spotted her sister. "I *knew* you wouldn't have the guts to wear that suit in public. What a waste of mom's money."

Veronica, wearing her usual T-shirt and surfer shorts, said nothing as she fixed her bathing cap in place. The thought of wearing nothing but her swimsuit in front of all these people, knowing that everyone watching wouldn't be able to resist comparing the bodies of the two girls standing side by side in identical swimsuits, had almost been enough to make her abandon her plan.

"You look extra fat today," Ashley said, projecting her voice like they taught in theater class. Around them, several kids laughed, enjoying her cruelty. "Are you going to be able to swim, or will you just bob like a fishing lure? Look out, Champ might get you!"

Anger steadied Veronica's nerves. "Oh, I'll be able to swim," she said, and pulled off her clothes to reveal the red swimsuit she wore underneath. She was peering hard at the platform floating way out on the waves. Was it just her imagination, or had she just seen a flipper waving, as if to say hello? "Best you can hope for is second place."

Ashley, eyeing the fit of Veronica's suit critically, opened her mouth to say something further. But when the race official blew his whistle, she only grimaced and got into a sprinter's crouch. The race was about to begin!

When the starting gun went off, a hundred screaming children dashed into the icy lake. Veronica was at the front of the pack, and as soon as she got knee deep she plunged headfirst and began swimming harder than she ever had in her life. She attacked the water, setting a pace no one could match . . . and one she couldn't maintain for long.

Seventy or so yards out, with the platform and its inflatable Champ looming near, she looked back to see that her closest competitor—Ashley, of course—was still trailing by ten yards. And Veronica stopped—just froze in the water. Back on shore, the crowd gasped. What had happened? Had she cramped up? Why was she thrashing around like that? The lifeguards stood on their towers and peered through their binoculars, wondering if they should stage a heroic rescue.

Treading water, Veronica watched her sister approach. "I knew you couldn't keep that up, lard ass!" Ashley huffed as she hurtled by.

"Wasn't planning on it," Veronica muttered. She reached down to tug her new fancy red swimsuit off, and then reached up to adjust a shoulder strap of the old blue swimsuit she'd been wearing underneath. Everything in place, she set off after her sister. Even at this leisurely pace, she was in no danger of losing to any of the rest of the kids, who were mostly swallowing water and dog-paddling in circles.

Up ahead, Ashley had just reached the floating platform. "Yes!" she cried, pumping her fist in the air. Spraying water droplets turned rainbow colors in the sun. "Yet again! Champ of Lake Champlain! A four-peat! A—"

And just like that she was gone.

Ten or so yards off to the east, there was a froth of white water, an occasional flick of dark flipper, and once, a pale flash of one of Ashley's long coltish thighs. In the distance, Veronica could hear people screaming and shouting. But, as if in a dream, she continued on, paddling until she reached the platform. Without too much difficulty she hauled herself up and stood there dripping. That was when her greatest enemy saw her.

"Mmmmf!" said Don Cornelius. His mouth was stretched very wide, wide enough to have engulfed the whole top half of Ashley. Her legs were still kicking and flailing, as if she were still swimming, and Don Cornelius had been right—her fancy swimsuit was the exact color of the oxygen-rich blood dripping from his doglike jaws. His mean old-man eyes were rolling in their sockets, wide and wild and full of hoodwinked fury. He looked like he very much wanted to spit Ashley back out, but she was stuck fast. *"Mmmmmffff!"*

"Like I said, too quick for the likes of you," Veronica told him.

Such hatred there was in Don Cornelius's poached-egg eyes that they seemed ready to burst from his skull. He began to cough, great ragged sobs, and inch by inch, Ashley began to slide free. He was coming back to the platform, and Veronica was unable to break free from his stare.

Fool me once, thame on you, his eyes said. *Fool my twice, thame on me! There'th no ethcape for you now, dearetht enemy mine!*

That was when they both became aware of the wasp buzz of the little Zodiac motorboat that had launched from the shore. In it were angry-looking men, lifeguards, firemen, and police officers cradling shotguns. Don Cornelius saw this, looked back at Veronica with implacable, timeless hatred, and then all that was left of him was the tip of his serpent's tail and swirling foam. A few seconds after that, there was nothing but the black water of Lake Champlain. In her head she could hear his aristocratic voice—*Honor can only be avenged with blood, even if it taketh lifetimeth*—and wondered if they were truly done with each other.

For days the Burlington Police Department and a special squad from the Cryptozoology Lab of the National Reconnaissance Office dropped dynamite into the lake. At first it seemed they were killing nothing but the thousands of pike and mackerel that floated to the surface and bloated in the strong summer sun, but finally, on the last day of the week, a great black eel washed ashore. It was almost fifty feet long, with the head of a beagle and the eyes of a cross (and very dead) old man. Of Ashley, no trace was ever found, and eventually everyone forgot about her, even her parents.

Despite the tragedy, Veronica was crowned Champ of Lake Champlain, and that summer she ate truly prodigious amounts of ice cream. But that was the last time she ventured out into the lake, and she never, ever wore red again.

I'd *like* to tell you she lived happily ever, that Veronica became a great athlete, and eventually went all the way to the Olympics—not as a swimmer, but a shot-put thrower. The truth is, though, she disappeared under mysterious circumstances while rafting down the Nile. But that's a story for another day.

NINA KIRIKI HOFFMAN

The Jewel of Abandon

ARIEL SLIPPED INTO AN ALCOVE IN THE HIGH-SCHOOL
corridor and lifted her palm so she could stare down at
her ring, whose large stone was turned inward in her hand. At
first the stone was clear, lucid as water, with rainbow hints and
chases. Then it clouded. In its cabochon surface she saw Trent
lean over Vera to murmur in her ear. Vera's pixie face flashed a
delighted smile. She nodded, her golden curls bobbing.

Ariel clenched her fist around the stone as though she
could crush the image out of reality. Trent had promised her
he wasn't fooling around with Vera. He had promised! But the
ring never lied. Sometimes it slanted things—well, all right, it
always slanted things. Since she had pricked her finger at sixteen
and bathed the ring's stone in her blood, it had always shown
the images most likely to hurt her heart. The images it showed
either *had* happened or would soon. She had never known the
ring to be wrong.

This was the sixth time the ring had shown her Trent with

Vera. Other times the ring had shown her Trent with another girl. She had teased out information, one way or another, to discover that the meeting was innocent. Trent was a helpful person; it was one of the things Ariel loved about him. That, and his gentleness, the crisp feel of his dark, curly hair against her palm when she pulled his head down so she could kiss him, the light that lived in his hazel eyes, how warm she felt when he put his arm around her. She loved all those things. She only wished he wasn't so kind to other girls.

She tightened the straps on her backpack and stepped into the stream of students flowing toward and away from classes. The cacophony of footsteps and chatter battered her. Disinfectant, perfume, stale sweat—the air was alive with odors. Ariel caromed off a tall boy's back and apologized when he snarled at her. She wasn't seeing too straight. She sniffed, wiped her eyes, and rejoined the student stream.

She dodged out of the hall and plopped down in her regular seat in Cultural Studies, near the back, between Trent's and Kevin's seats. Trent slid into his desk beside her. He was wearing the black T-shirt with the white skull sporting a red garden-lady hat she had seen in the vision, and the same dark curl flopped over his left eye. A rush of unwanted adoration washed through Ariel. He was so cute. He was so perfect. He was so—

—so toast. Either he'd whispered to Vera already or he would later in the day, and Vera would laugh, shake her curls, tilt her perfect little face toward him, smile that smile that showed her cute little pointy cat teeth.

Kevin, a tall skeleton of a boy with lank, streaky blond hair, a prominent nose, and an even more prominent chin, collapsed like a falling teepee into his desk, thudding his backpack down onto the desk's surface. "Oops." He unzipped the pack and gingerly removed his computer, shaking it to see if he'd knocked anything loose. "Whew."

"Good thing your dad got you the indestructible model," Ariel said.

"It crashes, but it doesn't break." He flipped open the laptop and the screen lit up. "Whew."

"Ariel," Trent said. He reached across the gap between their desks and laid his hand over hers. His thumb rubbed over the blank band of her ring, a habit he had established when he first touched her three months ago. He didn't know what the ring's hidden side looked like. Ariel had held hands with him as they walked down the hallway, and his fingers had touched the stone in the ring, but she'd never let him see it.

The ring had killed her mother, she suspected, and probably her grandmother before that. It had been handed down, mother to daughter, for generations, and all the mothers had led short lives. Ariel had noticed the fact when she did her family tree at eleven. Her family tree didn't look like anyone else's in her sixth-grade class. It had few branches. Each generation had produced one daughter who had married (or not, if you counted Ariel's great-grandmother, Pearl, who had had her daughter alone) just before or after her mother died.

Now that Ariel's mother was gone, would Ariel marry in the coming year, the way all her foremothers had? Would it just happen naturally? Who would she marry? Trent? Not if he kept talking to Vera that way.

Ariel used to ask her mother about their family history, but Judith would just shake her head and look sad. That was before Ariel stole the ring from her mother and discovered what it could do.

When Ariel was thirteen, she snuck into the bathroom while Judith was showering. The ring, that hateful thing her mom was always staring at, the one that made her sad all the time, sat on the bathroom counter in its own little blue-green bowl. Ariel knew about its special bowl from other times she'd peeked in. Judith wore the ring all day, but she didn't wear it at night or when she showered—it had its own small bowl by her bed, and this one in the bathroom.

If the ring were gone, Ariel thought, maybe her mom would look at her instead. So Ariel took it and hid it in the toe of a penguin sock from a pair whose images she loved, but the elastic was so tight it made her feet hurt to wear them. They stayed in her dresser drawer, rolled into a ball, and never went anywhere.

When Judith got out of the shower and found the ring gone, she didn't say anything. She came down for lunch, the same as always—except she smiled. Ariel made a joke while they were assembling peanut butter and jelly sandwiches, and her mom laughed. Judith chewed a carrot and sat back, her jaw still, her eyes shut, her face blissful.

The carrots were really good, Ariel thought, but were they good enough to make you smile as though they were chocolate?

That evening, her mom actually sang while she micro-waved dinner. She never mentioned the missing ring. Her dad was astonished when he got home. He had brought daisies that day—every day he brought Judith a different kind of flower—and her mom hugged them and kissed him, almost crushing

the flowers. "Oh, baby," Dad said, and they went upstairs to their bedroom and didn't come down until all the microwaved stuff had cooled too much to eat. They ordered out for pizza. Ariel couldn't remember her parents ever ordering pizza before, though she and her best friend Molly did it most Friday nights when they got together at Molly's house to watch movies.

It was the best afternoon and evening Ariel could remember.

Two days later, though, Judith was falling apart. Lines edged the corners of her eyes and mouth, and she had smudge marks like like bruises under her eyes. She made meals but didn't eat, and she never spoke except to answer questions, and then only a couple words at a time. The next morning, when Ariel's dad asked Judith how she had slept, she said, "I didn't."

On Day Five, Judith came to Ariel. "I need the ring back," she whispered. "I hoped I wouldn't, but I have to have it. Please give it back."

"What are you talking about?" Ariel asked.

Judith stared at her, then shook her head. "Oh, sweetie. I know you took it. You're the only one who could have."

"No, I didn't."

Her mom stared at her, and all the light leached from her eyes. She turned and left.

Ariel grabbed the penguin socks and went outside. She wandered down the street to Molly's house and climbed up in the big maple tree in the front yard. A safe height above the ground, where no one would think to look for her, Ariel unrolled the socks and pulled the ring out. Why did her mom need it so? It was just an ugly, clear stone like a marble, set in a dull silver band. What did her mom see when she looked at it?

The stone changed color while Ariel studied it, darkened, clouded. A tiny image flashed inside. Ariel lifted the ring and stared.

Judith was lying on her bed, weeping. She covered her eyes with her arm. Her shoulders shook.

Ariel nearly dropped the ring. Her hand jerked, but she gripped it with her other hand. What did her mom see when she looked in the ring? "Dad?" Ariel said.

The ring cleared, darkened, showed her another image. Her dad was in the reception area of his office, leaning over Joyce, his secretary. Was he really staring at her chest, or just reading over her shoulder? Ariel's hand jerked again.

Ariel slipped the ring onto her forefinger so she wouldn't drop it. "Molly," she murmured, and saw her friend lying on her bed in the ring. She glanced across toward Molly's bedroom window, which she could see from her perch in the tree. Molly was lying on her bed, reading a book, just as she did in the ring's image.

A shiver shook Ariel so hard she had to hold onto the branch with both hands to keep from falling.

She carefully climbed down out of the tree.

On her way home, she thought about the ring. It was like having a surveillance camera anywhere you wanted one, a tiny crystal ball that actually worked. If you could look at anybody you wanted anytime you wanted, and then suddenly you couldn't, wouldn't you feel as though you had been blinded? Her mom's haggard face loomed in Ariel's mind.

Ariel stood in the doorway of the master bedroom and studied her mother. She had rolled over on her stomach in the wrinkled middle of the king-sized brown bedspread. Her face rested on her hands. Her shoulders no longer shook, but she lay on the bed like something dropped there and discarded.

Ariel tiptoed into the room and slipped the ring into the little bedside table bowl. She fled.

After that, Judith's utter despair lightened. She stared at the ring often. She slept and ate, and sometimes she almost smiled. Ariel never heard her laugh again.

Three years later, Ariel's mother disappeared. Her dad said he knew where she had gone, but he wouldn't tell Ariel. Sometimes late at night, though, she heard him crying in his room with the light off.

He told Ariel that her mom wasn't coming back. To all Ariel's questions, that was all he said. The next morning, Ariel walked away, though it was raining. She walked all day in the rain, not caring how wet or cold she got. She thought maybe there were people on the sidewalk, people driving the cars that passed her, people behind the windows in the stores she walked past, but they were all invisible that day. She walked all the way to the ocean and stood a long time watching waves come in and go out.

It was dark by the time she got home. Not a single light was on in the house.

Her mom was gone.

That night, Ariel noticed that the ring in its blue-green bowl sat on the table next to her bed. It was wrapped in a note, written in her mom's handwriting: "Don't put it on. If you have to, it wants blood."

Ariel locked the ring in a drawer for months.

This term, she had finally taken the ring out again. It had stayed blank, no matter what she said to it, until finally she pricked a finger and touched her blood to the stone's surface.

She looked for her mom, but no images came.

She wanted to know where her dad was once in a while, she told herself, but she stopped looking in on him when she realized that he was more interested in his secretary's chest than in her work. Had her mom spied on him this way, seen him and Joyce go into his office in the middle of the afternoon, undress, and go at each other on the big leather couch? Was that what had made her vanish?

What if Mom left because she'd watched me do something? Ariel wondered. Steal that ten dollars from Dad's wallet? Shoplift the two lipsticks from Rite Aid? Kiss Alex Rodriguez with tongue under the bleachers during the football game, let him put his hand under her blouse?

But that was silly. Ariel could fight her horrible feelings about what her dad was doing by refusing to look at him. Mom could have stopped looking too, couldn't she?

When Trent asked her to be his girl, Ariel started wearing the ring to school.

She got no joy from it, though. Trent talked to too many girls. The ring delighted in showing Ariel moments when Trent's head was bent to listen to some blonde girl whisper something, or when he dropped a hand on some brunette's shoulder and smiled at her.

Ariel saw one telling moment in the ring where Trent and a girl named Stephanie put their heads into her locker together. The next minute, Ariel rounded a corner and saw the very scene in front of her. "Are you sure you lost it in here?" Trent asked.

"Positive," said Stephanie. "Wait, look. See the end of

the chain?" She stepped back, pointing, and Trent reached in, tugged on something, and pulled out a silver chain with a bent charm.

"Here you go." He handed it to her.

"Thanks, Trent. You're a lifesaver." Stephanie flashed him a wide grin, and Trent nodded and headed down the hall away from Ariel, his backpack bobbing. He hadn't even noticed she was there.

"What was that about?" Ariel asked Stephanie.

"It's my good luck charm," Stephanie said. "I always lose it. I can only find it if someone else looks for it. Maybe that means it's not so lucky, huh? But I'm trying out for the basketball team this afternoon, and I really wanted it. Trent was nearby when I needed another set of eyes." She fastened the charm around her neck.

"Good luck," Ariel said.

"Thanks," said Stephanie. She gave Ariel exactly the same width of smile she had given Trent, slammed her locker shut, grabbed her pack, and hustled down the hall.

Ariel tried locking the ring in a drawer in her desk at home, but those days she went to school without it, she felt naked and bereft.

She sat at the back of her Cultural Studies class while Mr. Whitman pulled down the screen so he could show slides. Trent held her hand, the pad of his thumb circling over the band of her ring. Warmth came from him. She closed her eyes and savored it. No matter what she saw Trent do, here he was with her, holding her hand as Mr. Whitman turned out the lights. She didn't have to look to know Trent was with her.

Light flickered as Mr. Whitman pressed the button on

the remote control, changing slides. Ariel opened her eyes and looked at images of Tibetan children, steep mountain landscapes, wedding-cake stone temples, women in dark dresses with bright sleeves and collars, men in flat-topped hats and serious expressions.

Everyone had the power to look at faraway things, but it didn't mean those things were more real than someone's hand holding yours.

She inched her desk sideways, closer to Trent's, and he edged closer to her. There was a reason they sat together in the back row. His arm went around her shoulders, and she pressed her lips to his. Behind her, Kevin tapped notes on his computer, but she didn't care. Kevin knew what they were up to. He'd share his notes later.

There, Vera, Ariel thought. Look in on this and come to your own conclusions. I'm the one Trent wants. I'm the one he asked to be his girl. Smile at him all you like. You're not coming between us.

Eventually, Kevin tapped her back, and she broke the kiss with Trent just before Mr. Whitman turned on the lights. Blinking, Ariel and Trent turned to face forward again. She jotted down the homework assignment, hugging warmth and certainty inside.

Outside the classroom, Trent kissed her one more time and fled. He had to get to football practice. Coach gave them all detention if any one of his players was late.

Ariel headed to homeroom. She studied for a while, then raised her hand for a hall pass to the bathroom. On her way back to class, she slipped into an alcove and stared down at her ring. Tibet, she thought.

Nothing happened.

The ring would only show her things that could hurt her.

Her mom had known. Her mom had dealt with the hurts caused by the images in the ring every day. Ariel remembered the first day after her mom lost the ring, how happy she had been, and then the sadness later. Judith was used to the pricks, but Ariel had only been using it a short time. Maybe she could stop before the tiny wounds grew so many that she couldn't live with them all.

Trent, she thought. There he was, in his football pads and jersey and helmet, no. 52, and there was Vera, in her cheerleading outfit, cocking her golden head and gazing up at him from too close. She tugged on his sleeve. He turned and smiled down at her.

He gave Vera the special smile Ariel had thought he saved just for her.

No. This was too hard. Ariel slipped the ring off her finger and zipped it into an outside compartment of her pack. Subdued, she went back to homeroom, opened her notebook and a textbook, and pretended to study.

When she got home that afternoon, Ariel dug through the bottom drawer of her desk, where she kept all her mementos. Here was the photo album she and her mom had put together last summer. They had gone through boxes of photo envelopes from the drugstore, pulled out the best pictures and put them in chronological order: The visit to the pumpkin patch when Ariel was five, so small her dad could seat her on a giant pumpkin and shoot her picture. The pony ride she'd gone on when she was seven. The family at the beach when Ariel was twelve. A drive they had taken to look at the autumn leaves two years ago.

Ariel opened the album, studied a picture of her and her mom. Ariel was eight, and dressed as a fairy with butterfly wings for Halloween. Her mom stood behind her, hands on her shoulder. The ring's plain band gleamed from the ring finger of Judith's right hand. She, too, had worn the stone inward.

Ariel set the album aside and pulled out the cigar box with letters in it. She didn't have very many: seven letters her mom had sent to her when Ariel was away at camp during two different summers; three postcards her dad had sent from business trips; and right on top, the note she had found wrapped around the ring.

She smoothed out the note and folded it into a small square. She found a ring box in a different drawer and set the note in the bottom, then slowly, she took the ring from her pack and put it in the box, then put the box in her pack.

She slept on her decision. She could always change her mind, she told herself while she ate breakfast and watched her dad read the paper. She didn't have to do this, she thought as she rode the bus to school, the ring box in her sweaty hand.

She didn't have to, but maybe she could.

Vera was standing near Trent's locker. Trent hadn't come yet.

"Hey," Ariel said to Vera. "I have something to show you."

She took Vera into an empty classroom and opened the ring box.

"What is it?" Vera asked.

"It's a magic ring." Ariel lifted the lid of the box and took out the ring, showed Vera the clear stone. "Watch carefully. Trent," she said, and the ring showed Trent in the front seat of his Volkswagen, his hair uncombed and his face harassed. In the passenger seat was a girl named Jenny. Her mouth was moving, and she twisted her ponytail around one finger.

"Wow," said Vera. "How does it do that? Is it like a mini-video iPod?"

"No. It's magic," Ariel said.

"Really? Do you believe in that weird occult stuff?"

"I do."

"Why do you have a movie of Trent and Jenny in your ring?"

"It's not a movie, Vera. This is what's happening now."

"Oh, go on. This is some kind of joke, isn't it?" Vera shook her head and smiled, revealing catlike teeth. "I know I must be getting on your nerves, Ari, because you know Trent likes me better. But I don't know why you think I'm going to fall for some weird trick that isn't even funny."

Ariel put the ring back in the box. "Come outside."

They went to the parking lot and waited. Trent pulled up in his blue Volkswagen bug, and there was Jenny in the passenger seat, chewing gum and twirling her hair. She popped out and came around as Trent emerged, grabbed his arm as though she owned him. He shook her off, reached in the back seat for his pack, and locked the car. In his anxiety to escape, he didn't look left or right, but headed for the entrance. He never noticed Vera and Ariel.

Vera's hand clamped onto Ariel's arm.

They watched Trent rush inside just as the first bell rang.

"How did it—" Vera began.

"I've seen a lot of things in the ring," Ariel said. Every time she had seen Trent with someone else, it had hurt. She was tired of believing the worst about him, especially when most times she had been able to check, he had an innocent reason for what he had done. Sometimes, she hadn't been able to ask. He didn't like jealous girls. That was why he'd broken up with his previous girlfriend.

She wouldn't be jealous if she couldn't see him all the time—she hoped.

Vera stared down at the ring and touched the tip of her tongue to her top lip. She looked hungry.

"I don't want it anymore," said Ariel. "Do you?"

Vera held out her hand and Ariel dropped the ring box into it. "First time you look, it's free," she whispered, "but then you have to feed it. There's a note."

Vera nodded.

Later, when Ariel and Trent kissed during Cultural Studies, Ariel wondered if Vera was watching. She hoped so.

JIM C. HINES

School Spirit

IN HER SHORT TIME AT OS-WEBRA, VEKA HAD ENDURED THE taunts and pranks of her fellow students with tremendous grace . . . for a goblin. In truth, the students here were amateurs compared to the goblins back home. A spider magically hidden in one's lunch was nothing. Where Veka grew up, that would be a tasty garnish, not to mention a courtship ritual.

Still, Veka was starting to think the humans were right. She didn't belong here. The stained robe she had brought with her from the lair smelled like stale mushrooms and barely covered her bulk. Blue skin peeked out through holes in the elbows. Back home, they laughed at her for being a fat, stuck-up goblin with delusions of wizardry. Here, they laughed at her for being a goblin.

Today though, she had more to worry about than mockery—things like old curses that killed students in particularly nasty ways.

Veka rubbed one of the curved fangs on her lower jaw as

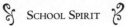

she stared at the sandstone wall of the mausoleum. The newest engraving read, *Theolyn of Salvati, Apprentice Magi.*

Theolyn had been a few years older than Veka. According to rumor, he had used a teleportation charm to remove various organs from his own body until he died.

Veka's oversized ears twitched, tracking whispers and footsteps in the hallway. Sound traveled strangely in Os-Webra, with its open passages and high walls. Her fingers tightened around her staff.

The door swung inward. A gangly, dark-skinned boy named Jimar stepped through, followed by several of his friends. "I told you she'd be here," Jimar said. Like most humans, he was taller than Veka, though she outmassed him. His robes were the finest silk, and he claimed the blue clan scars on his face marked him as a minor noble. Veka thought he looked like he had lost a fight with a woodpecker.

"What are you doing, goblin? Looking for leftovers?"

When Theolyn died, the humans had built an enormous pyre and placed his body at the center. How was she supposed to know humans cremated their dead instead of cooking them? She had figured it out quickly enough, but not before Jimar and his ilk had spotted her standing at the pyre, fork in hand.

Veka flattened her ears and bowed her head, trying to block out the memory of their taunts. Beads and bones rattled as the tangled braids of her black hair fell across her face. Back home, she had thought the trinkets in her braids made her look mysterious. These days, her hair was hopelessly snarled, but she wasn't quite ready to cut it all off.

"Be careful, Veka," said the girl behind Jimar. Veka couldn't remember her name. "Dakhan's curse could take you next, transforming you into a hideous monster. Oh, wait. . . ."

Veka inhaled the alien sweetness of the incense-burning braziers hanging from the walls. She tried to calm herself the way the Masters taught: Breathe in, breathe out. This was but a moment, and all moments ended.

"Theolyn was my friend, goblin," said Jimar. There was no humor in his words. Veka's ears perked, following his movements. "Letting a foul, filthy, fat monster in here is like spitting on his memory. I should—"

The end of Veka's staff cracked against Jimar's head. Jimar fell, whimpering.

All moments ended, but some needed to be helped along.

Veka gripped her staff with both hands and bared her fangs at the other humans. She counted four. Five, if you included Jimar. Several wore the light robes of advanced students, and they all looked angry enough to kill. Veka stepped back, wondering if they would use magic or simply rip her apart with their bare hands.

"Hey, who decided to throw a party in the mausoleum?" Veka would have known this human at once, even without the spectral gray cat that scampered at her feet. Young, cheerful, and graceful as a dancer, Melanie Lapan—Veka's roommate— slipped into the room.

"That goblin attacked me," Jimar said. "She wants to kill me!"

"We all want to kill you, Jimar." Mel reached down to help Jimar to his feet. "You're a jackass."

Jimar slapped her hand away. "This is no joke, Mel. She's a monster. Maybe the stench doesn't bother you, but wait until she slips into your cot some night for a midnight snack."

"Is that what you're worried about?" Mel laughed. "I

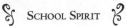

doubt Veka would eat *you*. There's barely enough meat on those bones to feed a baby goblin."

By now, everyone had forgotten about Veka. Their attention was on Mel and Jimar. Veka clenched her jaw. This was her fight, not Mel's.

But Mel actually *won* her fights. She tried to ignore that thought.

"You'd side with her?" Jimar asked.

"She's a new student. She hasn't even earned her novice robe. Why are you so afraid of her?"

"Afraid? Of that—"

"Or could all this bluster be a mask for something deeper?" Mel asked, winking at one of the girls. "Could the fierce desert noble be smitten with our blue-skinned beauty?"

"How dare you!" Jimar's hand went to his belt.

Mel raised a black wand with a beaded grip. "Lose something?" She flicked Jimar's wand a few times. Her ghost cat started to leap and bat at the end.

"Where I come from, thieves have their hands cut off," Jimar said, his gaze never leaving the wand.

Mel gave it a twitch, and Jimar's belt unknotted itself. He tried to grab it, but missed. The belt slithered out of the room like a serpent. Mel's cat pounced after the end.

Jimar raised his hands. "You arrogant little—"

Mel pointed the wand at his chest. "Try it."

The room went silent. Though she had only been here a year, Mel had already earned the blue robe of a third-year student. The only reason she still wore a burgundy robe was because it went better with her pale skin and dark hair.

Slowly, Jimar backed down. He bowed his head and

extended one hand. The other held his robe shut.

From his expression, it looked like the humiliation caused him physical pain. Either that or he was constipated. Veka still had trouble reading human expressions.

Mel slapped the wand into his hand. "Go quickly, before your belt crawls down a privy."

He left, followed by his friends, several of whom were laughing again. Mel had that effect on people. Everyone liked her. Time and again she was disciplined for some prank or minor theft, but where Veka's failings were seen as proof of her worthlessness, Mel's antics only made her more popular. The younger students worshipped her, even Jimar. After a few friendly words, and he'd be singing her praises as loudly as the rest.

Veka shoved past Mel and walked toward the door.

"You're welcome," said Mel.

"I didn't ask for your help, human."

"Sorry," Mel said. "Next time I'll let them pummel you."

Mel's cat raced back into the room. He scrambled right through Veka's leg, leaving her feeling as though she'd stepped into an icy pond. Stupid ghost cat.

"Hello, Snick." Mel snapped her fingers, and the cat leapt onto her shoulder. Mel always wore a scarf with her robe to protect her from Snick's spectral chill. "Jimar deserved a good thumping, but when you lash out, you're only proving to everyone that you're a monster."

Veka scowled. "I didn't ask for your advice either."

"What were you doing here? I didn't think you knew Theolyn."

"I wanted to know how he died," Veka said. "When you grow up in the tunnels, you have to be aware of things that can kill you."

"Dakhan's curse," Mel said. "It happens every year. Somebody gets cocky and decides he's the Prince of Os-Webra. Next thing you know, he's leaping from the wall or drowning himself in the cistern."

"Who's Dakhan?"

Mel stared. "You don't know?"

"People talk about me. They don't talk *to* me."

"Dakhan was a dark wizard. Os-Webra was his desert fortress centuries back, until he slept with the wrong local princess. There was a nasty war, and Dakhan was caught and executed. They dismembered him and scattered his body throughout the desert to prevent his resurrection. They say his last words were a prophecy."

Snick hopped to the ground as Mel drew up the hood of her robe. She lowered her voice and raised her shoulders. "'One day a wizard shall come, one whom even death fears. He shall call, and I shall place upon his brow my crown of fire. The Prince of Os-Webra shall know power unimagined by man or god.'"

Mel cleared her throat. "It goes on for a while. Lots of 'shalls' and 'whoms' and such. Dakhan was a wordy bastard. The curse is one of the disadvantages to building a school in the fortress of a dead madman. On the other hand, there's plenty of magic running through these walls."

Veka licked her lips. A long-dead wizard, one who could reach out from the grave . . .

"Veka?" Mel grabbed her arm, momentarily serious. "Everyone who's tried to claim Dakhan's power has died. Even the Masters. You can barely cast the simplest spells. You'd be crazy to try."

Veka shook herself free. "I cast a fair levitation charm."

"I'm sure that will be a great comfort when Dakhan's curse turns you inside out."

"Don't worry. I'm a goblin, remember?" Veka said. "We survive by running away from danger, not inviting it to kill us."

She slipped out of the room, her mind racing. Forget the stupid prophecy. Who wanted to wear a crown of fire anyway? Veka was more interested in the way Dakhan could still reach out after his death. He had been cut up and scattered to the desert, and he still survived to murder students.

That was a trick any goblin could appreciate.

Unfortunately, the only way Veka could think of to uncover whatever magic Dakhan had used to defeat death was to summon him. Given Theolyn's messy fate, she wasn't about to try it herself.

That was what roommates were for.

During dinner, she bribed one of the older students to share the spell for conjuring Dakhan. At first he laughed at her. Then he tried to scoff and laugh at the same time, and ended up coughing for several minutes. His face was still red as he wrote out the runes in exchange for Veka's dessert. Dessert, and the thought that Os-Webra would soon be rid of its lone nonhuman student.

Veka kept her ears flat, ignoring their jibes as she hurried away. She had what she wanted.

Mel always stayed out with her friends after dinner, which meant Veka had time to prepare the spell. For close to an hour, Veka crouched with her knife, carefully etching the runes of conjuration into the sandstone beneath Mel's bed.

Most students at Os-Webra had expensive, ornate knives

with handles carved of unicorn horn or a dragon's tooth, and engraved blades of mystical metal for spellcasting. The sheaths were even worse, brimming with beads and bells and other knickknacks. They dressed their weapons like little dolls.

Veka's knife was a goblin weapon, a piece of steel rubbed with a rock until it was sharp enough to kill, with leather wrapped around the handle.

She pressed her finger against the tip, then smeared blue blood into the runes. Blood of life to lure death.

Her plan was perfect. Mel would face Dakhan, and Veka would trace Dakhan's spell back to its source.

She busied herself with her spellbook, pretending to study when Mel finally arrived. She was sure she would be able to stop Mel from killing herself. Almost sure.

Six hours later, Mel was snoring on her bed, and Veka was no longer sure about anything.

Mel showed no sign of possession. The moonlight had crept across half the floor, and it was all Veka could do to stifle her own yawns.

She glared at Mel. What was the problem? Did Mel have some sort of magical ward to protect her?

More likely, Veka had messed up the runes. She lay back and sighed. Their beds were little more than holes carved into the stone walls, so that only a lip of stone protruded. The hard rock reminded her of home, but the reddish brown sandstone was so different from the obsidian walls of her lair.

Veka looked up at the ceiling, remembering those first awful days at Os-Webra. She had barely been able to convince the Masters to let her stay, even after giving them the meager coins she had swiped from some of the other goblins back home. And nobody wanted to room with her, especially after word spread of how human food affected her. Her stomach still gurgled at the mere thought of that dry, nasty stuff humans called bread.

The other goblins had said she was crazy to come here. A goblin becoming a wizard? What madness. Next thing you knew, rats would be demanding knighthood.

And they were right. She could barely follow the spells in her books, let alone cast them. Her potions turned into pasty sludge. Her runework was, in the words of Master Lia, "like the scratching of a diseased jackal."

She was a joke, and she didn't belong. She closed her eyes. The worst thing was, sooner or later, Mel would find the runes beneath her bed. Mel could be very forgiving of most things, but something like this . . .

Of course, there was a good chance Veka's runes would be so incomprehensible that Mel wouldn't realize what she had tried to do. It was bittersweet comfort at best.

Veka awoke to the sensation of needle-thin icicles jabbing her armpit. She jerked away so hard she fell out of bed. Her hip and elbow smacked the floor. Stupid humans, building their beds so high off the ground. Snick pounced after her, planting his feet squarely within her chest.

Veka squirmed and batted her hands through Snick's head until he got up. "I'm going to track down the biggest, meanest hunting dog I can find. Then I'm going to kill it so its ghost can spend eternity chasing yours."

Snick started to flee, then veered back to hide at the foot of Veka's cot.

"What's wrong with—"

"Silence, goblin." Mel stood by the window, her arms bare. Even Veka, for all of her struggles with magic, could feel the power crackling around Mel's body.

Veka reached for her staff.

Mel flicked her fingers, and Veka fell to the floor, gasping for air. "How shall I dispose of you?"

Veka couldn't have answered if she wanted to. She struggled to inhale, but every breath felt like she had swallowed water. She gagged and fought to keep from throwing up. Powerful as Mel was, this was another class of magic altogether. This was Dakhan.

Mel waved her hand through the moonbeam. Silver light sparked and danced at her touch. "This child has talent," she said, sounding both surprised and impressed.

Raw, burning envy swept Veka's fear aside. She wanted to cry. Melanie could *not* be the Prince of Os-Webra. It wasn't fair! She strained to break free of Mel's control, but it was useless. To make things worse, a red fire ant climbed up Veka's palm and sank its pincers into her thumb.

A second ant scurried beneath the door, followed by a third. Soft laughter told Veka this was no coincidence. Mel—no, Dakhan—was going to use the ants to kill her.

Veka's eyes watered, and her lungs were on fire. She struggled to contort her trembling hand into the proper position for a levitation spell. Trying to ignore the hammering of her heart, she reached out with her mind, feeling the lines of magical power that ran through the walls of the school. In this room, those lines all led to Mel. Veka struggled to divert the nearest one, like a child digging a tiny ditch at the edge of a stream. The power she touched was slight, but then, so was the target of her spell.

Her staff flipped into the air, and one end smacked the back of Mel's head.

Mel stumbled into the wall, and the spell holding Veka vanished. Veka gasped and pushed herself upright.

She wasn't fast enough. Strong hands caught her hair, yanking her off balance. Mel wrapped one arm around Veka's neck and squeezed.

"This is less elegant," Mel whispered, "but it's been so long since I've had the chance to kill with my bare hands."

Veka tried to levitate her staff again, but a stronger spell ripped it from her control. "Filthy, talentless goblin," Mel said. "You should learn not to interfere with your betters."

Veka sank her claws into Mel's forearm, wrenching it away long enough to shove her chin down. Then, before Mel could shift her grip, Veka bit her.

Veka's fangs weren't the sharpest or longest, but even goblin children had jaws strong enough to crack bone.

Veka's staff leapt into her hand as Mel tried to pry her arm free. A quick blow to the gut left Mel doubled over. A second strike knocked Mel to the ground. Veka sat on her for good measure.

"And you should learn not to shove meat in the face of a hungry goblin," Veka said, licking blood from her lips.

The only answer was a deep snore. Mel had fallen asleep.

Sunlight filled the room when Mel finally awoke. Veka sat on a folded blanket, her ritual dagger in one hand as she watched Mel stir.

Mel yawned and tried to sit up, only to choke on the rope looped around her neck. Her arms and legs were bound as well. A longer rope leashed her to the heavy trunk by the foot of her

bed. Veka knelt and pressed her knife to Mel's throat. If Mel was still possessed—

"They warned me this would happen if I roomed with a goblin," Mel said. She craned her neck to look at the crusted blood on her arm. "If you're hungry, you can always grab a snack from the dining hall. I would have swiped you a bowl of lamb and rice if you'd asked."

"You don't remember anything?"

"No." Mel hesitated. She clucked her tongue, and Snick hurried over to rub against her foot. "Which means you chomped my arm without waking me up. Care to explain how you did that?"

"Not really," Veka muttered. Snick scurried out of Veka's path as she walked to the bed. She kept her head down, hiding her face behind her hair. She yanked the blankets and mattress down to reveal Dakhan's runes.

"I see." For a long time, Mel said nothing more. Snick moved toward her bound hands, and she scratched his ears. "I think I'll have to kill you for this."

Veka shrugged and raised her knife.

"Wait! What are you doing?"

"Goblin rule of survival: When someone threatens you, kill them first."

"But I'm tied up!"

Veka nodded. "That makes it easier."

"Goblins." Mel shook her head, then slammed her legs against Veka's knees. Veka stumbled against the wall. The ropes around Mel's wrist unknotted themselves and dropped to the floor. Veka recognized the spell Mel had used on Jimar's belt, but this time, she was casting it without a wand.

Veka cursed. *Of course* Mel could fingercast her spells. She was better than Veka at everything else. Veka still needed a full staff to cast anything but a levitation spell, and even then her magic fizzled more often than not.

The ropes raced at Veka, coiling around her legs and reaching for her arms. She tried to cut them, but the ropes were too fast.

"I wasn't serious, you know," Mel said. "Humans don't kill each other on a whim."

"Dakhan was human," Veka said, trying not to fall. Her arms were lashed tight against her side.

"Fair enough. *I* don't kill on a whim." She plucked the knife from Veka's fingers and started to sit down on her bed. Then she glanced at the runes and moved to Veka's instead. She twirled the knife in her fingers. "I might maim on a whim, though, unless you can give me a good reason not to. Or maybe I should just let the Masters throw you out."

"It doesn't matter," Veka said. "We all know I shouldn't be here."

"Is that why you tried to summon Dakhan? Because you're having trouble learning on your own?" Mel shook her head. "Murderous wizards don't make the best tutors."

"I wanted to learn how he survived death," Veka said. "I thought I could stop him from killing you, then trace his magic back to the source of whatever spell he cast."

"How were you going to stop him?"

Veka's cheeks were hot. "I was going to hit you with my staff."

Mel tapped the tip of Veka's knife against her chin. "Brainless as that sounds, the overall idea isn't bad."

"It's not?" Veka stared, surprised.

Mel hurried back to her bed. Holding Veka's knife like a

quill, she began to scrape new symbols around Dakhan's rune. "This is a seal of slavery. It grants physical control of the body to another. I don't remember what happened, which means Dakhan took over my mind. If someone else has mastery of the body, Dakhan shouldn't be able to do anything."

She stepped back and brushed the knife on her robe. "There. Ready to uncover Dakhan's secret?"

Veka nodded. "You're sure that spell will keep Dakhan from controlling you?"

Mel's grin grew. "What do you mean, me?" She grabbed Veka by one fang and flung her onto the bed. "Don't worry, I'm pretty sure I'll be able to break Dakhan's control over—"

"It won't work." Veka's chest was heavy.

"You're criticizing my spellcasting?" Mel sniffed. "Strong words for someone who can't even mix an ever-glowing potion."

"My potion cast more light than anyone else's."

"Only because it set your desk on fire."

Veka shook her head. "It doesn't matter. Dakhan won't possess me."

"Why?"

Her throat felt like she had swallowed a rock. "He wants you. He said you had talent." Even long-dead evil wizards loved Melanie Lapan. "*You're* the Prince of Os-Webra."

"Princess. And that's ridiculous."

Veka shrugged and turned away. Ridiculous or not, she knew in her gut she was right. Mel was the heir to Dakhan's power, while Veka was . . . nothing.

Hours later, Mel was beginning to believe. She paced back and forth, each time stepping over Snick, who lay curled up in the sunbeam on the middle of the floor. "He didn't possess me right away either," Mel said.

"He won't come for me." Veka strained against the ropes. "You might as well let me go."

"Not yet."

"My bladder's about to burst. If you don't want goblin piss all over your bed—"

The ropes leapt aside, and Veka was free. She climbed to her feet, wincing as the blood pounded through her limbs. She picked up her staff and hobbled toward the door, only to stop midstep. She swayed, and then her leg lurched forward of its own accord.

"I told you the slavery seal would work," Mel said. She traced a circular rune in the air, ending the spell. "Come back when you're through, and we'll try again."

"If you want this to work, you shouldn't ask me for help," Veka said. "Go talk to one of your friends—someone who's not a complete failure as a wizard. Someone Dakhan might actually be interested in."

"I don't care that you're a failure," Mel said. She frowned. "Sorry, that came out wrong. Look, Veka, we can do this. We can find Dakhan's spell, and we can stop him from hurting anyone else. Even the Masters haven't been able to do that."

Veka hesitated.

"Besides," said Mel, giving a quick wink. "Think how Jimar will feel when he finds out a goblin helped destroy Dakhan's curse."

The next morning, Mel finally admitted Veka was right. Dakhan simply wasn't interested in a goblin with no real power.

So after breakfast, Mel altered the slavery seal, giving control of her body to Veka. "And before you get any ideas, I cast a second spell. If you try to eat me or anything like that, your insides will start leaking out of your ears."

Veka ignored her. Goblins made worse threats simply to greet one another. Besides, she was almost positive Mel was bluffing.

Dakhan took control of Mel the instant she touched the bed. The surge of magic felt like insects crawling over Veka's skin. Mel's body tensed, straining against the slavery spell. And then she simply stared, her eyes cool as she studied Veka. It was all Veka could to do keep from slitting Mel's throat right then, just to be safe.

Instead, she led Mel out into the passages of Os-Webra. They moved in unison, every step the same. It felt like she was carrying Mel on her back. Every step was twice as heavy, and every breath took twice the effort. A stronger wizard probably could have given Mel independent motion without walking her into a wall, but for Veka, it was all she could do to keep them both moving. She walked Mel into a few walls anyway, just on principle.

Halfway down the hallway, it hit Veka. She had conjured Dakhan. Not only that, but she and Mel had controlled him! Dakhan was her slave! Even the Masters had failed to accomplish so much.

Several students snickered and pointed as they passed the dining hall. "Careful," Jimar said, pointing to Mel. He thought Mel was mocking Veka's clumsy gait. "It's catching. Next thing you know, Mel's going to grow fangs!"

He grabbed two knives and held them to his jaw, mimicking goblin fangs.

Veka fought the urge to use a levitation spell to jab those knives up Jimar's nose. She concentrated, and Mel flashed an obscene gesture his way.

Snick slunk nervously in the shadows behind them. At least Dakhan's presence seemed to keep the ghost cat out from underfoot.

Veka flattened her ears and concentrated on tracking Dakhan's spell to its source. The power led down a narrow staircase that opened into a walled garden. The hot sun overhead made her squint, and her nose began to drip from the smell of the plants. Too-sweet flowering cacti bloomed pink and blue to either side of a dusty, tiled path. Stunted trees with bluish green leaves gave off a fruity smell.

Beyond the plants, the walls of Os-Webra spread in either direction. Large runes carved into the sandstone protected the school from outside magic.

"The spell is coming from here," Veka said. She could feel it, like a spider tossing line after line around Mel's body, each one pulling her closer. But pulling her *where?*

The gates of Os-Webra stood on the far side of the garden. They were heavy doors of smooth brown stone, balanced on iron hinges. This was one of the most tightly warded places in the school. They said the gods themselves would have to knock and ask permission before entering Os-Webra.

"The murderers of Dakhan carried his dismembered body along this very path," said Mel.

Veka's skin tingled. Mel shouldn't be able to talk at all. In typical goblin fashion, Veka's first thought was to flee. But where? Mel was behind her, and there was no way Veka could get through the gates. Snick was already racing between the cacti to hide.

There was an old goblin saying: When you can't run away,

at least anger your enemy into killing you quickly.

Veka swung her staff at Mel's head. The wood splintered in her hands, slivers driving deep into her palms. Blue beads of blood welled up on her skin.

"You're not as worthless as you appear, goblin," said Mel. She smiled as she inhaled the warm, dry air. "Fatally foolish, but no more so than scores of students before you."

Veka pulled her knife, only to have it ripped from her grasp. It flew into Mel's outstretched hand.

"The seal of slavery was clever," Mel said. "I assume that was the human's idea? But surely she couldn't believe she was the first to think of such a trick. Time and again they try, students and Masters both, always convinced their cleverness is a match for my own."

Humans talked too much. Veka backed away until she touched the doors. Dakhan's spell originated here. Not from the doors, but from the large tiles at her feet. This was the source of his magic.

"Grovel before me, goblin, and I may be persuaded to show mercy upon—"

Veka dropped to her knees.

Mel blinked. "No defiant speeches? How refreshing. And if I were to give you the choice of an honorable death or accepting the seal of slavery and helping me rid the defilers from my city?"

"Can we start with Jimar?" Veka asked. She kept her eyes down, feigning respect as she searched for the spell. The heavy tiles were worn smooth by generations of wizards and students. She saw no trace of runes or other enchantment, but the magic *was* here, pouring from the rock beneath her.

Mel chuckled. "I like you, goblin." She waved her hand, and it was as if an enormous stone had slammed into Veka's gut. Veka doubled over, struggling to breathe.

"Alas, I simply cannot allow you to live—not after your earlier defiance. But it gives me pleasure to know your blood will seep into the stones of my home."

As she lay there gasping for air, Veka spotted a line of fire ants crawling toward her face, creeping out of a tiny hole between the tiles. She wasn't even dead yet, and already they were preparing to feast. The stupid bugs were as bad as goblins!

"The ants are surprisingly efficient," Mel said. "In a few hours, only your bones will remain."

Veka tried to roll away, but another blow from Mel's magic knocked her flat. She groaned as she watched more ants pour up from the ground.

The ants . . . like goblins, they lived in tunnels. Goblin tunnels were a confusing maze of twists and turns, doubling back and crossing like the most chaotic runework.

That had to be it. She held her breath and traced a levitation spell with her fingers—the only spell she could cast without her wand—hiding the movement beneath her robe. Bits of sand began to rise away from the hole the ants were coming from.

"Stop that," Mel said. She reached for Veka.

Veka concentrated, and the sand flew into Mel's face. Veka poured her strength into the tile itself, struggling to rip it free. These tiles had been here for centuries. Surely time had loosened and cracked the mortar.

Mel clapped her hands, and Veka's robe tightened around her neck. She was hauled to her feet, then to her toes, and still her robe dragged her higher. Soon her frantic kicks touched nothing but air. She clawed at her robe, trying to tear the cloth, but all she managed to do was bloody her own neck.

Mel gestured with Veka's knife. "Farewell, goblin."

Veka switched the focus of her magic. She was rewarded by a crazed yowl. Caught by Veka's levitation spell, Snick tumbled head over feet through the air, his tail lashing like a snake. He passed right through Mel's head and shoulders, flying much faster than Veka had intended.

Mel gasped and stumbled back, clutching her head. Veka dropped to the ground. She placed both hands on the tile. She could do this. She had levitated stone before. Sure, those were loose pebbles and rocks, and this tile was a good two feet wide and who knew how thick, but she could do this. The ants had dug through the mortar, weakening it. All she had to do was concentrate and remember her lessons. A calm mind and cool, precise control would—

"Cursed goblin," Mel said. "I'll bind you to this life until the last bit of flesh is consumed from your bones. Your death will last for hours, but it shall feel like an eternity!"

Sometimes panic and terror worked better than calmness and control. Veka plunged all of her strength into the ground. The tile ripped free, and she used her magic to fling it at Mel.

It exploded into dust. Mel coughed and waved her hands, completely untouched. A breeze swept the dust aside.

Veka watched the ants scurry deeper into the stone, and wished she was small enough to do the same. The exposed tunnels formed familiar patterns, but she wasn't a good enough student to identify the runes.

"Well done, goblin." Mel's hand clamped onto Veka's neck. "As they carried my dismembered body from my fortress, they dropped my left hand. In that hand, I held a single ant that slipped away before anyone noticed. That ant began to carve the spell that would one day return me to glory. In return, the descendants of that ant will feast on goblin flesh."

She forced Veka's head to the ground, so her face pressed against the ridged tunnels. "You wished to discover my spell. I grant you that wish."

Tiny mandibles stabbed Veka's forehead. She wrenched her head to the side, momentarily dislodging the ants. But more were already pouring from the tunnels, biting her scalp. Perhaps Dakhan was controlling them, or maybe they were just hungry. They really did remind her of goblins swarming over larger prey.

But goblins had bigger teeth. Wrenching her jaw open, Veka jabbed her left fang into the rock and dragged it across the tunnels. Human teeth were small and frail, but Veka's fang punched through the thin walls of the tunnels, etching a new line through the runes.

Mel gasped, and her fingers loosened. Veka squirmed free and kicked her, knocking her down. Then she leapt to her feet and began to smash the ants on her forehead.

"What happened?" Mel asked. Her nose was bleeding where Veka had kicked her.

Veka rubbed her tooth. She had chipped the tip and her mouth was gritty with sand, not to mention a squirming ant or two. She grimaced and spat. "You know me," Veka said, pointing to the tunnels. "Always messing up the complex runes."

Veka watched as Mel used her magic to scrub the runes from her bed. Mel flicked her wand at tiny sand elementals who darted back and forth, grinding the stone smooth. Several

ragged lines showed where Dakhan's ants had chewed through one of the outer runes, breaking the seal of slavery and freeing him from Veka's control.

"It's not fair," Veka muttered. "All that magic, destroyed."

Not that Veka would ever have been able to learn it. Dakhan's spell had been far too complex. When the Masters finished excavating the ants' nest, they had found runes extending ten feet into the rock and stretching nearly six feet across.

All that remained now was an ugly pit by the gates. A pit, and a lot of angry, homeless ants that had crept into the school and infested everything.

Veka stared at the ground. The other students didn't know what had happened, and the Masters weren't talking. Even if Veka told them, who would ever believe a goblin had helped destroy Dakhan's curse?

Mel clapped her hands, banishing the elementals, then sat down on the edge of the bed.

Veka walked toward the window. The movement startled Snick, who had been dozing in the sun. The ghost cat hissed and fled.

"What's wrong with him?" Mel asked. "He's been scared of you ever since we came back."

"How should I know?" Veka snapped. Mel didn't remember much about the fight, but Snick certainly did. Apparently he hadn't appreciated being levitated through Mel's head.

"Veka . . ." Mel bit her lip. "It's cloudy, but I remember you using magic to rip open the floor and expose Dakhan's spell. You saved me. Thank you."

Veka didn't answer. She didn't know how. No human had ever thanked her before, and goblins didn't talk to one another like this. "I saved *me*."

"Either way, I'm glad you were there." Mel stared into the distance until a shudder snapped her attention back to Veka. Even Veka could tell Mel's smile was forced. "I guess Dakhan's curse was no match for a goblin's fangs."

"That prophecy was nothing but a trick to get people to summon him," Veka said. She scraped her claws along her forehead. A cluster of ant bites spread across her brow.

"Maybe." Mel cocked her head. "Tell me, how are those bites doing?"

"They burn," Veka said.

"Almost like a crown of fire?"

Veka stopped in midscratch as she realized what Mel was saying. "You're mad."

Mel's lips quirked in a grin. "And have you noticed how scared Snick is of you?"

"The prophecy said *death* would fear the Prince of Os-Webra. Not a dead cat."

Mel shrugged. "These things are hard to translate precisely. And that was quite a powerful levitation spell. You've got potential, Veka."

Veka didn't answer. Mel was mocking her, the same as the rest of the humans.

Only her voice didn't have that nasty edge. And she was still smiling, baring those pitiful human teeth.

Veka? The Prince of Os-Webra? It was sheer madness. Almost as mad as a goblin trying to be a wizard. "You really believe that?"

"Come on," said Mel. "There are some aloe plants growing behind the school. The milk from the leaves should soothe those bites. There's just one stop we'll have to make on the way so I can teach you a spell."

"Why?"

"It's a simple summoning, one that should lure a few of those fire ants into a single spot." Mel's smile widened. "Unless the Prince of Os-Webra is too busy to learn a spell from a mere human?"

"Princess," Veka whispered. She shook her head. "The Masters dug up the hole. Let them clean it up."

"Even if we lure the ants into Jimar's bedsheets?" Mel asked.

Veka grinned so hard her fangs dented her cheeks. Mel had a wicked streak worthy of a goblin.

"A princess is responsible for the welfare of her kingdom," Mel added.

And Veka *had* come to Os-Webra to learn. She rose and headed for the door. "Let the lesson begin!"

Blackwater Baby

THE BUILDING'S SCREAMS STOPPED FATHER JOSEPH AS HE admired how the breeze brought blood to the cheeks of the passing crowd. He looked up at the pink stucco walls of Charleston's slave market. Sharp shadows fell through the early November afternoon. Friezes of laurel wreaths twined through goat skulls above the market building's crumbling columns. He listened for the scream again and followed its echo toward a side yard. Piercing as any baby's howls, they swelled to an inhuman register that set his spine aching with recognition. He shook his head. Not this time.

No, he thought. I am done . . . with the Fey, with the Council, with all of it. If I must roam for an eternity alone, I am done.

The baby's cries were suddenly muffled, as if someone had put a hand over its mouth. The silence drew Father Joseph more than the screams. In the side yard, a small crowd milled around a man in a ragged top hat. Father Joseph could see the bundle the man held in his arms.

No. He looked back toward the docks, toward the way to an eternity of peace and solitude.

"This baby was born out of a water lily, right straight out of the blackwater!" The man's voice was cut off by a strange, strangled sound.

Turning again, the priest saw the man shaking a finger as though the child had bitten him. The baby resumed its screams. Some of the people waved their hands in dismissal and walked away, but the majority stayed.

"Look," the man said. "Look if you don't believe me!"

He held the baby up for all to see, letting the blankets fall to the ground. Her skin was black as the water from which she'd reputedly come, but there was a sheen to it, like gold dust, that Father Joseph doubted anyone else could see.

The light drew him closer, through the open iron gate and into the crowd. He saw the tiny webs of skin between her fingers and toes. He made his choice. If he did not take the baby from this man, come twilight everyone in this yard—the entire slave market, even—would be marked for death. The Fey, particularly the Unhallowed Ones, would not abide humans stealing a child of theirs and selling her into slavery.

"Born right out of the marsh," the man yelled again. "Perfect for a carnival show! You know you'd love to add her to your collection! Who'll bid first?"

A man with a long handlebar mustache and watery blue eyes raised his hand. Then, a woman's went up.

Father Joseph signaled to the auctioneer.

"A priest?" The man laughed. He shoved his top hat back with his bloody finger and grinned.

People began muttering about "unholy devilry"

and "snake oil salesmen." A few women turned away and brushed past, lifting their crepe skirts above the red dust of the ground. Father Joseph went closer to the front of the dispersing crowd.

As the auction continued, the mustached man persisted in trying to outbid him.

"What do you want with her?" he snarled once. "You're a priest."

When the baby opened her mouth wider to scream, Father Joseph saw the tiny points of her canines. There was no doubt. He bid the last of the money he had taken from the Council.

The mustached man threw up his hands and walked away.

The auctioneer retrieved the dirty blanket and swaddled the baby with it. "She's your'n," he said. "The green stuff, Father." He held out a grime-encrusted hand.

The priest dug into the beaten leather knapsack he carried. He scraped all the money together, sighing as he handed it over. He could have easily persuaded the man to give him to her, no questions asked, but he had sworn after he left the Council to use magic only if the direst circumstances warranted it." Thank you kindly," the man said, putting the baby in Father Joseph's arms. "I don't know why you want her, but she's sure to bring in more than you paid once she's all growed up. A good investment. Wish I could find another one like her. Think there'll be more where this one came from?"

The priest stared at him. "Stay away from the swamp or you will suffer a fate more terrible than you can imagine."

The man laughed and shoved the money in his pockets. "This don't seem like such a terrible fate to me."

Father Joseph shook his head and walked away, the baby howling against his ribs.

The nearest monastery was a few streets over from

Chalmers Street, close enough to the water that he could smell its tidal stench as he rang the bell. The novice gave him immediate entry, glancing at the baby but remaining silent until they reached a row of cells off the courtyard.

The novice stopped before a rickety door. "This is your cell, Father . . . ?"

"Joseph," he replied. "Of the Order of St. Fillan."

The novice bowed. He glanced at the still-screaming baby. "Shall I take the child to the nunnery? It's only two streets farther."

"No." Father Joseph said. Then more quietly, "No. She must stay with me for a time."

"As you wish, Father," the novice said. "Will you take meals with us or remain in seclusion here?"

"I will remain in seclusion. The baby cannot be left alone."

"May I bring you anything before vespers, then?"

Father Joseph was about to shake his head. Then he said, "Bring warm milk."

The novice nodded and went away.

Father Joseph unrolled the thin mattress over the rope bed with one arm, then laid the baby down on it. Salt from the baby's tears made white tracks across her face, like the crystalline shores of his long-abandoned home.

"Mara is your name," he said to her. "It means 'bitter sea.'"

When the novice returned with a bladder of warm milk, Father Joseph tried feeding it to Mara, holding her in one hand while fumbling with the bladder with the other. A little milk managed to get into her mouth between her screams, but much of it poured down her neck and soaked the dirty blanket. The screams became deafening, so piercing that he knew the Unhallowed could hear them from miles away. He could feel them waking from the shadows of the live oaks, creeping out of the cypress trees.

The sun threw red rays through the bars of his cell. It would not be much longer before they came.

He looked down at Mara as she fretted and punched at him. He set the bladder aside and dabbed at her lips with an edge of the blanket. Her lips swelled, red welts streaking from her mouth, down the sides of her neck, and he saw, as he pulled the blanket aside, across her chest.

"Mary, Mother of God," he said. *How did they do this?* Long ago, such children had been quite common, and the Unhallowed had sought means of begetting more. The Council then cursed the Unhallowed with barrenness and worked to exterminate the remaining children. Turn and turn about. The secret war between mortals and Fey escalated, and the stakes had become too high. This was one of the reasons he had left. He was tired of murdering children. But how had the Marsh King managed to sire a child? Were the Council's curses, set so long ago, finally unraveling? The thoughts made his bones cold. He had thought he was done with it. Yet, it appeared that this terrible business was not done with him.

With the failing sun, he heard the Unhallowed howl from beyond the city's edge, bent on retrieving the stolen child of their lord. He thought of the auctioneer and shook his head. If they found him, the man would learn quite painfully how little money was worth compared to the crime of stealing the Marsh King's daughter.

"What shall we do?" he asked, rocking the baby softly

as her screams fell into weak, echoing cries. He wasn't fooled. The Unhallowed could still hear her.

Her breath hiccupped and stopped.

"Oh, Lord," he whispered. He had hoped she was a bit more human than she seemed.

He saw the choices clearly: He could let her die, and the Unhallowed would still exact their vengeance upon him, especially when they discovered who he was, whom he had betrayed. They would revel in their capture. He had known their torments before. But at least the abomination would have ended before she could do anyone harm. If Mara grew to her full power, the Unhallowed would have the dark champion they sought so desperately. She would be filled with all the power of her human and Fey ancestry; Half-Born, she would walk between worlds, claiming them all for her own.

Her death would spare the mortal world much difficulty. Babies died easily. No one had blamed him before.

Gills bloomed briefly at her throat, as though her body thought she had fallen underwater.

Or he could let her live. She would be a powerful weapon; she would open doors and magics that had been shut to the Council. Where the humans who served the Council failed because of their paltry blood, Mara would unite and lead them, magic pouring from her fingertips like the blackwater from which she came.

He leaned close, blew across the gills, watched their feathery fluttering. Her eyes were glassy and dilating, but they followed him still, all her cries choked deep in her throat. But perhaps there was another choice . . .

He pulled the knife from his knapsack and laid the baby

across his knees. She was turning blue. The priest felt for her tiny, beating heart. That, at least, was something they shared in common.

He raised the knife and cut a deep red crease across his index finger, then set the finger against her lips. She suckled weakly at first, then with greater force as she regained some of her strength. The sun fell beneath the window, and the blue tinge left her skin.

In that moment, he felt her body shift across his knees. A giant black toad regarded him mournfully. He snatched his finger out of its mouth. It watched him with such a human expression that he couldn't bear to return its gaze. However the King had managed to get her, she was not entirely one thing or the other. The curse, warped though it might be, still held.

A tiny, black voice spoke in his mind. *Take me to the root.* An image of vultures soaring over a barren field sailed through his internal vision.

The Unhallowed circled ever closer, like the vultures in his mind.

He remembered that he had denied all of these things. That he had meant to find a ship and sail south, as far south as he could go.

I vowed I was done with this. When he left the Council's school in Virginia, he had sworn to have no further dealings with the Unhallowed or the Council. He would live out an eternity alone somewhere, away from the curses and talismans, away from mortal sorrows and immortal vengeance. Even if the Council summoned him, he wouldn't heed the call. He had lived long enough to see the fruitlessness of all their schemes.

But . . . He pondered whether or not his aimless wandering had drawn him here, to find this Half-Born child, to take her to safety.

The toad stared at him, unblinking. *Take me . . .*

No. I am done. He picked her up, opened his cell door, and tossed her out into the night. Moisture from her skin clung to his hands.

He shut the door and listened to the silence, feeling the creatures that had been bearing down on the church veer away. Without her cries to guide them, the Unhallowed had lost track of her. Father Joseph wiped the froggy dampness onto his cassock. He glanced at the cross and prayed briefly that he would find a ship before anything else intruded on his peace.

There was no trace of the toad in the morning or rumor of the baby all that day. By afternoon, Father Joseph had booked passage on a merchant vessel that would leave at high tide after midnight. It had been easy to make the ship's captain believe he needed a priest to attend to the spiritual life of the crew in lieu of payment for passage. Much as it galled Father Joseph, such petty magic had its uses.

He returned to the monastery to wait. Thankfully, no one had questioned him about the baby. He was sure they assumed he'd taken her to an orphanage or to the nunnery a few streets over. Late afternoon came, and the novice brought the bread and water of seclusion. Though he ate, he could feel the hunger gnawing at him, a hunger that could not be filled by bread alone. It was nearly twilight, but still a long time before he was to arrive at the docks. The bread sat in his belly like a stone.

When this hunger had come on him before, he had often abated it by going to a butcher's shop. But tonight, it seemed that would not do. He needed something fresher, warmer. He opened his door and looked out on the court-yard, where the Spanish moss ghosted down from the trees. Compulsion thrummed in the air, like the murmur of locusts just beginning in the live oaks. The Unhallowed had felt his magic. They had set the trap, knowing he would be unable to resist. He tried to speak a charm against it, but it died against his lips. They were close. He would have to go where the compulsion bade and hope he could resist the hunger as he had often done before.

As he walked down the street, he knew those he passed saw only a pensive priest. He cursed the Unhallowed under his breath and crossed himself afterwards. He would not say aloud the name of the Unhallowed witch who had done this to him, who had made him half-mortal and half-Unhallowed—half-human and half-vampire. For her, there were not enough curses in all the world.

He hunted through the back alleys, ignoring the prostitutes who unwittingly tried to lure him to their own deaths. He walked past the heavies outside the shuttered taverns, the skinny white quartermasters sousing away their sorrows in another pint. Something very special called him.

He entered the back alley as the twilight fractured the palmetto leaves into black spines. He heard the low hum of a spiritual before he saw the woman, her cap crisply white against her dark skin. She spoke to the little boy who played in the dirt, then started toward the house. She hadn't seen him.

Father Joseph waited, wishing he hadn't come this way, unable to resist the lure. The locusts chewed the dusk into tiny, singing scraps. The boy sat by himself, making piles in the red clay. Father Joseph slipped through the back gate, the prickly palmettos.

Only a little, he promised himself. His hands shook. He

thought he heard the witch laughing, as he always did at these times when the hunger overpowered him.

As Father Joseph emerged, the boy shrank back a little. Rusted patches of clay smeared his worn cotton shirt and britches.

"Come here," the priest said. His voice stretched thin as a wire. It was not his voice at all, but the voice of the Half-Born, the voice of the panther's hunger, the compulsion of the stinging wasp.

The boy rose and came toward him, shedding red dust from his clothes. Father Joseph squatted so he could look into the boy's face. He put his hands on the boy's shoulders.

"Only a little," Father Joe whispered. He opened his mouth and fangs erupted with their usual pain, like a thorn thicket growing through his gums. The boy didn't move, but stared beyond him into the moving darkness of the palms.

Father Joseph saw the minute whorls in the boy's skin, the warm life pulsing between sinew and bone. His teeth sank through the dark patterns. The boy trembled a little, but didn't cry out. Before the membrane could close over his eyes, the priest saw something squatting by the cabin, a sad puddle of shadow.

Take me to the root. A black buzzard circled through his mind.

Father Joseph pushed the boy away from him. The protective second lids snapped back under his eyelids.

He went to the toad. Tears left salt tracks down her knobby chin, splashing down at her webbed toes in the dust.

"It was you," he said. "You called me."

The toad bobbed her head, and all his excuses and vows fell into dust.

Take me to the root, she said again. A flock of vultures wheeled. Where?

She had said this before and he didn't know what she

meant. Back to the swamp to return her to her father? No. He wouldn't do that. Perhaps it was still not too late to rid her of her Unhallowed half. When he had been turned, there had been a chance for him to regain his mortality. That was why the witch had kept him chained with ironwood and thorn to her throne. That, and the humiliation, of course.

He scooped the toad up and placed her in the knapsack. He turned and saw the little boy watching him, thin trails of blood leaking down his neck. The priest went toward him, but the boy, as if he'd finally woken from his obedient trance, screamed and ran around the corner of the cabin.

Father Joseph hurried back through the palms into the alley. The sun was gone. The Unhallowed would have sensed what he had done. Such acts of feeding always drew them.

Though he had intended to return to the monastery to wait, he wouldn't risk the lives of the other monks by bringing the Unhallowed there. He wandered the alleys of Charleston for several hours instead, sweeping ever closer to the docks, muttering charms and casting them behind him to boggle their pursuit. The Unhallowed were uncomfortable in the city with its iron gates and kegs of powder and shot. They crept out of the swamps cautiously, all the more angered for being unrooted. He could only imagine how much power had gone into Mara's making—so much that precious little had been left to protect her.

When he finally came to the docks, he waited in the shadows until it seemed safe to enter the flickering circles of the gaslights. He could sense the Fey boiling all around him, frustrated by the barriers he'd thrown up, working at the riddles and charms he'd laid, assured now that he was the one they sought.

The merchant clipper's masts rocked above him in the darkness. He stepped out through the light and went up the gangplank. He still was unsure what he would do with Mara. He remembered those vulnerable days of his own rebirth, but this was much different. He had not been sired by the Unhallowed in quite the way Mara had. He longed for the Council library with its vast collection of grimoires and spell ingredients, but that way was closed to him. He would have to find another path.

And he would have to find it soon. When the sun came, she would revert to her human form and she would need blood. She was certainly weak; he knew she couldn't have fed since he had given her his own blood. A few sheep milled about on the deck as the deckhands worked to get them below; the sheep would be the only source of food if his plans failed.

Half-Born!

The voices of the Unhallowed whined in his ears like a nest of metallic hornets. No one else on the ship had heard it; such voices were beyond the range of normal mortal ears. But he felt the toad hunkering down in the sack on his shoulder as though in pain.

Father Joseph looked back toward the dock and saw one of the Unhallowed step out of the alley. It was a mass of twisted oaken bone and trailing lianas, sparkling with witchlight. The face that emerged from the collar of bone and branches resembled a panther's, but it shifted into something resembling a human face every now and then. It was a seneschal, probably the King's second-in-command. A gory green tide crested the buildings on the dock. The Unhallowed danced on the rooftops, battering the gables with their twiggy fingers, smearing shop signs with their excrement.

Half-Born, the Unhallowed seneschal said. *Give back the Marsh King's daughter!*

"Ah, Father, good to see you aboard," the ship's captain said behind him.

Father Joseph turned, nearly knocking the toad in the sack against the boat.

"Captain," he said, "are we ready to cast off?" He tried to project a veneer of calm.

"Well . . ." The captain was obviously perplexed by the request. "We've all the merchandise on board, but high tide's not for another hour yet."

Father Joseph slid his eyes to the dock. The Unhallowed seneschal's hooves clicked across the warped boards, the army of minions dancing after it.

"Might we at least pull up the gangplank then?" Father Joseph said. He looked deeply into the captain's eyes, saw the pupils go round and empty for the second he needed.

"Yes," the captain whispered.

"Good." Father Joseph nodded and turned back to the docks. The seneschal and his minions were nearly to the edge.

"Haul up the gangplank," shouted the captain.

Some of the deckhands looked at him in confusion, then began hauling the gangplank up from the dock. One Unhallowed had already put a cloven hoof on its edge. Father Joseph watched as the sailors strained and grunted at the weight, then finally pulled the gangplank off the dock. The satyr slipped and fell into the slice of harbor between ship and dock. An oily stain spread on the water.

These Unhallowed, bound as they were to the marsh, could not cross even the smallest bit of ocean. They could call their ocean kin, the mermaids and telkhines who swam the depths, but bargains would have to be made, and those would take time. He hoped by then either to be far enough away or to have somehow expunged Mara of her Unhallowed parentage.

Half-Born, the seneschal growled.

Father Joseph watched it lean forward, but refused to speak to it directly. He spoke a charm of warding under his breath as the ship rocked outward on the swelling tide.

If you would steal the Marsh King's daughter, then bear thy curse. It chanted words he had known all too well—the curse he had set upon the Unhallowed long ago:

> *Cursed be thy hand, sinew unto bone.*
> *Cursed be thy heart, blood into stone.*
> *May all your days to darkness turn,*
> *All your loves your lovers spurn,*
> *All your great works fall to dust,*
> *All your life's hope fade to rust.*

The last word coiled across the water. Father Joseph felt its noose slide down over him and tighten. He tried to speak against it, but his tongue was numb. The power in him drained away, killing any chance he might have had for making Mara human on his own. He would need the Council now, whether he wished it or not.

I will not go back . . .

The tide beckoned the ship as it lifted and strained at its moorings. The seneschal nodded, drew its cloak of vines and witchlight about it. It turned and walked into the fog, which boiled with leaping minions as it passed.

Father Joseph went into his tiny cabin—yet another treasure he'd wrested easily from the captain's mind—and shut the door behind him. He put the knapsack on the floor and the toad crawled from it. She hauled herself into a corner and sat trembling. The lamplight threw her shadow mercilessly against the wall.

"Mara," he said, when he could. The toad looked at him. She knew her name.

He didn't know what more to say. I wanted to save you. And now, I can't, he thought.

"I can't go back," he said. There was nothing left but the endless bickering of mortals drowning in secrets far too dark and deep for them. They didn't know the full truth of what he was, didn't dream of the danger he represented. None of them understood that the time for patience was long past. He had warned them to move against the Unhallowed in whatever way they could, but they were unwilling. Here was the result of their dawdling. Somehow, despite his efforts to free himself from it all, he had been tossed squarely into the middle of it again.

He imagined the witch who had captured him so many centuries ago. How the golden bells of her laughter would chime when an emissary told her that the Marsh King's seneschal had thrown his own curse back at him!

He shook his head. At the next port, he would have to disembark, find a ship headed north, return to the Council school . . .

He looked at the toad. He saw empathy in her eyes, a deep understanding that he had seldom experienced from any human being. *Take me to the root . . .*

"If only I could," he said, before the buzzards could circle again.

The cracking of giant bones all around him woke Father Joseph from a troubled sleep. He looked around, but could see nothing in the pitch dark. Had the Unhallowed somehow managed to take the ship after all? He couldn't believe the Marsh King could have made a bargain so quickly with the mermaids, telkhines, and other creatures of the deep. They were fractious by nature, and had their own revels to attend.

Shouting preceded the shattering of his cabin door. He covered his face as the water curled in. Images of burning masts and forms running and pulling ropes in the darkness flashed behind his eyelids. Sheep screamed from the hold.

"Mara!" He searched through the cabin, falling against the wall and floor as the ship shuddered. The hammock tangled about him as he fumbled through the sloshing water for the toad. She was nowhere to be found.

He pushed out of his cabin. He could see the faintest red light of dawn on the horizon. The toad sat on the bow with witchlight glowing around her as the ship dashed itself to pieces on the low reef near an island's mangrove-shadowed shore.

"Mara!" he cried. He forced his way down the deck as it broke beneath his feet. "Mara! What have you done?"

Going to the root, the small, dark voice said in his mind.

And just as the sun threatened to tear through the ship's rigging, the toad leaped from the bow.

Father Joseph didn't think. He dived off the railing after her, the sounds of the dying ship stinging his ears as he plummeted to the water.

The tide threatened to suck him away, but he struck out after the black bump of the toad struggling through the water. He snatched her just as the transformation came, just as she would have sunken beneath the waves, all the Marsh King's precious power lost like a galleon at sea.

He held her to his chest as she choked and tried to scream. But the waves slapped her silent. She writhed at their touch. She was so thin and wasted; he didn't know how she had survived this long.

At last he made the mangroves. He waded through their twisted, fingerling roots until the land rose a bit more and he pushed through saw grass, the hem of his cassock dragging through the mud. When he at last climbed onto steady, sandy ground, his legs were trembling, his arms sore from cradling the baby.

In the late afternoon, he came through the live oaks to a drowned, barren field. He decided to rest under a live oak before going farther. Spanish moss blew in the fitful November breeze above him. The baby's skin was clammy and nearly transparent.

He had lost his knife, his knapsack, everything but his filthy clothes. He closed his eyes and put his wrist to his mouth, felt his canines puncture his skin, the second eyelids sliding down as he tore.

He set his wrist against her mouth, barely able to see through the protective membranes. They receded as his body realized he had no prey. She roused to the warmth against her lips, gurgling softly. He felt her draining him slowly and steadily, while the golden light crept back across her darkening skin. He looked around, praying deeply that this truly was an island, that no Unhallowed had somehow been transported here. Though he had seen much, these few days alone were enough to convince him that anything was possible.

When he first saw how the man stepped from the shadows, Father Joseph guessed they had not found an island after all. The blackness of the man's skin, the way he blended so easily with the darkness between oak and palmetto, was akin to the Unhallowed of the marsh when at their full power.

Father Joseph removed his wrist from the baby's mouth and tried to hide the self-inflicted wound with his sleeve. Mara screamed. He reached deep for the magic within, although he knew it was bound, rendered useless by the Unhallowed curse.

"No use in dat," said the man, as he came closer.

His face was scarred with years of sun and disease, years of working the island's rice fields. Father Joseph saw that the man's long dreadlocks, drawn back in a tie at his nape, were silver at the roots.

Movement above the canopy caught Father Joseph's eye. Buzzards circled, their black wings stretched against the sunset.

"You can't take her where you goin'," the man said.

"What?"

"You think you take her up north, up to your people," the man said.

Father Joseph was too tired to argue. He nodded, pressing at his wrist with his other hand as he balanced the sobbing baby on his knees.

The man shook his head. "But you ain't got no root to protect her. You ain't got nothin' that will keep de ole King and his people from findin' her."

No root . . .

Take me to the root . . .

"I have people—we know ways to keep her safe," Father Joseph said, trying to muster up some defiance.

The man came forward and picked up the crying child.

"You ain't got nothin'."

Father Joseph pushed himself to his feet, but exhaustion countermanded argument. Even as the darkness grew, light played around the man. He saw how Mara lifted her hands to the glow, how she fed and grew stronger from it than she had even from his immortal blood. She laughed.

"I'se Dr. Buzzard, the biggest root doctor 'round here. I got roots to protect her. What you got?"

Nothing. But he said, "She said to take her to the root."

"She know I can help her. You can't change her, preacher-man. You can try to take the baby out of the black-water, but you can't take the blackwater out of the baby."

Father Joseph nodded. "But there may come a time . . ."

"You'll come back," the man said as Mara reached for one of the ties of his shirt. "But it'll be her choosin' to go."

"Fair enough. And until then . . ."

"We keep her here where she belong, and teach her the roots her mammy knew. We teach her how to be human *and* haint."

Father Joseph smiled to himself at the use of the word "haint." He hadn't heard that term for the Unhallowed in an age. Father Joseph knew Dr. Buzzard told the truth; his power was evident.

"And you'll keep her safe? You won't let the Marsh King have her?"

"Son, I been puttin' roots down for maybe as long as you been walking this earth. De Marsh King knows to fear me. He don't mess with me."

Father Joseph looked at him more closely, then understood that the recognition he'd felt earlier was for one of his own. Yet another Half-Born—one who seemed to know where he belonged, who had perhaps conquered the hunger for mortal blood. Father Joseph felt a flicker of self-pity. He wished that he could be cured of his eternal hunger. But it was his burden, just as it was the burden of Mara and Dr. Buzzard.

When he looked again at Dr. Buzzard, the root doctor's gaze was distant and hard. Father Joseph could see that the man knew how the hunger had driven him. Dr. Buzzard shifted Mara into the crook of his arm and pointed to the darkness beyond the rice field.

"Dey's a boat yonder. Leave our children, or dat curse feel like a bitty sting compared to what I lay on you in return."

Father Joseph nodded. He started for the field, then turned for one last glimpse. Witchlight encircled Mara in Dr. Buzzard's arms. She watched him as he went, her eyes black as the waters of her birth.

J.D. Everyhope

Old Crimes

It happened at the restaurant down the road, the one with the guitarist who'd trained a Guatemalan parrot to sing. May's father demanded a table on the balcony overlooking the white beach. He dropped his keys on the table and sat with his back to the sea. May's mother sat next to him, angling her head and gazing at the ceiling. That was how she pretended to be sick. May and her brother Ethan sat across from them, her brother hunched over his AP American Government textbook.

May's father caught her eyes and asked, "Well, how're you doing in school?"

"Fine," May lied. If he was asking, he hadn't looked at her report card. Her father stared at her until she became uncomfortable and looked away.

"You're a junior, right? What classes are you taking?"

May shook her head. "I'm a sophomore. I'm taking standard sophomore classes like every other sophomore."

"I put May's report card in your inbox. Be sure to take a look at it whenever you're home." Her mother stood, her chair clanging against the banister. "Where's the waiter?"

May closed her eyes. Sometimes, she thought that she'd imagined her life because surely, no one real would act so badly. But then her mother and her father did.

"Un momento, por favor!" A young waitress smiled and hurried past, carrying a tray of mixed drinks. Five Texan undergrads whistled as she approached, applauding when she handed out misshapen and bright-colored glasses. Rushing to May's mother, the waitress said, "Yes, senora?"

"I'd like lime soup." May's mother sat and unfolded her napkin, smoothing it across her lap. "I'm not feeling well."

"Of course." The waitress smiled.

May ordered black beans with rice and Ethan ordered a beef enchilada. Her father ordered the most expensive dish on the menu: shrimps in tamarind sauce, flame-broiled with tequila. Her father watched the waitress walk away. Her mother watched her father.

"We ought to tip her. She's very busy but she got right to us," her father said. "I ought to tip her well."

May knew where this was going.

"Oh, *that's* the reason you want to tip her." Her mother slammed the water glass down. "I can't believe you. You get the most expensive thing on the menu as if I don't know what you really like spending your money on."

It always happened like this.

"I know you know." Her father smiled. "I like that you do."

"Son of a . . ." her mother said. She grabbed the keys and stomped away. The Texans stared. Ethan was still reading. She hated that he could sit there as if nothing had happened, as if he didn't care. He waited until his enchilada came and ate it in five minutes. May wasn't even halfway done with her beans and rice when he stood to leave. She was going with him. She stood up but her father grabbed her hand.

"Sit down. I don't eat alone."

May looked at Ethan. He was standing by the stairs, looking at her and their father. He shook his head and left.

May's jaw clenched. Her face hurt. She looked at the Texans and saw that they were watching. Tensing up, she sat down.

"Good." Her father smiled at the waitress. May ate, wishing he'd choke on his shrimp. Whenever the waitress walked by, her father wheedled and smiled. He asked about mainland Mexico. Smiling and coy, the waitress sidled closer. Her father nodded. The waitress whispered in her father's ear. Her father's attention now taken by the waitress, May excused herself.

May left the restaurant and walked down the old dirt road toward their hotel. Fireflies glowed in the grasses and far away, the wild dogs barked.

Her father had first brought a woman home when she was three or four. The woman had pinched May's arms and fed her animal cookies. When May was in second grade, her mother left and her father never noticed. Hungry, May had opened her father's wallet, taken two hundred dollars, and gotten in trouble for stealing and suspended for having lice. Only a year ago, May had walked in on her father with two women in her bedroom. May had taken her bed apart and dumped it in the alley behind her house.

Her father did not come back to their hotel that night. Her mother turned on all the lights and remade her bed again

and again. Ethan was able to finish his chapter, turn over, and go to sleep. But May couldn't block out her mother. She grabbed some blankets. Though she wanted to, she couldn't lock the bathroom door. She slept in the bathtub. She woke up stiff in the morning, with one foot damp from the faucet drip. Dim light seeped through the window and the mating toucans croaked on the roof.

May left for the beach. She walked across the Mexican sand, her feet sinking in. The warm sea washed away her footprints. On the far end of the beach, a limestone outcropping jutted from the sea. She climbed along the spiny rocks beneath the ledge. There was a fissure in the stone. Curious, May peered inside. It looked like it led to a large cave, so she climbed through.

She stared. A writhing serpent was carved into the limestone. It was twenty feet long, maybe longer, curling around the cave in loops. Its pug-nosed snout protruded from the wall, and a collar of carved feathers extended down the beast's back. The scales were painted red and yellow, and the feathers were colored green and blue. Gleaming obsidian chips were embedded in the eyes.

"You have come." It was a soft and leathery voice. Underlying it were other sounds, guttural words and popping consonants, like it was speaking another language but she could understand it anyway. "You will free me from my thousand-year imprisonment and together, we will take revenge."

May looked around, expecting to see a nook where her brother could've set up his iPod speakers. He liked to mock her for reading fantasy novels. May kicked the conch shells and the obsidian littering the floor, looking for something in the debris. "Revenge, huh?"

"You aren't what I was expecting," the voice said. "I am called Topiltzin, and once I was a great king. I ruled a city called Tollan, the capital of the Toltec nation. It was a time of plenty. My mother, Cihuacoatl, ran the forest sometimes as a woman, sometimes as a deer. Mixcoatl Totepeuh, the priest-king of Quetzalcoatl saw her. Her swiftness enchanted him. He chased her and she, falling in love, was captured. I was conceived. Within a mortal skin, the god Quetzalcoatl was born."

May wondered if her parents had been in love when she and her brother were conceived—if they had ever been in love at all. She decided that this wasn't her brother's iPod. She sifted her fingers through the sand, half- listening to the story now.

"But birthing a god is arduous. When my mother heaved out the afterbirth, she saw that jaguars had encircled her. She hid me, and the jaguars bred my brother on her. He was the god Tezcatlipoca. We were raised like ordinary boys but we wandered the jungle like learning gods. He ate the maggots out of corpses and I sang feathers off the wings of quetzal birds. We were as different as can be. Nonetheless, we were good brothers."

"That's good," May said. She'd never had anything like that with her brother. Ethan did whatever he wanted, and he wanted nothing to do with her.

"It didn't last. When I was sixteen, the bond between us broke. We came home and saw mother with a man."

The statue had responded to her, like this was *real*.

"It was my father, Mixcoatl Totepeuh. His first son, Ihuitimal, had died and he'd sought me out to inherit his throne. My brother and mother came with me to live in the palace, where tame ocelots played with blue parrots. My mother

attended the dying king and happily conceived my little sister Hatsutsil. But my brother was not so happy. He desired my throne, though he had no right to it."

"Well," May said, "that's how families seem to work."

"Royal families in particular—if only we had stayed brothers! When I finally inherited the throne, my brother began to work against me as the Yaotl, the perpetual enemy. I tamed alligators and poisonous snakes with my flute, and my brother told the people I was allied with the beasts. When I opened schools, my brother said it was an act of egotism. When I abolished blood sacrifice, he said that I was trying to bring the apocalypse. Whatever good I did, he twisted into evil.

"Finally, he began rumors about Hatsustil, my sister. I confronted him in the street. There, we fought. I cut off his left foot. Gushing blood, Tezcatlipoca limped into the crowd. Despite his grievous wound, he did not die. Bitter, he watched the bright lives of my family in his dark obsidian glass. He schemed. When he returned to us, begging us to take him in, my sister prepared his chocolate with her own hands. We lay garlands across the lintels, invited musicians and dancers. He gave me a drink he'd invented, called *pulque*. And, I drank it. Soon the room spun. The floor swayed beneath my feet. I remember little: getting angry, standing blood-soaked in the cool night air. Tezcatlipoca had betrayed me."

"This is true, isn't it?" May asked.

"To my misery, yes. You don't know the worst yet, for in the morning my brother said I'd killed my beautiful Hatsustil. He told me he'd drugged me, and laughing, he dumped a jug of pulque over me. I buried my sister that day and walked into exile. Some among my court and some among my subjects, unconquered by my brother's lies, joined my escort. But Tezcatlipoca wouldn't let us go; he wanted me to suffer."

"Why are people like that?" May asked. She'd wondered this when her parents fought, but she never knew anyone who she could ask.

"My brother is like that because he is Tezcatlipoca, and that is what Tezcatlipoca does. He eats innocents in the night and sends plagues through his smoking mirror. I want him to suffer as I did, and know the meaning of justice. He followed me into the mountains, slaughtering my friends and throwing their carcasses to the jaguars. Soon, my mother and I were alone, weak with hunger. He stabbed a spear through her. He was so consumed by his hatred that he'd forgotten she was his mother too."

Could May kill her family? Could she kill anyone? Sometimes, she imagined what it would be like, how she would do it if it was a stranger, a friend, someone she loved and knew.

"He bound my magic with her blood. Then, he carried me to this cave, carved this shape, and cut my throat. But you cannot kill a god. When he saw my spirit escaping as the wind, he imbedded me in the stone. To mock me, he decorated my prison with a colorful paste made from my bones. Tezcatlipoca left the conch shells so that I may hear an untouchable, outside world. He promised that if I could break my morals and shed the precious water, then I would be free."

"From your prison," May mused. "You're trapped, and you can't free yourself because of what's been done to you."

"Yes," the statue said.

"Maybe I'm going crazy or maybe I'm dreaming," May whispered, and the statue did not reply. "I want to tell you

things I've never said aloud. Sometimes talking makes whatever you're saying real, and if it's real, I'd have to do something. But I don't know what to do."

"Speaking is the only way I am real," Topiltzin said.

May shook her head. Words stuck in her throat. She walked over to the statue and leaned on its carved head. She imagined that she could feel the buried life beneath her fingertips, that the roughness of the paint was not sand but bones.

"You understand me," Topiltzin said.

"No," she said, then, "well, yes." May told him about yesterday at the restaurant, how her father had gripped her wrist and how he had treated the waitress. She told him about how her mother never stopped talking. May knew her mother's rant so well she could recite the names of her father's mistresses, too: Tristina, Kaitlin, Janelle, the maid, and did it go on or what. She told him that her mother always said after that, "Sometimes, I don't know why I bother staying with this man." May didn't know. If she had the choice, she would leave. But she was too young to go and old enough to know what happened to girls who left home.

"When I was seven, Dana came to my house. I'd seen her before, in the marketing department, one of my father's girls. She came into my bedroom and dumped my school stuff out of my backpack, shoved clothes in, grabbed my wrist, and pulled me downstairs. My brother was sitting in the living room watching TV. He stood at the door when she put me in her hatchback. His eyes looked like dead fish eyes and he just stood there. He watched her take me away."

May took a deep breath. "They say I was missing. I don't remember much. My father was going on a date with Dana, and by accident, he found me locked in her closet. They sent me to a child psychologist. The sound of locks still makes me hyperventilate. My brother knew who Dana was. He knew where I was. He knew the whole entire time but he didn't say anything. Why didn't he tell anyone?"

"Your past has captured you. Your brother, your father, and your mother have woven you into these events. There was nothing you could do," Topiltzin said.

"Stop it. You can't say things like that to me. It wasn't my dad's fault, or my mother's. They're only betraying each other. My brother, he must have been trying to hurt me. Why else wouldn't he tell? He never protected me—never did what older brothers are supposed to do."

"You could change it," Topiltzin said.

"Oh, yeah right." May realized that she was rolling her eyes at a Toltec god trapped in a talking statue. She stopped doing it.

"You could shed the precious water and break my spell. Blood shed for justice and a just cause." His voice was a whisper now, and lower.

"You want me to *kill* him," May said. He was her brother! She couldn't do something like that. He did have something coming to him, though.

"Yes," Topiltzin said. "You need to free me so that I can avenge my sister and my mother, and retake my people. My brother is an evil god, and I need to stop him."

"You didn't stop him before. If I sacrifice someone, what makes you think you could, like, get your revenge?"

"I will emerge from the stone in my godlike form." Topiltzin was angry. "I am no longer weak with grief. I am strong with hatred."

May nodded. She wondered if she could do it and if he

really, really deserved it. Could anyone deserve to die at all? Would she regret not doing it more than doing it? She probably would always wonder if she didn't.

"Do you want revenge like I want revenge?" Topiltzin's voice was soft, almost wistful. He sounded like he'd be okay with her saying no.

"I don't want him to suffer." May wondered if she could do it. She was afraid of how tall he was, how he'd always watched her with his forehead smooth. "You said you need the precious water to break the spell."

Topiltzin told her how it must be done. Then, she walked back along the beach, sand fleas beneath her feet. A man smoked a cigarette, his hand dangling from the balcony rail. She could feel his eyes smolder as he watched her.

She climbed the stairs and opened the door. Her father was kneeling on the floor, folding his light-colored slacks. Books with pages torn out, chunks of coral, and a squished bottle of sunscreen were scattered about. He put the slacks on the bed, next to his polo shirts.

"What happened?" May asked.

Ethan, sitting at the table, looked up from his book. Bands of light stretched from the lamp and across his forehead. "Mother decided that this vacation was useless, that she was going home. She thought of taking you with her, but I told her you were busy."

"What?" May didn't know if she was more shocked that her mother had left or that her mother had wanted to bring her along. "Why did you say that?"

Ethan shrugged and went back to reading.

"She'll be back," her father said. "She always comes back. May, get over here and clean this up. I need to get this fixed.

It's not supposed to be like this."

"No," May said. "It is like this, so just deal with it. I'm not going to pick up your stuff for you. Ethan, why do you say things like that?"

"May, don't push me," her father said.

But May was looking at Ethan. "Seriously, Ethan."

Her father stood. He unplugged the telephone very delicately and threw it at her head. May ducked. The phone banged into the door and fell on the floor. The ringer purred at her heels. "May. Get over here. Now."

May stepped forward, jerkily. Her heart pounded. She could feel her father's anger. It was as if the air had clenched around her. Her father grabbed her wrists and pressed them into her stomach. He loomed into her, forcing her to meet his eyes. His eyes were bloodshot and thirsty.

Her father said, "Ethan. Get out."

Ethan stood, holding his book in one hand, his index finger marking the page. He looked at May, his eyes lingering on her captured wrists. He looked at his father. He shrugged and left. Just like that, he left.

"It's not supposed to be like this," her father said again. "Women don't leave me. Just like your mother, you want me to take care of you." He was rubbing her wrists now, his grip tight enough to make her fingers curl.

"Get away from me." May stomped on his feet. He recoiled, reeling onto the bed. "It's all going to change now. Understand that," she said and went outside.

Ethan was standing on the balcony, his book balanced on the rail. Some light from inside seeped through the curtains, but it wasn't enough to read by. She stood next to him and looked into the moving palms. Across the way, the tip of a cigarette glowed

cherry-red. The man with the smoldering eyes was watching them.

"What?" Ethan said. He was probably irritated by her silence.

"Why didn't you say anything?" She still wanted to know.

"I don't know," he said. "Sometimes I think something's wrong with me."

"You think?" May said. Hilarity welled within her. Something was wrong with him. Something had to be wrong with him, with all of them, and she couldn't fix it. She could change something, though. Perhaps she was changing the way the world worked. "Never mind. I don't want to be here anymore, not after that."

Ethan stared into the moving darkness.

"I'm going down to the cave." May went to the stairs and pretended to hesitate. "You might want to see it."

"What cave?" Ethan asked.

"It's the one with the . . . you know . . . carving. Down by the sea, under the rocks. I thought you might want to see it, so that you can tell me if it's real or not."

"What's it of?" He was interested now.

"I don't know. It's not like I know anything about the Aztecs. Only that my history teacher said they followed an eagle, then founded Mexico City.'."

"Those were the Chichimecs," Ethan corrected automatically. "They only became the Aztecs after they founded Tenochtitlan. Your history teacher was misinformed at best."

May shrugged. "Well, I'm going to go."

"I'll come." Ethan brought out his keychain and clicked on his miniature flashlight. They walked past the smoking man and down the beach. Ethan stayed behind her so they wouldn't have to talk. Right behind her, he climbed onto the butte, cursing as he stubbed his knee balancing book and flashlight. The beam bounced wildly on the rocks and the flashing sea.

"I'm going in now," May said. Her brother followed her through the roaring waves. May touched the damp rock and crawled into the fissure. She licked the salt spray from her lips. Deep inside, May crouched over obsidian shards. She breathed and told herself, Make a decision now. Conch shells clattered.

The wind, the sea, and the walls around her whispered, "Yes."

GREGORY FROST

The Fortunate Dream

THERE ONCE WAS A POOR YOUNG MAN WHO HAD NO hope. His name was Loctrean, and he lived in an old, dilapidated house with his parents and sister in the city of Guhnavra, which lay on a narrow peninsula on the far side of a great desert. He lived with his father and mother and sister.

His father was a dreamer, a teller of tales who was very popular at the local tavern because he always had a story to share and always had enough coin to buy his audience a round. And if they disbelieved his adventures, the free drink bought their complaisance.

The father claimed to have been a sailor on board the ship of the infamous Captain Sindebad, to have walked in exotic lands, seen impossible monsters, and sailed to the very edge of the world and back. At home he told the same tales to his children, filling their heads with dazzling images, breathtaking

adventures, and often promising that one day they would all be terribly rich. But when he was off fishing, their mother would say, "The truth is, your father hasn't been anywhere at all. The only place *he's* sailed is inside his head." They would have preferred not to know, but they were children and at the mercy of the adults. Loctrean in particular wanted his father to be the adventurer of the stories.

Loctrean's life might have gone on like that forever, except that one evening his father didn't return from the day's fishing, and no one knew at first what had befallen him. Eventually, other sailors found his father's boat and dragged it into the cracked and broken courtyard of the house. The keel had been shattered as if upon a sharp point of rock, and the sailors left it overturned in the courtyard across from the dusty, dried-up fountain. Of his father they had found no sign. Loctrean overheard the superstitious sailors whispering that God had killed his father for all of the lies he'd told, and Loctrean burst upon them, shouting, "He didn't lie! He did travel far! He *did* have adventures!" But despite his defense, he was ashamed, though whether for himself or for his father, he didn't know.

It wasn't long after that before his mother succumbed to a wasting disease. Paying for her medicine cost the family nearly everything they had. Before she died, she clutched her son close and whispered that she'd lied about his father because she was jealous. "He never took me on a single one of his adventures," she said. "They all happened in his youth, and he said he was done with that, and that I was pestering him when I asked. He hurt me, but he didn't lie to you." Now, she said, she was embarking on her own adventure—her last. Then she closed her eyes and died.

In short order then, Loctrean lost both of his parents and found himself suddenly an orphan with a sister to care for.

Loctrean inherited his father's house and the fishing boat, which is to say he had inherited his father's many debts. The house fell into further disrepair. He couldn't afford even to replace the wine-colored striped awning over the door, which was too threadbare to keep even light rain from spilling through.

His father's boat remained in the courtyard. Its smashed planks grew so rotten that the boat would never be seaworthy again. He felt like that boat, as if a hole had been punched through him, never to be healed.

All he knew how to do was fish, but he could not repair the boat, nor could he afford to buy a new one. There were few fishing crews in the town and none of them would hire him either, as they believed he was the same as his father, a dreamer who would be a danger to the others in their crew. Even the kindest of them explained to him that they couldn't take a chance on him.

The only good news came when his sister married a neighboring grocer. The grocer made just enough money for the two of them and had nothing left over to help with the debts their father had left, but at least his sister was looked after, and Loctrean took solace in that.

He accepted that he was going to lose his father's house and there was nothing he could do about it. He determined that he must sell the property for whatever he could get, pay off all the debts, and use whatever was left over to start again somewhere else.

The night he made this decision, however, Loctrean's father appeared to him in a dream. "You must close up the house," said the ghost, "but not sell it. Then travel to the city of Perla. There you will find your fortune."

"So, it's true and you are dead," Loctrean said sadly.

"I drowned. It wasn't any fun."

"And how is mother?" he asked.

"No longer in pain," his father's shade replied. "You were a good son to her. A good brother to your sister too."

"Thank you," he said, and a longing to embrace his father welled up inside him. He wanted to reach out and hug his father, but in the dream he seemed unable to do anything but stand and observe.

"Never mind all that," his father admonished him. "Just wake up and go!" With that the ghost vanished and Loctrean awoke.

Well, he thought, I suppose it's no worse an idea than what I was *going* to do. I wish, though, I'd asked him to tell me one of his stories. That would have been nice.

As instructed, Loctrean closed up the house, and with his remaining coins, he set out for Perla.

That city lay far away across the broad inland sea and up the wide Black River. It had a reputation as a dark place, surrounded by marshes and swamps, ghostly lights and pirates. The air was tinged with the stink of sulphur long before the city came into view. It had a thoroughly unwholesome reputation to match the smell, and Loctrean wondered why his father would have sent him there, or even how his father might have been familiar with the place. Still, he could not refuse to obey the wishes of his father's shade. He booked passage on a ship that took him part of the way to Perla, but had to sign on as a member of the crew to make most of the journey. The captain of that ship worked him hard too. He learned to tack and wear, to sound depths, and even to bake biscuits for the crew. There was no job aboard ship that he didn't learn well before they entered the mouth of the Black River.

Long before they arrived in Perla, the crew smelled the noxious city. Strange, ghostly lights danced in the mists upon both shores. Some of the crew cowered at the sight of them, but Loctrean was unimpressed. He'd heard of far scarier things at his father's knee than bobbing lights in the fog. Besides, his father's ghost had told him to go to Perla, and so he knew no harm would come to him on the journey. There was a reason he was here, and he had to find it.

Once the boat arrived and was tied up at the wharf, Loctrean took his leave.

Of course, he didn't know what to do now that he had arrived. His father had not been specific at all about what to do once he got to Perla, only that he should come.

He walked the whole length of the city, and as anyone who's been there can attest, it's a long, narrow place, trapped between swamps on the one side and mountains on the other. Loctrean had walked to the far outskirts of Perla. He was penniless and hungry, and had no idea what to look for or where to look for it.

Rain began to fall. First it merely drizzled, and then the skies opened up and a torrent poured down as if upon him alone.

An ancient, domed temple stood at the edge of the city, on the last street before the city wall. Multiple rows of columns lined the front of the old temple, all of them gouged and pocked from centuries of bitter sulfurous rain. Loctrean hid beneath the roof that the columns supported, and while there he looked inside.

The interior was dark and quiet and cool, filled with

still more slender columns, like a forest thick with trees. Small rugs were strewn everywhere. No rain dripped there. In fact, dust hung in the air, yet no one was praying or attending. He couldn't fathom to what deity the temple had been built in the first place. All the icons and statues appeared to have been removed. But it was dry and offered protection from the rain. He found a secluded alcove, curled up, and went to sleep. He hoped his father would show up again and tell him what to do.

Instead, while penniless Loctrean slept, a group of thieves crept into the shrine. They had been coming there nightly for weeks. Each night they chiseled and loosened the mortar around a stone that, once removed, would give them access to a usurer's shop that abutted the old temple wall. The moneylender was a true fiend, but was known to be enormously wealthy. The thieves intended to kill him and rob him of his obscene fortune.

The previous night they had succeeded in removing a large stone on which they'd been working for weeks, lifting it from the wall of the temple. Now they worked even more cautiously but urgently to remove the smaller bricks from the wall of the adjoining house. What they failed to take into account was the usurer's penchant for staying up late into the night to count his fortune. He had blacked all the windows where he kept the money so that no one could see inside. To the thieves it appeared that he'd retired for the night.

Thus the evil usurer, sitting in the very room they intended to plunder, was alerted to their intrusion. He blew out his candle and waited.

At last, the thieves removed enough smaller bricks in his wall for one man to slide through. Triumphantly, their leader stuck his head through the hole, only to find a cackling madman awaiting him on the other side and brandishing a scimitar.

When the thief's feet frantically kicked out, his friends hauled him back into the temple only to discover that his head had been lopped off. But the alarm was sounded—the usurer had rushed into the street and was shouting for the police. The thieves dropped the corpse of their leader and fled.

Poor Loctrean awoke to their commotion. He stumbled from his alcove just as the authorities arrived.

"Here's one!" shouted a deputy, and the police fell upon him and beat him senseless. Of the gang they found only the headless body. They dragged Loctrean to the jail and threw him inside.

The following day, he was hauled before the chief magistrate. Bloody and bruised, he could only insist that he knew nothing of any robbery beyond what they themselves knew. The usurer of course demanded Loctrean's execution on the spot, but that only infuriated the magistrate toward more leniency than he might otherwise have shown his suspect.

"If I were a thief," Loctrean explained, "would I have waited to be captured, sir? Did you capture any others of this gang waiting in the dark? Any who still have their heads, I mean. Why would I have lingered?"

The magistrate sensed that he was hearing the truth. "What were you doing there, then?" he asked. "No one has worshipped in that temple for years."

So Loctrean explained his situation, his poverty, and how his father's ghost had appeared in a dream and advised him to seek his fortune here.

"You mean to say you sailed all the way from Guhnavra because of a dream? You're crazy, do you know that? Acting upon such things. I myself was visited just the other night in my dreams by a woman who told me she knew of a house where a great treasure lay buried."

"Did you find the house?" asked Loctrean.

The magistrate sighed. "You haven't been paying attention, fool. The woman and her treasure aren't *real*. To begin with, this house doesn't even exist in Perla. It looks nothing like houses here. It was a square-topped place with an old, purple-striped awning, and a rotted boat in one corner of the courtyard and a dried-up, broken old fountain in another. Crumbling old place. Furthermore, and even more ludicrous, she insisted that the hidden treasure had come from the legendary Captain Sindebad. Well, I mean, really. It's a fairy tale, isn't it? Something recalled from my childhood, no doubt and brought back by some bad turnips or something."

Excited, Loctrean asked, "This treasure, where was it hidden?"

"How should I know that? I woke up, didn't I? Haven't you been listening? This isn't . . . oh, never mind." The magistrate saw that the matter was hopeless. He had a simpleton here who could neither have robbed the usurer nor comprehended that the world did not operate via magical dreams.

"Listen, the best thing you can do, fellow, is go home and stop attending to these fantasies. Learn a trade. Establish yourself." He took out a small purse and placed two coins on the table. "Here." he said. "Because we beat you and I'm certain you're innocent—naïve, gullible, but innocent. Go home, my friend."

Loctrean thanked the magistrate and limped stiffly out of the police barracks.

He used the coins to buy part of his passage home on the same ship that had brought him. As before it wasn't enough, but the crew was happy to have him because his cooking had proved better than anyone else's. All the same, they taunted him. "Didn't find that treasure after all?" they asked. "No magic beans, no geese laying eggs of gold?" Loctrean hardly paid them any mind because he was fearful that something might have happened to his house meanwhile.

However, it awaited him as he had left it, save for a few more rodents as tenants in the holes of its walls. The awning had finally split in two and hung down in shreds.

Loctrean entered the house and began searching everywhere. The woman in the magistrate's dream—surely it was his mother—had said that the treasure was buried, and he pulled up every stone in every room only to find dirt or sand or mice beneath. Exhausted, he went out and collapsed in the courtyard against the boat.

From there he found himself staring directly at the fountain pedestal. Hadn't the magistrate made mention of the fountain?

Even as he watched, the stones beneath it cracked, and the fountain tilted slowly to one side.

He got up and climbed over the retaining wall and into the dustbowl that had once been a shallow pond. He grabbed the pedestal and began wrenching it back and forth until it came away completely.

Pushing it aside he stared into a dry hole where, presumably, water had once been channeled. He knelt and then lay amidst the rubble and reached his arm down into the hole. His fingers touched the sides of a cloth bag. He clutched it and dragged it up out of the hole. It was heavy and thick, the neck tied with a cord. The outer layer of cloth had frayed but there were at least two more layers beneath it. He heard the coins before he saw them. They were huge, so big that he couldn't circle his fingers around them. They had strange writing on them, and faces of some foreign gods or emperors stamped into one side. Loctrean had never seen any coins like them. One bag must be worth a fortune. He lay on the tiles again and reached into the hole, and his fingers touched another bag. He drew it out, and this one contained gems: rubies and sapphires, diamonds and emeralds. It was a fortune fit for a king.

Kneeling there in the dust he praised his father for telling the truth, even though no one had ever believed him. He *had* sailed with the mythical Sindebad. Here was the proof.

That night Loctrean had another dream. In it his father apologized for not telling him about the fortune years earlier. "I kept it hidden," he said, "because I wanted you and your sister to grow up unspoiled by riches, to know what it was like to have to work, to earn your way, the way almost everyone must."

After that, Loctrean saw both his parents from time to time in his dreams. His mother would tell him some incredible tale of the afterlife—how grapes grew as big as her head or how animals talked—and his father would explain, "She's lying. It's nothing like that at all here, let me tell you."

Loctrean paid off his debts. He had the house refurbished from top to bottom and hung a bright new awning over the door. He bought a fleet of fishing boats but left his father's decrepit craft in a corner of the yard as a shrine. He showered his sister and her husband with gifts and ensured that they would never want for anything.

Eventually he sailed back to Perla on the ship he now owned.

There he gave the dismayed magistrate a generous sum in thanks for showing him compassion, adding, "Had I not listened to you, I wouldn't have found my fortune."

When finally he married (and with his riches he was a very desirable catch), he doted on his wife, keeping her and their children happy every day—mostly by telling them fantastic stories of the glorious adventures of their grandfather, who had sailed to the ends of the world and faced every peril imaginable. And if the children didn't believe him, well, it hardly mattered, after all.

E. Sedia

Out of Her Element

LETICIA WINDHAM DID NOT EXPECT TO SEE A SALAMANDER emerging from the flames in the fireplace of her parents' drawing room. And yet, here it was, still surrounded by a lingering halo of afterflames, smelling of brimstone, and looking over Leticia with queer black eyes that reflected nothing back.

"That is strange," said Mrs. Wilkes, the housekeeper, and shifted in Leticia's mother's deep chair, rearranging her sizeable derriere to greater comfort. "But these things spend winter in rotten logs, so I suppose the heat woke it up."

Leticia nodded, but tucked her legs under her skirts more thoroughly. She was sitting on the floor in front of the fire, and not far from the salamander's path.

"You shouldn't sit on the floor, young lady," Mrs. Wilkes said. "You'll catch a fever again."

Leticia smiled and remained sitting. It was just a ritual they exchanged often. Everything felt like a ritual when her parents weren't here: Mrs. Wilkes and she went through the motions in the big echoing house, brushing against each other like figurines in the great clock in the living room, but never really connecting. Both were too wrapped up in what it meant that Mr. and Mrs. Windham weren't there. Everything was hollow without them, and Leticia and the servants retreated into themselves every time Leticia's parents left.

The salamander paused and moved its head side to side, as if considering the best possible egress. Leticia doubted it would be able to survive long outside in London's drizzly November blown through with cold, cutting winds. She envied her parents, who were somewhere deep in warm Egypt. *Really, she thought, if they were so concerned about my health, they would've taken me with them.* At least it was dry and hot and marvelous there, and much more interesting than London, but her parents always said that the travel would be too much for her. She wondered why they couldn't stay here with her, but never dared to ask it out loud.

"Can I keep him?" Leticia pointed at the salamander and shot Mrs. Wilkes a pleading look. "He'll die outside."

Mrs. Wilkes looked up from the embroidery that had been consuming her attention. "As long as he doesn't go running through the house."

"He won't," Leticia promised and jumped to her feet a bit too fast—she was still weak, and her head spun. She stood a moment, and the salamander had progressed all the way down the hall before she felt well enough to run after him and scoop him up. As soon as she did that she yelped in pain—the dry skin of the creature burned her fingers.

"I do not think you're supposed to be that warm, Mr. Salamander," Leticia said, and carefully transferred her infernal pet into the folds of her apron. "Why, I think you're running a fever.

I would ask Dr. Greenaway to put leeches on you, but I doubt you would enjoy that." Leticia ran to her room, even though she grew winded quickly, and when she grew winded, she coughed. Her coughing fits always made Mrs. Wilkes frown and her parents whisper in dark tones. She tried not to cough, and hid every blood-stained handkerchief as well as she could. Maybe they wouldn't leave quite as often if she could just get better.

She had situated Mr. Salamander in one of the elaborate dollhouses that sprouted in her room ever since she first fell ill. Her parents seemed to believe that death would get confounded in the tiny hallways and tangled in lifelike draperies. Leticia imagined her room filling with dollhouses until bursting, when there would be no more place left for her among the delicate airy miniature architecture. Then, she imagined, she would perish. Or perhaps she would become miniaturized and would explore the town of three-storied mansions and castles and fake lawns without a concern in the world, with no one to tell her not to exert herself too much, or to spend a day in bed. She especially looked forward to investigating the depth of the lake, swimming with white swans cleverly made of wax and chicken down, even though the lake was just a small mirror kindly donated by her mother and that still smelled of lilac perfume, just like everything Leticia's mother ever touched.

The salamander seemed to enjoy his new surroundings. He eagerly ambled among the tiny chairs with tall backs and knocked down a few miniature shepherdesses that seemed in awe of their opulent surroundings. The salamander settled on a velvet couch, callously displacing a few miniature sheep that took residence there.

"I wonder what you eat," Leticia said.

The salamander's black eyes met hers. *Fire*, the answer came to her.

"Did you just say that?"

The salamander did not answer, and Leticia dismissed it as her imagination. She decided to ask the gardener next time he came by to tend to the anemic indoor garden on the back veranda. He probably knew what salamanders ate.

Her train of thought was interrupted by a thunderous thumping of the door knocker, followed by a desperate dinging of the doorbell. She startled at the sounds—it was certainly too late for visitors, even if they were expecting any visitors at all. When her parents were gone, the only people who came and went were the maids, who used the servants' entrance, and Leticia's music tutor.

She crept to the top of the stairs and listened to the commotion in the hall. She heard Mr. Bresson, the butler, open the door, and another male voice inquiring if he could come in. Bresson said something in his subdued but forceful tone, and the visitor's voice changed to pleading. There was some rustling of paper and banging of heavy objects.

From her post at the top of the stairs, Leticia saw a man wrapped into entirely too many scarves, overcoats, and cloaks enter. He was dragging a heavy chest with brass corners by the handle. His free hand held a crumpled piece of paper that apparently gained his admittance. It had to be a powerful talisman to pacify Bresson and to induce him to allow entry to a stranger, especially so late at night.

Bresson huffed and grabbed the other handle of the chest. "Follow me, sir," he said with his usual hostility. "I'll show you to your room and notify the housekeeper that you are in need of a bed. The cook has left for the day, so I hope you're not hungry."

The two of them proceeded down the hallway toward the

visitors' rooms. Leticia remained at her post as Mrs. Wilkes bustled to the visitor's' quarters, exiling the new arrival to the drawing room while she commanded the maid to remove the covers from everything and to prepare the visitor's bed.

Bresson retired to his room, stooping over more than usual. Leticia pitied him just like he pitied the housekeeper and the cook, and even herself—all of them abandoned by her parents, left to coexist without those who held them all together.

Leticia had grown bold enough for a closer look at the visitor and tiptoed to the drawing room, where the guest, now relieved of his coats and scarves, stood in front of the fire, desperately rubbing his thin, bluing hands right next to the flames.

"Good evening," Leticia said.

The guest spun around, his face of a pale greenish hue expressing great alarm. At the sight of Leticia, his face relaxed, and he smiled. "You must be the young Miss Windham," he said. "Your parents always speak fondly of you."

Leticia's heart squeezed in her chest. "You've seen them?"

"I know them," the visitor replied. He extracted the much folded and refolded piece of paper from his vest pocket and handed it to Leticia. "An invitation to visit—I met them in Egypt. Unfortunately, the letter took so long to reach me that by the time I got here they have left again."

"Your name is Richard Stanton," Leticia observed, glancing at the letter. "Are you going to stay here?"

"For a little while," he said, apologetically. "If you don't mind, of course. I have just returned to England, and I have to look for proper lodgings.'"

"You can stay," Leticia permitted. "You wouldn't happen

to know anything about salamanders, would you?"

His eyes went wide with surprise. "Salamanders? Why would you ask that?"

"I just found one, sir," Leticia said. "He came from this very fireplace. And now I don't know what to feed him."

Richard Stanton hesitated. "You wouldn't mind me taking a look at this remarkable creature, would you?"

"Not at all," Leticia said. "Come along and I'll show you."

The salamander had taken to his new home and seemed to enjoy investigating the elaborate hallways and convoluted passages of the dollhouses and the grounds around them. Leticia did not have much to do but to watch him—her music tutor rarely came by since her health grew worse, and the weather was too dreadful to leave the house.

When not playing with her dollhouses or reading her parents' books, Leticia liked to slide through the hallways on her feet clad in thick stockings, silent as shadow, and to listen to the noises of the house. The kitchen was always awash in the heat and reddish light from the stove, and the cook rarely saw Leticia poking her head into the kitchen realm. The cook spent most of the time standing facing the stove, her hands hanging idly by her sides as if she were lost in deep reverie. Sometimes Leticia wanted to ask what she was thinking about, but never quite had the courage.

Mrs. Wilkes kept quiet too, when she wasn't ordering the maids around. She sat in her drawing room with a half laid out game of solitaire in front of her. Sometimes her candle burned down, and she did not move to light a new one. Her thoughts were a mystery to Leticia, and she wondered if it would be possible to truly understand another soul.

The only times when any of them came together were at mealtimes, when Mrs. Wilkes presided over the table and Leticia and Richard Stanton tried to avoid staring at each other across the wide, cold expanse of the tablecloth. Leticia snuck occasional peeks at the mysterious visitor and quickly looked away if he was looking back. He asked after the salamander occasionally, but kept to himself otherwise.

"You see, Mr. Salamander," she explained to her new friend, "when my parents are not here, everything changes. I know that they have important work to do, and I don't want to be selfish, but I so wish they were here. For one, my father would certainly know what you eat. Or what you are, for that matter.

"And I wish their friend Mr. Stanton would talk to me a little. I think he knows more than he says. And also I wish he would tell me about my parents. They spend so much time in Egypt, he probably knows more about them than I do."

The salamander listened, his unblinking eyes fixed on Leticia's. She got a feeling that he was really paying attention, and that was enough to earn him her gratitude. The houseguest was another matter.

Richard Stanton was an irregular visitor, at least according to Mrs. Wilkes. She disapproved of his habit of staying up all night and sleeping until noon, and complained bitterly of the strange smells and colored smokes seeping from under the door of his room. She was especially displeased by the proliferation of strange pictures, charts, and books in Mr. Stanton's room.

"Downright unchristian," she told Leticia after describing a particularly ghastly figurine that was the last to emerge from Mr. Stanton's chest. "That's what it is. He lived among heathens for so long, he has converted to their ways."

Leticia grew concerned about her parents' spiritual well-being and decided to question Mr. Stanton at the first opportunity. However, Leticia Windham was not the girl to wait for opportunities—she marched straight to Mr. Stanton's room and swung the door open without waiting for his response to her knock. "Are the Egyptians unchristian?" she demanded.

Stanton looked up from his alembic, which was heating on the flame of a small gas burner, and smiled. "Most of them, yes. But some are Christians. I spent a lot of time with Coptic Christians, and I assure you that they are as devout as you or me. And some of these charts and paintings are also Coptic, if that's what you're asking."

"Oh." Leticia watched Stanton carefully measure some blue and white powders into a small crucible and fit a porcelain vessel open on both ends on top of it. "What are you doing?"

"Experimenting."

Leticia noticed that the entire side table had been converted to a makeshift laboratory, and a variety of metal and ceramic vessels, tongs, tiny anvils, and glass retorts crowded its surface. "What kind of experiments?"

"I'm a doctor," Stanton said, "of sorts."

Leticia's suspicions flared up. "Is this why my parents asked you to visit us? Are you going to put leeches on me?"

"No leeches," Stanton promised. His olive face briefly expressed great sadness, quickly replaced by his usual dead-pan mien. "I'm not that kind of a doctor, Leticia. I'm not even a good one. I wish that I were, but with consumption . . . the only things that help are sanatoria, and even those are not always effective."

"I know," Leticia said. "I didn't really think you'd be able to help me, sir."

"I'm sorry," Stanton repeated. "Here, why don't you lend me a hand. I'll heat up this aludel, and as you see little crystals forming in the top vessel, I want you to pour this liquid over them." He pointed at the vessel open at both ends, stacked on top of another one

Leticia was always eager to play with things that bubbled and hissed, and she happily poured liquids, added powders, and mixed solutions with a glass rod at Stanton's instructions. The mixture changed color a few times and exuded colorful and fragrant steam. Leticia couldn't hold back a squeal of delight as large golden crystals shaped like giant marzipan snowflakes filled the top vessel, falling out of the steam cloud one by one.

Stanton picked up one of the crystals with a set of tongs and held it up against the light of the burner so that it shimmered and sparkled with hidden life. "Pretty, isn't it?"

"Yes, very," Leticia said. "What is it for?"

"I'm not really sure yet," Stanton replied.

Leticia made a face. "Than what's the use of your experiments?"

Stanton put down the crystal and tucked his thumbs in the pockets of his severe black jacket. He looked almost magical in this darkened room, which was concealed from the drizzle and soot outside by a set of heavy draperies. "I'm certain there is one," he said rather defensively. "The usefulness of something does not have to be apparent right away. By this logic, your salamander has no use at all."

Something in his voice sounded strange to Leticia. She shot him a penetrating look. "Oh? Do you know something about my salamander?"

"He's a lot like this crystal," Stanton admitted. "I'm sure

there's a use, but I don't know what it is yet. Figuring out hidden uses is what I do. Understand?"

Leticia did. She remembered how long it took the doctors to find the cause of her fatigue, frequent fevers, and the cough that wouldn't go away. She supposed that some mysteries had better resolutions than others.

She left Stanton to his contemplation of the marzipan crystals and went to investigate his books and charts that had so upset Mrs. Wilkes. The charts all seemed similar—they depicted strange symbols, among which Leticia recognized the sun, the crescent moon, and Venus and Mars.

The books were more puzzling—most had strange squiggles instead of letters, and those that were written with real letters were all in Latin. Leticia knew very little Latin, but even with this scant knowledge she could see that the books were about alchemy. This discovery compelled her to squint in Stanton's direction skeptically. "You believe in alchemy?"

"I practice it," Stanton said in his most earnest tone. "I know that your parents are dismissive of my chosen field, but please be assured that I follow the great Paracelsus rather than less . . . scientific authorities."

"Paracelsus was a doctor," Leticia said. "I've heard of him."

"You are a well-educated young lady," Stanton said. "Although I'm not surprised, knowing your parents. Your mother is the only lady scientist I have ever met."

"It's not because of them, sir," Leticia said. "It's because they have a library and are never around. I rarely do anything rather than stay home and read."

Stanton nodded sympathetically. "I do appreciate your help in the laboratory," he said. "You're welcome to stop by any time."

"Thank you," Leticia said. "I will."

She kept her promise and visited the laboratory almost every day. Though they spoke about little besides Paracelsus and salamanders, Leticia felt a growing fondness for the visitor. Among his alembics and the retorts, time passed quickly, and Leticia sometimes forgot about her illness altogether.

The salamander still resided in the dollhouse and remained too hot to touch. But despite Leticia's entreaties, he showed no desire to eat anything offered to him—not even pieces of roast beef tied to a string and wriggling like real worms. The dry heat emanating from his fading black and red-spotted skin grew less intense as the salamander refused food and his eyes grew dull. He barely moved off his toy velvet couch.

"I'm concerned about the salamander," Leticia told Stanton, who had become her new confidant, since he was more interested in Egypt and salamanders than Mrs. Wilkes could ever hope to be. He also had a sympathetic demeanor. Even though Leticia would be embarrassed to accept downright pity, she appreciated his willingness to let her help him. It was almost like having her father around. And she suspected that he enjoyed her presence rather more than he let on; his face always crinkled into a smile when she entered his room.

Stanton paid the salamander a visit and gave him a thorough look over. "According to some old alchemical traditions, which I do not follow, these are purported to be elementals of fire. But he seems to be growing colder."

"He did come out of the fire," Leticia said. "Do you think you can cure him, sir? I'm so afraid he will die."

"I can try." Stanton reached into the dollhouse and picked up the couch with the salamander. "Come along, little fellow. Let's see what my books think about you."

"I'm coming too," Leticia said. "He is mine."

Stanton gave her a fond look. "You of course have every right to supervise the treatment of your dependent."

Leticia followed Stanton and the salamander down the stairs and into Stanton's quarters. Stanton set the miniature couch onto the laboratory bench.

The salamander looked around, and for the first time in days his beadlike eyes lit up with enthusiasm. He quickly ambled up to the burner, and stood by it expectantly, as if waiting for someone to light it.

"I think he wants fire," Leticia said. "He told me that on the first night, only I thought I imagined it."

Stanton lit the burner, a narrow copper spout connected to a small reservoir of alcohol. Blue flames shot up from the nozzle, and the salamander ran up and lapped at the tongues of flame eagerly.

Leticia gasped in amazement as the colors of the salamander's skin revived as if by magic—the red spots flared with scarlet brilliance, the same bright color as the flames in the fireplace and spots on Leticia's handkerchiefs. The black background deepened into the blackness of coals, shot through with the afterimages of orange sparks that disappeared quicker than the eye could see. The formerly dull eyes of the salamander blazed with the blue of the flames reflected from the burner.

Stanton let the salamander slake his fire thirst and turned his attention to Leticia. "You are the most remarkable young lady I have ever met," he said with an expression Leticia couldn't quite place. "That salamander came and spoke to you, and you understood him."

"I suppose," Leticia said modestly. "But he could've

appeared anywhere. It was mere luck."

"Not so," Stanton said. "The experiment you helped me with—remember that? I could never make those crystals before. Only when you added the copper salts and the *aqua fortis* to the aludel did it actually go the way it was supposed to."

"According to Paracelsus?" Leticia asked skeptically.

"Other philosophers," Stanton admitted. His dark face assumed an embarrassed expression. "Paracelsus learned from the Egyptians too. The old things I learned in Egypt don't always agree with modern science in method, but in intent—to heal, not to do childish magic or greedy metal transformations. Paracelsus talked about curing powers of alchemy, of how it can be used to transform human body to health. And the Coptic alchemists also wrote of healing magic—of *aqua vitae* and philosopher's stone, of finding knowledge enough to heal every disease."

"So what were those crystals really for?"

Stanton sighed. "They're supposed to be an intermediary stage for something very important—the panacea, a substance that would cure any disease. I've never believed in it, but after meeting you I decided that I have to try."

Leticia's eyes filled with sudden hot tears, and she turned around and ran to her room, forgetting the salamander. She knocked over one of the dollhouses, kicked its delicate walls apart, and threw herself on her bed, sobbing. For the first time in her life she wept about her illness. She was angry with Stanton for offering her false hope—everyone knew that there was no cure for consumption, that she could only hope to live a bit longer by sparing herself any kind of excitement and spending summers in the Alps. It was simply too cruel, she thought. One did not talk about things like panacea in the presence of ill girls. It was hard enough for her to kill her hope in the first place.

It took Leticia a few days to regain her composure. Mrs. Wilkes was quite relieved to have Leticia free of Stanton's heretical influences, and didn't mind when Leticia asked for her meals to be served in her room.

"Just stay in bed, dear," Mrs. Wilkes said. "I'll keep you company if you want."

"Please," Leticia said. It was the desperation in Mrs. Wilkes' voice that prompted her. "I'd like it if you stayed with me."

Mrs. Wilkes sat heavily on the chair by Leticia's bed and started on her interminable cross-stitching. "You poor thing," she told Leticia, looking down at her work. "It's a shame when a young one suffers."

"Why don't you have any children, Mrs. Wilkes?"

Mrs. Wilkes shook her head. "I was married once, only he was killed in a war, far away. I went from a bride to a widow in two months. No time for children there."

Leticia did not know how to express that she knew how short a life was. She could only mumble, "Oh, I am sorry to hear that."

Mrs. Wilkes shrugged and went back to her stitching, her gaze studiously focused on her hands. Leticia got a distinct impression that Mrs. Wilkes would not meet her eyes.

The weather had grown worse. The freezing rain knocked against the window like bony fingers, and even the thick draperies could not keep the drafts out.

Leticia couldn't sleep at night, and she wandered through the echo-filled hallways, the candle flame that flailed in the draft her only companion. There was no light in Mrs. Wilkes room, but Leticia imagined her sitting upright in her wooden chair by the covered window, in the dark, not moving, and not really aware of the empty darkness around her, lost somewhere in the memories from a time very long ago.

She stopped by Bresson's door. There was light spilling out from under it, and Leticia pressed her ear against the wooden planks, listening to the shuffling footsteps inside, and to the old man's cough and sighs, which sounded almost like strangled sobs.

She moved away carefully, stepping without making a sound, and crept down the hallway toward the guest rooms. There was light in Stanton's room as well, and his door stood open. The light bisected the gloom of the hallway with a golden wedge. The fire crackled inside, and the glassware clinked. Leticia blew out her candle and peered inside cautiously.

Her salamander slept, curled up around the spout of the burner. She was reassured to see that he was well and brilliant in color.

Stanton was preoccupied with making something in his alembics. Leticia watched as he mixed red and blue powders and muttered to himself in a strange, glottal tongue. Coptic, Leticia assumed.

A fire flared in one of the alembics, and Stanton tried to blow it out, but the flame grew until it filled the entire vessel and cracked it, spilling the contents on the bench. The salamander woke up, ran up to the puddle of the flaming liquid, and lapped it up like a cat would lap up spilled milk.

Stanton watched the salamander, his lips pressed together, his forehead traversed by wrinkles. Leticia retreated into the shadows by the door, peeking inside with one eye. But Stanton would not have seen her even if she were standing right in front of him—he seemed to stare somewhere far beyond the salamander and the fire. She wondered if he could see the very essence of things, if he still thought about the cure. The thought tightened Leticia's throat and she ran to her room, the weight of her misery quadrupled on her shoulders.

Leticia did not wander about the house anymore, and stayed under the covers, the fireplace in her room always lit. She kept the flames lively by feeding them the toy furniture, the waxen dolls in expensive brocade gowns, the walls of her dollhouses, and the lush artificial trees.

She raided her parents' library and read everything she could find about Egypt, the pharaohs, and their pyramids. There was nothing about the Copts or the Gnostics.

A few days after her voluntary cloistering there was a knock on the door. She pulled the covers up to her chin. "Come in," she said.

Stanton entered, the miniature couch in his hands, and the much-revitalized salamander riding upon it like some ancient royalty. "I brought you your salamander back," Stanton said.

"Thank you."

Stanton stared at the denuded floor of her room and the single dollhouse that still remained standing. "What happened?"

"I burned the rest," Leticia said. "I just kept this one, and the lake and the orchard, so that Mr. Salamander has a place to live."

"I'm sorry I upset you—"

"It is not your fault, sir," Leticia interrupted. "But I would rather not talk about cures."

Stanton set the couch and the salamander inside the doll-house. "That is unfortunate," he said. "I brought you something to read, but if you don't want to—"

"I can't read any of your books anyway," Leticia said.

"It's not a book, but my journal, with some of the things I tried to talk to you about." He put it at the foot of Leticia's bed. "I will let you rest now."

As soon as the door closed behind him, Leticia jumped up and grabbed the leather-bound and much worn journal. She flipped through the pages, frowning at Stanton's chicken-scratch handwriting. There were many more symbols she didn't understand, and strange recipes that included saltpeter, *aqua regis*, and pure mercury. Stanton mentioned Nag Hammadi Library and Pistis Sophia, which, as far as Leticia was able to determine, was the source of the dangerous and forbidden books. There were also lovingly transcribed passages from Paracelsus. Leticia paused over one particular passage:

> The Egyptians, Chaldeans, and Persians often mistook the salamanders for gods, because of their radiant splendor and great power. The Greeks, following the example of earlier nations, deified the fire spirits and in their honor kept incense and altar fire, burning perpetually.
>
> — Paracelsus'
> *Auslegung von 30 magischen Figuren.*

Leticia skipped along, to learn more about elementals.

> They live in the four elements: the Nymphæ in the element of water, the Sylphes in that of the air, the Pigmies in the earth, and the

Salamanders in fire. They are also called
Undinæ, Sylvestres, Gnomi, Vulcani, etc. To each
elemental being the element in which it lives
is transparent, invisible and respirable, as the
atmosphere is to ourselves.

—*Philosophia Occulta*

Leticia noted that her salamander seemed quite comfortable outside of its element and felt a bit of satisfaction at the
thought that she knew some things better than the ancient
wizards. She stopped smiling once she got to the part that
was not a quote from some obscure text, but read as a feverish
translation of Stanton's own thoughts:

> The elementals possess their own essence
> akin to phlogiston, but filled with more eso-
> teric energy. As such, I believe the elemental
> essence contained in their blood, lungs, and
> hearts has the ability to increase the potency
> of any spell. The crystallized life essence (p.
> 15) has failed to exhibit sufficient curative
> properties, but I have a reason to believe that
> if combined with the elemental essence it can
> be transmuted to panacea.

Leticia closed the journal carefully, as if afraid that the
loathsome secrets contained within would spill out and stain
her, like her bloodstained white handkerchiefs, which were
meticulously washed by the maids. She wrapped a sheet around
herself and padded over to the surviving sliver of her demolished
toy empire by the fireplace.

The salamander basked close enough to the fireplace to glow like the embers in it.

"You better be careful, Mr. Salamander," Leticia said. "You're getting so hot and fiery, you'll set your house aflame. Where would you live then?"

The salamander listened. *Fire*, came to Leticia. He retreated away from the flames into the shade of the miniature trees by the shores of the mirror lake. His heat had already melted the swans into shapeless clumps of wax and feathers. Leticia picked one up and rolled it on her palm. Her skin was paler than wax, the color of tallow, and almost as translucent, showing the periwinkle veins etched just under it.

And yet, she knew that the salamander crouched by the dollhouse like a miniature dragon had the power to infuse her skin with color again, and to stop bright red flowers from blooming on her pillow every morning. The problem was, the salamander would have to part with his heart and lungs.

Leticia got dressed and went to see Stanton. He sat in his darkened room, draperies drawn tightly as always, reading by a sole white candle.

"Are elementals spirits?" Leticia asked.

Stanton smiled. "You do not bother with preambles, do you?"

Leticia shook her head and remained waiting for the answer.

"No, they are not spirits. They are flesh and blood and bones, just like you and me. They just live in fire or other elements, which are to them as air is to us."

Leticia had thought as much. "So they can die?"

"Yes," Stanton said. "While you were sequestering yourself, I was here, looking at your salamander gobbling up all the fire from my burners and candles, and I thought about how his blood and heart could save your life. The reason panacea has not been discovered yet is because no one has ever seen a live elemental of any kind. And I thought that there must be a reason why the salamander came to you. What if it was meant to be so? There are forces in the world that want you to live, that want me to cure you—to find a way to cure all the ill people in the world."

"But you didn't hurt him," Leticia said. She was moved that Stanton, as dedicated as he was to his art, had enough kindness to consider her feelings.

Stanton shrugged. "He is yours. It would've been rude of me to presume and use him without your permission. But now that you know the use of my crystal and your salamander, may I have your kind permission to make panacea?"

Leticia did not need to think about her answer. "No." She turned around and exited Stanton's quarters without as much as a backward glance.

"Wait!" Stanton ran after her, great surprise and confusion in his voice. He grabbed her sleeve. "Perhaps you do not understand."

"I understand," Leticia said. "I just don't think it is right to destroy something so magical, even if your intentions are noble and good."

"But you . . . you will . . . " He couldn't finish the sentence.

"I know." She carefully freed her sleeve from Stanton's fingers. "It still isn't right. Mr. Salamander is my friend, and what sort of person would I be to make him into medicine? Sorry, Mr. Stanton, but you will have to find yourself another elemental."

She left Stanton standing in the dark hallway, amidst the wood paneling and the pale light of the wall sconces.

She came to her room and collapsed by the fire, exhausted by all the excitement. The salamander ambled out of the dollhouse and rested by Leticia's side. *Fire.*

"Do not worry, Mr. Salamander," Leticia said. "I won't let anyone hurt you. You can stay here as long as you want. I know why you came to me. You knew I would never let any harm come to you."

The blue eyes of the salamander looked into hers with great sympathy and understanding.

"You recognized me, didn't you? You knew that I, too, was out of my element." Leticia thought a bit. "I wish I could go somewhere else, somewhere other than earth. I wonder if it's cold down there. If I were a fire elemental—"

I shall go home soon. His voice sounded in Leticia's mind.

"I will miss you. Thank you for coming to me."

The salamander remained sitting by her side, staring into the ghostly landscapes that flared within the fireplace for just a moment and disappeared. If Leticia squinted, she, too, could discern red and amber and orange trees and dark paths laden with ash, tall spires, and throngs of fiery salamanders. Leticia watched the flames and the images within them leap from log to log, the sparks exploding in spectacular clouds and fading again. When all the logs had burned out and crumbled into gray ash, and only a few red sparks still streaked among them, the salamander stirred and headed for the fireplace grate.

Leticia pushed away the screen that guarded the fireplace's interior and tossed the melted swan into the dying embers. The wax flared briefly, and she fed the nascent flames with tiny artificial trees and the toy furniture—tall-backed chairs, tiny dining tables, and the velvet couch.

The dollhouse was the last to go into the flames. Its interior lit up in alarming yellow and orange as the hungry flames licked its walls, puckering and peeling the blue wallpaper.

Leticia heard Stanton enter the room, but she did not turn around. She was too busy watching the fire shoot up, sending the fountains of sparks up the chimney as the dollhouse charred and twisted.

The salamander crawled up the grating and into the fireplace, and stood among the flames shining so brightly, Leticia had to shield her eyes from the brilliance. The wave of heat wrapped around her as the salamander's gaze gripped hers. *Thank you.*

The dollhouse peeled, flamed, and crumbled around him until consumed by the fire. As the flames died down, the fiery landscapes within the fire faded, and the image of the salamander grew paler and shimmered until it was gone, extinguished with the flames.

Only then did Leticia turn to face Stanton. "He has gone home."

"So I see." Stanton sat down on the floor next to Leticia in front of the cooling fireplace.

"I hope he comes back to visit me some time," Leticia said.

Stanton nodded. "Of course he will. Every time there is a candle flame or a burning fireplace, he will be watching over you."

"Did Paracelsus tell you that?" Leticia said with a smile.

Stanton's hand hesitated before carefully smoothing her hair. "No. One does not need a prophet to recognize friendship."

Stanton was right, she thought. Mr. Salamander was her friend, and friends always looked out for each other. "Thank you for letting him go."

Stanton sighed. "It was not my choice, Leticia. I hope you realize what you have done."

Leticia nodded, smiling. "Yes, sir. But I do wonder what will happen to me when I die."

"I don't know," Stanton said. "What would you like to happen?"

"I would like to become an elemental," Leticia said. "Like Mr. Salamander. I think I would enjoy living in the fire—I look into it, and it is always different, and always pretty and warm."

"Gnostics say we all return to our origins after death." Stanton thought for a while until he noticed Leticia's shivering. "Are you cold?"

She nodded.

Stanton blew on the remaining embers and fed them kindling until a kernel of flame bloomed in the fireplace amid the ashes. He stoked the flames with logs Bresson had stacked by the fireplace, and settled next to Leticia to watch the fire.

Leticia had forgotten that Stanton was there as she peered into the growing and spreading flames, to their brightest hottest center where elementals and their towns rose and fell before her eyes with every movement of the fire. She watched the spires made of sparks and vast flaming rivers, and the spotted hides of salamanders slithering among the constantly shifting outlines of the buildings.

Leticia reached toward the flames and felt their warmth on her fingertips. They seemed always a living thing, and Leticia sighed, imagining herself among the salamanders playing in the deepest golden flames, far away from the cold drizzle outside and the sorrowful house surrounding them.

HOLLY BLACK

Virgin

L ET ME TELL YOU SOMETHING ABOUT UNICORNS—THEY'RE
faeries and faeries aren't to be trusted. Read your story-
books. But maybe you can't get past the rainbows and pastels
crap. That's your problem.

Zachary told me once why the old stories say that mortals
who eat faerie food can't leave Faerie. That's a bunch of rot too,
but at least there's some truth in it. You see, they *can* leave—they
just won't ever be able to find another food they'll want to eat.
Normal food tastes like ashes, so they starve. Zachary should
have listened to his own stories.

I met him the summer I was squatting in an old building
with my friend Tanya and her boyfriend. I'd run away from my
last foster family, mostly because there didn't seem to be any
point in staying. I was humoring myself into thinking I could
live indefinitely like this.

Tanya had one prosthetic leg made from this shiny pink
plastic stuff, so she looked like she was part Barbie doll, part

girl. She loved to wear short, tight skirts and platform shoes to show her leg off. She knew the name of every boy who hung out in LOVE park—so called for the word sculpture, but known for all the skaters that hung around. It was Tanya who introduced us.

My first impression of Zachary was that he was a beautiful junkie. He wasn't handsome.; he was pretty, the kind of boy that girls draw obsessively in the corners of their notebooks. Tall, great cheekbones, and reddish black hair rolling down the sides of his face in fat curls. He was juggling a tennis ball, a fork, and three spoons. A cardboard sign next to his feet had "will juggle anything for food" written on it in an unsteady hand. *Anything* had been underlined shakily, twice. Junkie, I thought. I wondered if Tanya had ever slept with him. I wanted to ask her what it was like.

After he was done and had collected a little cash in a paper cup, he walked around with us for a while, mostly listening to Tanya tell him about her band. He had a bag over his shoulder and walked solemnly, hands in the pockets of his black jeans. He didn't look at her, although sometimes he nodded along with what she was saying, and he didn't look at me. He bought us ginger beer with the coins people had thrown at him, and that's when I knew he wasn't a junkie, because no junkie who looked as hard up as he did would spend his last quarters on anything but getting what he needed.

The next time I saw Zachary, it was at the public library. All us street kids would go there when we got cold. Sometimes I would go alone to read sections of *The Two Towers*, jotting down the page where I stopped on the inside hem of my jeans. I found him sitting on the floor between the mythology and psychiatry shelves. He looked up when I started walking down the aisle and we just stared at one another for a moment, like we'd been found doing something illicit. Then he grinned and I grinned. I sat down on the floor next to him.

"Just looking," I said. "What are you reading?" I had just run half the way to the library and could feel the sweat on my scalp. I knew I looked really awful. He looked dry, even cold. His skin was pale, as if he had never spent a day in the park.

He lifted up the book spread open across his lap: *Faerie Folktales of Europe.*

I was used to people who wouldn't shut up. I wasn't used to making conversation.

"You're Zachary, right?" I asked like an ass.

He looked up again. "Mmhmm. You're Jen, Tanya's friend."

"I didn't think you'd remember," I said, then felt stupid. He just smiled at me.

"What are you reading?" I stumbled over the words, realizing halfway through the sentence I'd already asked that. "I mean, what *part* are you reading?"

"I'm reading about unicorns," he said, "but there's not much here."

"They like virgins," I volunteered.

He sighed. "Yeah. They'd send out girls into the woods in front of the hunts to lure out the unicorn, get it to lie down, to sleep. Then they'd ride up and shoot it or stab it or slice off its horn. Can you imagine how that girl must have felt? The sharp horn pressing against her stomach, her ears straining to listen for the hounds."

I shifted uncomfortably. I didn't know anyone who talked like that. "You looking for something else about them?"

"I don't even know." He tucked some curls behind one ear. Then he grinned at me again.

All that summer was a fever dream, restless and achy. He was a part of it, meeting me in the park or at the library. I told him about my last foster home and about the one before that, the one that had been really awful. I told him about the boys I met and where we went to drink—up on rooftops. We talked about where pigeons spent their winters and where we were going to spend ours. When it was his turn to talk, he told stories. He told me ones I knew and old-sounding ones I had never heard. It didn't matter that I spent the rest of the time begging for cigarettes and hanging with hoodlums. When I was with Zachary, everything seemed different.

Then one day, when it was kind of rainy and cold and we were scrounging in our pockets for money for hot tea, I asked him where he slept.

"Outside the city, near the zoo."

"It must stink." I found another sticky dime in the folds of my backpack and put it on the concrete ledge with our other change.

"Not so much. When the wind's right."

"So how come you live all the way out there? Do you live with someone?" It felt strange that I didn't know.

He put some lint-encrusted pennies down and looked at me hard. His mouth parted a little and he looked so intent that for a moment, I thought he was going to kiss me.

Instead he said, "Can I tell you something crazy? I mean totally insane."

"Sure. I've told you weird stuff before."

"Not like this. Really not like this."

"OK," I said.

And that's when he told me about her—a unicorn. His unicorn, whom he lived with in a forest between two highways just outside the city, who waited for him at night, and who ran free, hanging out with the forest animals or doing whatever it is unicorns do all day long, while Zachary told me stories and scrounged for tea money.

"My mother . . . she was pretty screwed up. She sold drugs for some guys and then she sold information on those guys to the cops. So one day when this car pulled up and told us to get in, I guess I wasn't all that surprised. Her friend, Gina, was already sitting in the back and she looked like she'd been crying. The car smelled bad, like old frying oil.

"Mom kept begging them to drop me off and they kept silent, just driving. I don't think I was really scared until we got on the highway.

"They made us get out of the car near some woods and then walk for a really long time. The forest was huge. We were lost. I was tired. My mother dragged me along by my hand. I kept falling over branches. Thorns wiped along my face.

"Then there was a loud pop and I started screaming from the sound even before my mother fell. Gina puked."

I didn't know what to do, so I put my hand on his shoulder. His body was warm underneath his thin T-shirt. He didn't even look at me as he talked.

"There isn't much more. They left me alone there with my dead mom in the dark. Her eyes glistened in the moonlight. I wailed. You can imagine. It was awful. I guess I remember a lot, really. I mean, it's vivid but trivial.

"After a long time, I saw this light coming through the trees. At first I thought it was the men coming back. Then I saw the horn—like bleached bone. Amazing, Jen. So amazing. I lifted up my hand to pet her side and blood spread across her flank. I forgot everything but that moment, everything but the white pelt, for a long, long while. It was like the whole world went white."

His face was flushed. We bought one big cup of tea with tons of honey and walked in the rain, passing the cup between us. He moved more restlessly than usual, but was quieter too.

"Tell me some more, Zachary," I said.

"I shouldn't have said what I did."

We walked silently for a while 'til the rain got too hard and we had to duck into the foyer of a church to wait it out.

"I believe you," I said.

He frowned. "What's wrong with you? What kind of idiot believes a story like that?"

I hadn't really considered whether I believed him or not. Sometimes people just tell you things and you have to accept that *they* believe them. It doesn't always matter if the stories are true.

I turned away and lit a cigarette. "So you lied?"

"No, of course not. Can we just talk about something else for a while?" he asked.

"Sure," I said, searching for something good. "I've been thinking about going home."

"To your jerk of a foster father and your slutty foster sisters?"

"The very ones. Where am I going to stay come winter otherwise?"

He mulled that over for a few minutes, watching the rain pound some illegally parked cars.

"How 'bout you squat libraries?" he said, grinning.

I grinned back. "I could find an elderly, distinguished, gentlemanly professor and totally throw myself at him. Offer to be his Lolita."

We stood awhile more before I said, "Maybe you should hang with people, even if they're assholes. You could stay with me tonight."

He shook his head, looking at the concrete.

And that was that.

I told Tanya about Zachary and the unicorn that night while we waited for Bobby Diablo to come over. Telling it, the story became a lot funnier than it had been with Zachary's somber black eyes on mine. Tanya and I laughed so hard that I started to choke.

"Look," she said. "Zach's entertainingly crazy. Everybody loves him. But he's craz-*az*-azy. Like last summer, he said that he could tell if it was going to rain by how many times he dropped stuff." She grinned. "Besides, he looks like a girl."

"And he's into unicorns." I thought about how I'd felt when I thought he was about to kiss me. "Maybe I like girly."

She pointed to a paperback of *The Hobbit* with a dragon on the torn remains of the cover. "Maybe you like crazy."

I rolled my eyes.

"Seriously," she said. "Reading that stuff would depress me. People like us, we're not in those kinds of books. They're not *for* us."

I stared at her. It might have been the worst thing anybody had ever said to me, because no matter how much I thought about it, I couldn't make it feel any less true.

But when I was around Zachary, it had seemed possible that those stories were for me; it didn't matter where I came from, as if there were something heroic and special and magical about living on the street. Right then, I hated him for being crazy—hated him more than I hated Tanya, who was just pointing out the obvious.

"What do you think really happened?" I asked finally, because I had to say something eventually. "With his mom? Why would he tell me a story about a *unicorn?*"

She shrugged. She wasn't big on introspection. "He just needs to get laid."

Later on, while Bobby Diablo tried to put his hands up Tanya's halter top before her boyfriend came back from the store and I tried to pretend I didn't hear her giggling yelps, while the whiskey burned my throat raw and smooth, I had a black epiphany. There were rules to things, even to delusions. And if you broke those rules, there were consequences. I lied down on the stinking rug and breathed in cigarette smoke and incense, measuring out my miracle.

The next afternoon, I left Tanya and her boyfriend tangled around one another. The cold gray sky hung over me. Zachary was going to hate me, I thought, but that only made me walk faster through the gates to the park. When I finally found him, he was throwing bits of bread to some wet rats. The rodents scattered when I got close.

"I thought those things were bold as hustlers," I said.

"No, they're shy." He tossed the remaining pieces in the air, juggling them. Each throw was higher than the last.

"You're a virgin, aren't you?"

He looked at me like I'd hit him. The bits of bread

kept moving though, as if his hands were separate from the rest of him.

That night I followed Zachary home through the winding urine-stained tunnels of the subway and the crowded trains themselves. I was always one car behind, watching him through the milky, scratched glass between the cars. I followed him as he changed trains, hiding behind a newspaper like a cheesy TV cop. I followed him all the way from the park through the edge of a huge cemetery where the stink of the zoo carried in the breeze. By then, I couldn't understand how he didn't hear me rustling behind him, what with the newspaper long gone and me hiking up my backpack every ten minutes. But Zachary doesn't exactly live in the here and now, and for once I had to be glad for that.

Then we came to a patch of woods and I hesitated. It reminded me of where my foster family lived, where the trees always seemed a menacing border to every strip mall. There were weird sounds all around and it was impossible to walk quietly. I forced myself to crunch along behind him in the very dark dark.

Finally, we stopped. A canopy of thick branches hung in front of him, their leaves dragging on the forest floor. I couldn't see anything much there, but it did seem like there was a slight light. He turned, either reflexively or because he had heard me after all, but his face stayed blank. He parted the branches with his hands and ducked under them. My heart was beating madly in my chest, that too-much-caffeine drumming. I crept up and tried not to think too hard, because right then I wished I were in Tanya's apartment watching her snort whatever, the way you're supposed to wish for mom's apple pie.

I wasn't cold; I had brought Tanya's boyfriend's thick jacket. I fumbled around in the pocket and found a big, dirty knife, which I opened and closed to make myself feel safer. I thought about walking back, but if I got lost I would absolutely freak out. I thought about going under the branches into Zachary's house, but I didn't know what to expect, and for some reason that scared me more than the darkness.

He came out then, looked around, and whispered, "Jen."

I stood up. I was so relieved that I didn't even hesitate. His eyes were red-rimmed, as if he had been crying. He extended one hand to me.

"God, it's scary out here," I said.

He put one finger to his lips.

He didn't ask me why I'd followed him; he just took my hand and led me farther into the forest. When we stopped, he just looked at me. He swallowed as if his throat were sore. This was my idea, I reminded myself.

"Sit down," I said and smiled.

"You want me to sit?" He sounded reassuringly like himself.

"Well, take off your pants first."

He looked at me incredulously, but he started to do it.

"Underwear too," I said. I was nervous. Oh boy, was I nervous. Mostly I had been drunk all the times before, or I had done what was expected of me. Never, never had I seduced a boy. I started to unlace my work boots.

"I can't," he said, looking toward the faint light.

"You don't want to?" I took one of his hands and set it on my hip.

His fingers dug into my skin, pulling me closer.

"Why are you doing this?" His voice sounded husky.

I didn't answer. I couldn't. It didn't seem to matter anyway. His hands—those juggling hands that didn't seem to care what he was thinking—fumbled with the buttons of my jeans. We didn't kiss. He didn't close his eyes.

Leaves rustled and I could smell that rich, wet storm smell in the air. The wind picked up around us.

Zachary looked up at me and then past my face. His features stiffened. I turned and saw a white horse with muddy hooves. For a moment, it seemed funny. It was just a horse. Then she bolted. She cut through the forest so fast that all I could see was a shape—a cutout of white paper—still running.

I could feel his breath on my mouth. It was the closest our faces had ever been. His eyes stared at nothing, watching for another flash of white.

"Do you want to get your stuff?" I asked, stepping back from him.

He shook his head.

"What about your clothes?"

"It doesn't matter."

"I'll get them," I said, starting for the tree.

"No, don't," he said, so I didn't.

"Let's go back." I said.

He nodded, but he was still looking after where she had run.

We walked back, through the forest, and then the graveyard, back, back to the comforting stink of urine and cigarettes. Back to the sulfur of buses that run all night. Back to people who hassle you because you forgot your work boots in the enchanted forest where you cursed your best friend to live a life as small as your own.

I brought Zachary back to Tanya's. She was used to extra

people crashed out there, so she didn't pay us any mind. Besides, Bobby was over. That night Zachary couldn't eat much, and what he did eat wouldn't stay down. I watched him, bent over her toilet, puking his guts out. After, he sat by the window, watching the swirling patterns of traffic while I huddled in the corner, letting numbness overtake me. Bobby and Tanya were rolling on the floor, wrestling. Finally Bobby pulled off Tanya's shorts right in front of the both of us. Zachary watched them in horrified fascination. He just stared. Then he started to cry, just a little, in his fist.

I fell asleep sometime around that.

When I woke up, he was juggling books, making them seem like they were flying. Tanya came in and gave him a tiny, plastic unicorn.

"Juggle this," she said.

He dropped the books. One hit me on the shin, but I didn't make a sound. When he looked at me, his face was empty, as if he wasn't even surprised to be betrayed. I felt sick.

Three days he lived there with me. Bobby taught him how to roll a joint perfectly and smoke without coughing. Tanya's boyfriend let him borrow his old guitar and Zachary screwed around with it all that second day. He laughed when we did, but always a little late, as though it were an afterthought. The next night, he told me he was leaving.

"But the unicorn's gone," I said.

"I'll find her."

"You're going to hunt her? Like one of those guys in the unicorn tapestries?" I tried to keep my voice from shaking. "She doesn't want you anymore."

He shook his head, but he didn't look at me, as if I were the crazy one, the one with the problem.

I took a deep breath. "Unicorns don't exist. I saw her. She was a horse. A white horse. She didn't have a horn."

"Of course she did," he said and kissed me. It was a quick kiss, an awful kiss really—his teeth bumped mine and his lips were chapped—but I still remember every bit of it.

That fall, I took my stuff and went back to my foster home. They yelled at me and demanded to know where I'd been, but in the end they let me stay. I didn't tell them anything.

I went back to school sometime around Halloween. I still read a lot, but now I'm careful about the books I choose. I don't let myself think about Zachary. I turn on the television. I turn it up loud. I force my dinner out of cardboard boxes and swallow it down. Never mind that it turns to ash in my mouth.

Pig, Crane, Fox: Three Hearts Unfolding

DON'T GET ME WRONG, BUT YEAH, I KNOW EVERYTHING I need to and a little bit more. I can tell you who built Lóng City, and why it's got the Hundred Sewers. I know about the first kings, the Interregnum, and why our Guild Council let Prince Xiang back on the throne. Oh, and I can show you sixty-five dagger strikes and where to find the best meat pies. I even know . . .

Okay, I flunked astrology, and my trigonometry sucks the Celestial Wind, according to my Mā mī, who runs a tutoring shop for conjuration and mathematics. Ai ya, does she remind me—at least six times a day.

Today was no different.

"Where are your homework papers, Kai-my-son?" she asked.

"Which papers?" I asked, sweet as sugarcane.

Mā mī's bright black eyes narrowed to slits. She said nothing, but tapped her ink-stained fingers against the neat stacks of rice paper where she was adding up her accounts. My mother was tiny and whisper thin, but when she studied me like that, she reminded me of the vast and hungry watch demons that patrolled Lóng City's streets come dark. Behind me, Chen snorfled and grunted, invisible. Smart pig spirit, I thought, wishing I could disappear too.

"You leave, you sleep outside tonight with the watch demons," Mā mī said mildly. "Let us see if you are more obedient after a few days running from *them*."

I swallowed. Mā mī never bluffed. "I . . . I wrote out three problems."

"Then you have six left. Do them now, please."

"But Mā mī, I need to find Yue and Danzu and—"

"Those miserable street rats you call your friends cannot help you with simple arithmetic, much less calculus or divination."

That last was not entirely true. Yue could twiddle formulas nearly as well as Mā mī, but now was not a good time to argue. I tried again. "Mā mī, I really must go. It's important. It's about the king."

That got her attention. "What do you mean?"

I opened my mouth, but nothing came out.

"I know what you mean. You stupid boy. You—"

I gasped. "Lya! Mā mī, what is that behind you?"

Mā mī rolled her eyes. "If you think . . ."

She was already reaching for the bamboo switch when a crackling noise stopped her. Before she could turn around, a stinky yellow cloud that smelled worse than rotten eggs and gargoyle dung exploded in the air over her head. Chen and his magic tricks. Right on time, as always.

Mā mī gave a yelp of dismay. I didn't wait to hear the rest. I darted out the curtain doorway. Chickens flew up, scattering black and white feathers, as I pelted through the tiny courtyard and down the nearest alleyway. I heard old man Kang cursing me, but I kept running, round and down the stairs, through the tunnel and into the main boulevard, dodging carts and bicycles and those new auto-wagons that ran on magic and electricity.

It was only when I reached the lane behind Golden Market that I dared to slow down. I ducked into the closest noodle shop, where I drew a deep breath of curry and garlic, bitter-strong tea, and the sharp tang of burning magic. The room itself was a dingy old hole—dust covered its red-tiled floor and the bamboo paintings on the wall looked cracked and faded. I heard a tinny radio coughing out old-fashioned flute music from the kitchen. Two old men huddled over steaming bowls of tea, but the shop was otherwise empty. Luckily, I hadn't come here for the company or the food.

A greasy old waiter hurried toward me. "Five minutes, on-time," I told him. "And a ginger soda."

He grunted something that sounded like "yassur." A minute later and ten yuan poorer, I shut the cubicle's wooden door and plugged my talk-phone's cable into the wall socket. Blue sparks burst from the socket, and I wrinkled my nose at the metallic smell. Bad connection, but typical for a shop like this one. Still, no time to waste. I tapped in Yue's number and gulped down a swig of my ginger soda to clear my dust-clogged throat. Oh ya. Sessions with Mā mī were often like that. We argued, I ran, she always took me back. So far, at least.

Three chimes. Five. Yue never took this long to answer. Just when I started to worry, the flux buzzed up a couple notches and the talk-phone clicked over to connect.

"Kai."

Yue's husky voice sounded breathless, as if she'd been running.

"Waterfront docks," I told her. "Everyone."

"Everyone?" There was just a hint of surprise in her voice, which made me wonder. Yue usually knew everything before I did. That's what made her a good second-in-command for the posse.

"Ya, everyone."

"Same-old, same-old, then."

"No."

I clicked off before the meter ran out. Yue would know what I meant. We always talked in code, just in case the king's wizards had spiked the lines. I wished, for the thousandth time, I had one of those sweet new talk-phones with no-wires and video screens, but those cost five hundred yuan.

Maybe I can after all—if things go right.

With a sputter and a pop, Chen materialized inside my cubicle. He was dark brown, with shiny black eyes, four neatly split hooves, and a row of pointy blades down his spine. He'd shrunk himself to miniature form so he could fit; at this size, his tusks looked silly, but I knew better. Chen was one fierce pig.

The wizards spike the no-wire talk-phones too, you know.

I know. But I could use it just for fun times, not business.

Chen tilted his bristly head and studied me with bright eyes that reminded me uncomfortably of Mā mī. He had first burst into my head and my life when I was six—two years past the usual age when companion spirits appear—but that was the first and only time he was ever late.

Have you figured out how to get past the king's guards? he asked.

Not yet. I will.

Chen snorted and vanished. I finished off my ginger soda and went to find Yue and the rest of my posse.

Waterfront meant uptown. *Docks* meant the warehouses behind the Pots-and-Kettle bazaar. *Everyone* meant . . . well, everyone.

I set off for Pots-and-Kettle as fast as I could, but Lóng City covers half a mountainside. By the time I zigzagged my way to the wind-and-magic-powered lifts, then jogged around the terrace to the warehouse district, the clock towers were clanging the next hour. I slipped between two tall buildings and down a muddy alleyway to a rusty iron door.

I gave an up-and-down whistle. The door creaked open and Danzu poked his bony face out. "Huh, it's you. Took long enough."

"So what? I'm here now."

I shoved past him into the dark cavern of the warehouse. Once upon a time, rich merchants had stored bundles of silks, flax, and other trinkets they imported from the distant Phoenix Empire here. But a few years of bad luck and high taxes meant they had to sell the building. The new owners had worse luck when a pack of ghost dragons invaded the premises. It was Yue who discovered the hideout and bargained with the ghost dragons to let us use the basement-below-the-basement for posse meetings.

Danzu had left the trap door open. I swung down onto the rope and wooden ladder. Far below, light leaked through the floorboards above our hideout. I sniffed smoke from a lamp, the sweaty damp from earth and stones, and something like the fresh, green scent of mountain pines—human and earth scents. Others I couldn't identify. If I heard any strange scrabbling noises around me, I ignored them and moved faster. It was Lóng City, after all. Rats, demons, ghost dragons, and other strange creatures had their own kingdoms alongside ours. As long as you ignored them, you were okay. Usually.

The others were already there, waiting for me. Jing-mei and Gan sat on the floor, playing cards for small change. Yue leaned against a wooden post and tossed her belt knife in a complicated pattern. Light from the oil lamp glanced off the blade as she caught the knife and sent it spinning in new directions.

I landed on the dirt floor with a thud. Right away, a skinny foot-long ghost dragon coalesced from the air and curled around me, making me twitch. He was tiny, as ghost dragons go, but little didn't mean harmless. Legend said that ghost dragons could smother you with their breath, and their bite was more poisonous than a drink of pure magic flux. I didn't want to find out if those legends were right.

Yue snickered. "Hey, Bixi, none of that."

She stuck the knife in her belt and extracted a sugarcane stick from her jacket pocket. Right away, the ghost dragon's whiskers poked forward and its translucent eyes glowed. Yue waggled the sugarcane at the dragon. With a flick of its tail, it shot past Yue. The cane vanished, and so did the dragon.

I shuddered. "Creepy."

"They say the same thing about you. What's up, Kai?"

"Yeah, what's up that we all had to run here?" Danzu landed behind me and gave me a push in payback for the one I gave him upstairs. He grinned and flicked his long, black hair out of his eyes. "Me, I was busy. Lady wanted my opinion about some diamonds."

"You mean you wanted to nick her jewels," said Gan with a bored roll of his eyes. He swept up the playing cards from the floor and slid them into a jacket pocket.

"We don't nick jewels, remember?" Jing-mei said. "Too risky."
She shook a few extra cards from her sleeves and gave them back
to Gan, who shot her an exasperated look.

"That's right," Yue said. "But we do trade news and favors."
She folded her arms and gave me a suspicious sidelong glance.
"Like now. Kai has some news he'd like to share with us."

"Not exactly news," I said. "Talk. Big talk."

The others frowned, puzzled. Yue's eyes were bright with
suppressed laughter. "Oh, *big* talk is it? You must mean the
king's proclamation."

Ai ya, I thought. Of course she knew about it. Everyone
did, what with the radio broadcasts and the posters in every
square. Fifty thousand yuan, plus the hand of his daughter,
Princess Lian, to the man who satisfied three impossible
wishes. Still, I hadn't expected Yue to figure me out so
quickly.

It's not so hard, Chen said. *Qi says Yue guessed last week you would
do something stupid.*

Qi was Yue's companion spirit. I hadn't noticed her
around, but crane spirits are hard to spot unless they want
you to see them.

I'm not stupid, I said fiercely to Chen.

Not always, Chen agreed. He popped away, probably to
share jokes with the other companion spirits.

"You're right," I said to Yue, as though I didn't care. "This
proclamation is what my Mā mī calls an opportunity."

"You want to marry the princess?" Yue asked.

Her voice had a breathy catch, as though I'd surprised
her. "No, no," I said. "I just want the money. I figure we can
split the prize among us."

Danzu smirked. "Good luck. None of us can enter that contest—only princes are allowed."

"Yeah, well, I have a plan."

And I did. Sort of. One I'd thought of on the way here.

"What about those impossible tasks?" Gan asked.

I waved a hand. "Oh, you know me. I'll think of something."

Danzu looked unconvinced. "Why talk to us, then?"

"Because, we're brothers and sisters—"

"You mean, because your plan stinks and you want me to think up a better one," Danzu said.

"Hah. As if you could think at all."

Danzu launched himself at me with a curse, but Gan grabbed him before either of us landed more than a punch. Yue took me by the shoulders and shoved me against the wall. "Shut up," she hissed. "Now. The ghost dragons hate it when we fight."

Lamplight reflected from her eyes like tiny golden sparks. If Mā mī was a watch demon, Yue was a dragon. She jabbed a finger at me, then Danzu. "You are both idiots. Now, Kai says he has a plan. Let him talk. If his plan stinks, we make it better."

"Why?" Danzu said sulkily.

"Because we all want the money. Right?"

Reluctantly he nodded. So did Jing-mei, but with more enthusiasm, as though she were already counting her share of the prize. Gan shrugged, but I knew he would listen before he would say yes or no.

"I do have a plan," I told my posse. "But I need some help. See, I already know how to get past the guards—"

"How?" Jing-mei demanded. "You aren't a prince."

"But I am. Wait." I held up my hand to stop the flood

of arguments. "Let me explain. I am a prince—a prince of the streets."

Everyone blinked in surprise—everyone except Yue, who was studying me with an odd expression caught between amusement and something else I couldn't quite pinpoint.

"You're kidding," Gan said finally.

"No. I figure what I need is a certificate."

"A certificate?" Jing-mei's voice scaled up in disbelief.

"Ya, a piece of paper with my name and fancy seals and such. And my title—Prince of the Streets. It just has to look good."

"That's not enough," Danzu said. "The king, everyone knows he's got those magical calculor-gadgets. Your fancy certificate has to have more than the right seals and stamps. It needs special codes and wires and that invisible ink—"

"No invisible ink," Yue said. "But Danzu is right about one thing. You can't just wave a piece of paper at the guards, Kai. You need a real certificate. And I know where I can get you one."

We all stared at her.

"You can?" I whispered. "How?"

"Why should you care? That's why you came to us, Kai. So we could help." She glanced at each of us in turn, her gaze cool and remote, as though she were fifty and a princess and not a fifteen-year-old street rat dressed in patched brown hand-me-downs and scuffed slippers.

Yue's lips puffed in soundless laughter. "Come, my brothers and my sisters. Why so miserable? Kai has a plan, of sorts, and I have the means to make it work."

"Yes, but—"

She swiveled around to face me. "But what?"

"Nothing," I muttered.

"Good," she said. "Now, here is what else you must do . . ."

Mā mī kept her word. When I got back to our house, I found the doors locked, the windows barred, and the ladder steps to our second-story apartment hauled up and out of reach. Through the slats in one shutter, I could just make out the faint blue glow from the calculor machine on her desk. No sign of Mā mī herself, however.

I blew out a breath, scared. When Mā mī closed the shop early, it meant she was more furious than an army of thunder and rock demons blowing up volcanoes.

If I could just talk to her . . .

Chen's presence tickled my brain. *Later. The sun is going down.*

No sooner did he say that than the sun slid downward another notch, the light darkened, and a twilight breeze ruffled my hair. I shivered. Chen was right. I needed a safe place, and soon. Well, maybe Mā mī would take me back once I collected my prize. With a last glance at the blank walls and windows of our house, I jogged off to find shelter.

The next two days I spent dodging around Lóng City, checking in with my posse, scouting the palace's outer perimeter, scrounging meals, and badgering Yue for that cursed certificate.

"You smell like horse turds," she told me late on the second day.

"Gan found me a room in his uncle's stables." It was a tiny closet filled with horse tack and musty blankets, but I wasn't going to mention that part.

"Lovely. You will need to bathe before you present yourself to the king."

"I know that. What about your friend? Has he even started making the certificate?"

Yue favored me with a smile. "All in good time. But, Kai-my-brother, if you pester me again, I will beat you with a stick and feed you to the ghost dragons."

The third day, which felt more like the three hundredth, Gan tracked me down and gave me some extra cash (he didn't say where he got it) and a note from Yue written on rice paper so the wizards could not spike our lines. Even before I unfolded the note, I had guessed its contents. My heart did a drum dance as I read the two short lines: *We have our certificate. Meet me at the palace gates tomorrow morning, at ten o'clock. Remember to take a hot bath and wear clean clothes.*

Stupid girl. But I could tell Gan had read the note, so I kept my face blank and my voice happy. "Excellent. Please let Yue know that I shall follow her suggestions precisely."

And I did. Almost. Early the next morning, after a cheap breakfast and lots of hot tea, I visited the nearest bathhouse, where I spent three yuan on extra soap and hot water and scrubbed myself until my skin turned ruddy brown. Two more yuan got me a haircut and my fingernails trimmed. My clothes were hopeless—dusty and stained—but I brushed them hard to remove the worst of the dirt. Besides, I didn't want to look *too* prosperous, not if I were a genuine Prince of the Streets. Once I'd plaited my hair tight and smoothed out my tunic, I scanned the results in the bathhouse mirror. Not bad, I thought.

Chen popped into view, a huge hairy image in the mirror. *Pretty boy.*

"Be nice," I muttered.

Nervous?

Shut up.

Don't you want to know that you're late?

Stupid pig, I'm not—

Just then, the clock towers starting striking the hour. I yelped, slapped down the money on the counter, and ran out the door. Luckily, I knew six shortcuts between the bathhouse and the palace—a couple twists and turns, a scramble over a fence and through a private courtyard, and I had reached Lóng City's grandest public square even before the last loud gong faded away. Yue waited for me in the shadow of a very ugly statue, next to a useless-looking water fountain.

"You're late," she said.

"Not exactly," I snapped back.

"Hah. You *are* nervous. Good. Here's your certificate."

She handed me a leather scroll case. It was heavier than I would have guessed, capped at both ends with gold-plated discs embossed with impressive designs and the latest connector interfaces. I hefted the case in one hand. The dark red leather felt cool and slick against my palm. There were patterns tooled into the leather too, and I recognized some of the official guild patterns. "How much did this cost?"

"I bargained my friend down."

"That's no answer."

She shrugged. "Of course not. Now go, before the palace guards arrest us for loitering."

Right. Time to make my bid—our bid—for the prize. "Wish me luck."

"Break a leg," Yue said. She disappeared into the crowds.

Break your head, Chen added. With a pop, he, too, vanished.

Comedians, I thought, as I crossed the last distance to the palace gates.

Six hundred years ago, when they decided to build a royal palace over the old fortress, the ancient kings of Lóng City had hired the finest architects from the Phoenix Empire. It took thirty years, nine different kings, and half the treasury before the architects finished what Mā mǐ called the golden egg crate. Dozens of fat towers, all of them connected by walkways and low buildings, rose up from behind a thick wall that looped around for six miles, interrupted every so often by watch towers and guard posts. I felt like a small, annoyed flea as I approached the gates, which were twice as tall as any man, and decorated with beaten gold that blazed in the sun.

Twelve guards flanked those gates. They were all dressed in gray tunics and trousers trimmed with scarlet embroidery, with the royal insignia of a screaming dragon over their hearts. These weren't just dress guards either, because they carried scimitars and stun pistols in their belts, and fancy wireless talk-phones strapped to their wrists.

I stopped in front of the guard in the middle. He looked older, grayer than the others, and he wore more badges plus a row of tiny jewels above his insignia. To him, I held out my scroll.

He glanced down. Didn't move.

"Take it," I said. "Those are my credentials."

"For what? Sweeping the stables?"

"No," I said, trying to keep my voice steady. "For the king's challenge."

Old Guard lifted an eyebrow. "You know the rules."

With a shock, I realized his left eye was fake. Gold wires made a hatch pattern beneath the translucent lens, and when he blinked, red and silver particles whirled past, making my stomach go flip-flop. I swallowed and managed a shaky smile. "Sure. I can prove I'm a prince. It's right here."

Still with that disbelieving expression, he took my scroll case and ran his fingers over the leather. Squinted at the patterns and seals with that weird eye and nodded. That done, he drew a shiny metal disc from beneath his tunic and laid it against the connector plate. I heard a loud snick. With a flick of his thumb, the guard opened the case and tilted it. My heart gave a bad thump. All of a sudden, I wished I'd checked its contents. But no, Yue and her friend had not played any tricks. A thick, tightly coiled scroll slid into Old Guard's waiting hand. He unwound it—all three feet of heavy parchment—and I could see that everything was perfect, right down to the embedded copper-wire pattern in the lower right-hand corner.

"Prince of the Streets," said Old Guard. "Your credentials appear valid, Your Highness, but my orders require me to perform a few more checks. Please follow me."

He unlocked a small door next to the gates and ushered me into the guardhouse.

I stepped into a long narrow room built into the perimeter wall. A dented wooden desk occupied one entire side, its surface lost beneath stacks of logbooks and several strange devices that reeked of magic flux. Silk screens suspended from the ceiling flickered between views of the palace gates and the crowded square outside. The air felt close, and my skin itched from nerves and imminent magic.

Old Guard locked the outer door and went to the desk. He cleared a spot and laid out my expensive fake certificate underneath an ugly gray lamp that coiled over the desk like a cobra.

A bright blue flash lit up the room. I squawked and nearly fell over. "What's that?"

Ignoring me, Old Guard flipped open his talk-phone and listened a minute. "Yes, my lord. Very well, my lord." To me, "We may proceed, Your Highness. This way."

He indicated another door. I started to pick up my certificate, but Old Guard stopped me. "Please do not encumber yourself during your audience, Your Highness."

"But I—"

I shut up. Old Guard's expression made me think arguing was a bad idea. That, and the stun pistol at his belt. Besides, he'd said the magic word: audience. Maybe they didn't quite believe I was a prince, but they were letting me see the king.

On the other side of the guardhouse, we crossed an immense courtyard stuffed with runners and pages and lackeys and more. Off to one side, a dozen handlers were coaxing an elephant to kneel, while a squad of mounted guards maneuvered toward the gates. Old Guard would not let me stare. He hurried me through the crowds to a pair of doors flanked by more guards. When he gave a funny hand signal, like a twist of a doorknob, the two guards made stiff bows. A third man dressed in a fancy blue tunic and robe appeared out of nowhere and swept the doors open.

I am a prince, I told myself as I marched through, Old Guard close behind. I'm used to servants and guards and palaces that go on forever.

But it was hard not to goggle. Beyond the doors, an enormous entry hall lined with bronze statues of elder gods, ghost dragons, and the first kings extended in all directions. Then we were off again, through more corridors and gates and locked doors, up three flights of stairs and along a

balcony that overlooked an enormous garden with bright
scarlet flower beds. A sweet perfume drifted through the
air. Someone was singing, accompanied by chimes and lutes
and drums. It was as though I'd fallen into another world
where money flowed like the spring floods. I wasn't sure I
liked it. I wasn't sure I didn't.

Finally, just when I thought my scruffy sandals would fall
into bits, we arrived at a small enameled door set deep into the
wall. A single guard stood outside. Unlike the others, he carried
no weapons. Instead a small ghost dragon lay coiled at his feet, its
scaly wings and tail overlapping his boots. Its presence surprised
me. Ghost dragons were not pets or slaves, I knew. It raised its
head and studied me with silvery eyes.

"You are to wait here, my lord," said Old Guard. "The
king's steward will fetch you for your interview."

He executed a crisp about-face. The other guard opened the
doors and bowed. With a last glance at Old Guard's retreating
back, I stepped inside.

This had to be the only medium-sized room in the whole
palace, I thought. Extra fancy, like everywhere else, but comfortable
too. Silk rugs covered the marble floors. A silk screen covered
another entire wall; it flickered with dancing images from one
of the popular broadcast troupes. Off to one side, three carved
chairs circled a miniature waterfall that burbled softly. My skin
prickled from all the magic. Protection spells—lots of them. I'd
sensed the magic flux throughout the palace, but here it flowed
thick and strong.

And I wasn't alone. A young man slouched in the biggest
chair. He was bone thin and wore his hair shaved close like
blue-black velvet. When he tilted his head in my direction, tiny
points of light glittered from his skull. I'd heard of that new

fashion, where the rich paid huge sums to have magic highlights decorating their hair or skin or even their eyes. His gaze flicked toward me and away, as though he'd seen a bug. Right then, I felt like one.

I settled into the chair next to Skinny. As soon as I did, one of the marble tiles slid open, and a tiny teakwood table with a teapot, cups, and cloth napkins rose up beside me. Steam trickled from the teapot's spout, filling the air with a summer-sweet scent. I poured myself a cup and pulled out a packet of apricots to chew. That helped with the waiting and the not knowing what came next. Skinny wrinkled up his nose but didn't say anything.

"Want some?" I offered him the packet.

Skinny coughed delicately.

I tried again. "What's your name?"

No answer, except that his mouth thinned.

"Come on. Tell me, or I'll have to call you Stick Man."

Skinny glared at me and his mouth got even thinner. "My name," he said in a tight voice, "is Prince Fei-hsien of Crescent Moon."

Oho. Crescent Moon was the city-kingdom the next mountain over. Small and rich, but not as rich as Lóng City. So Fei-hsien came to hunt a fortune. I grinned. So had I.

"Mine is Kai," I said to him. "I'm a Prince of the Streets."

"I hardly think that you—"

The air inside the room shimmered. Without warning, an arched passageway appeared on the wall opposite the entrance. A man stalked through in a whirlwind of black silks and jewels. I glimpsed a dark red face set in a ferocious scowl before he disappeared through the outer doors. The doors slammed shut. Magic buzzed in the air, and for a moment, the video screen went blank. Fei-hsien and I stared at each other. He looked as pale and shaky as I felt.

"Who was that?" I whispered.

"Prince Tso-lin," he whispered, and when I showed I didn't understand, he added, "Prince of a minor house in the Phoenix Empire. A clever man. I heard. . . ." He paused to glance around. "I heard he finished two impossible tasks in less than a day."

But not the third, obviously.

"How about you?" I said casually. "Done anything impossible yet?"

That got me a suspicious glance. "Not yet. I—"

Once more the archway shuddered into view. A soberly dressed man entered the room. He had pale gray eyes, gray hair that was slicked back into a tight queue, and a gray tunic—even the screaming dragon insignia looked more subdued on this man. This had to be the king's steward. "My lord and prince," he said with a deferential bow to Fei-hsien. "A thousand apologies for the delay. The king would invite you into his presence now."

Fei-hsien gulped and jumped to his feet. With a swipe of his hand, he smoothed his glittering hair before following the steward through the passageway.

That took away my appetite. I crumpled up my remaining apricots in their wax paper. A tiny emerald lizard appeared from nowhere to pluck the paper from my hands. It vanished back into the walls, and the back of my neck prickled. Somewhere, a guard, maybe even Old Guard, might be watching me from a video screen. Nervous, I poured myself another cup of tea, trying to act as though I didn't care. How long before the king summoned me? What kind of tasks would he choose? And why? That was the real question. Only now did I remember what Mā mī always said, "Kings have their reasons, and queens do too. If you can't see why at first, it's because they don't want you to. One thing you can be sure of, humans or demons, it's all politics in Lóng City."

Bang!

Fei-hsien burst through the suddenly apparent archway. His face was flushed, his eyes had narrowed to angry slits, and he had one hand clenched in a fist as though he wanted to punch someone. Uh oh.

"What happened?" I asked.

Fei-hsien paused to glare at me. "Nothing," he hissed.

"What do you mean, nothing?"

"I mean nothing, oh Beggar Prince. He wanted *nothing.*"

He flung the outer doors open and stalked through, his robes swirling behind him.

I blew out a breath. Nothing? The king wanted *nothing?* That didn't make sense. What kind of impossible task—

"Your Highness."

The king's steward had reappeared.

"My turn?"

He gave me the briefest of bows in answer.

My mouth went paper-dry. The king wanted nothing. I had nothing to give. I—

It was true. I had *nothing* to give.

I stood up with a grin. "I'm ready. Show me the way."

Whatever his thoughts, the king's steward betrayed no surprise. He took me through a series of ever-larger rooms to a grander archway flanked by six guards and three whisper-lean ghost dragons. Beyond, I glimpsed a huge chamber with a dais that filled the entire opposite wall. On that dais stood a throne built of jewels and rare polished metals, so elaborate it looked ugly and beautiful at the same time. I nearly missed the bent old man who occupied it, but not the young woman beside him, whose slim blue robes gleamed like a summer sky.

His Royal Highness, Wencheng Li. His daughter, the Princess Lian.

Before I could lose my nerve, I marched across the room to the edge of the dais and knelt with my hands cupped together. "Your Majesties, I have brought you the item you requested."

Princess and king stared. He looked old and weary and out of temper. She . . . Her eyes were like rare black pearls, her skin like honey-colored silk, and her mouth as red and soft as a fresh-plucked peach. She looked smart and dangerous and ready to order my execution if I said one wrong word.

The king's steward hurried to my side and seized my arm. "You must follow protocol," he whispered.

"I did. I am," I whispered back.

"Let him speak," said the princess. "I wish to know how this young man fulfilled a task no one gave him."

Her voice was cool as a snow-fed stream. I kept my gaze lowered away from those bright eyes that reminded me of mountain eagles. "Your Majesty," I said. "I *have* presumed I know. But let me say only that I spent the past several days and nights considering what impossible tasks a king might demand for his daughter's hand. What could possibly equate to your rank? Your loveliness—"

She cut me off with a gesture. "Stop the pretty words and answer my question."

Right. Okay. I tried again. "Your Highness, what I said before is both pretty and true. Mostly." (Here, the princess's lips quirked.) "Your father *cannot* demand anything that compares with you or any of his possessions. And because nothing could, I bring . . . nothing."

Standing, I uncupped my empty hands, as though presenting a gift.

A heavy silence followed, during which the magic flux eddied around me, and I considered all the sins of my too-short life.

Then the princess laughed. "He is right, my father, my king."

"He is not," the king said harshly. "You know he is not."

"I do *not* know that," she retorted. "Consider this, my dear royal father. He demonstrated as much cleverness as Prince Tso-lin. More, because he had to acquire a certificate and brave the guards' examination. Let us call that two impossible tasks accomplished. No?"

"No!"

"Ah, but that leaves us with our problem unsolved."

Mā mī was right about kings, and princesses too, I thought, wishing myself far away from this battle that had nothing to do with me or any other prince. Before I could stir, however, the king signaled to the steward, who relaxed his hold on my arm. Princess Lian gave me a tiny smile. "Prince Kai, I declare that you have completed the first two tasks to our satisfaction. Do you wish to continue?"

"Won't you chop off my head if I say no?"

"No." Laughter rippled beneath her voice. "To fail is punishment enough."

I swallowed, remembering Yue and her debts. This Lian might be arrogant, but she was right. I had to win this challenge, and not just for my own sake. "Go on. Tell me what comes next."

Princess Lian and her father exchanged a glance. The king shook his head as though to say it was her decision. "Very well," said the princess. "I give you the same task I gave to Prince

Tso-lin. Bring me my heart's desire."

"You have three days," the king added. "Now go."

"Her what?" Gan said.

"Her heart's desire," I repeated.

I'd called everyone to our backup hideout as soon as I had left the palace. *Uptown, downtown, notown,* were the code words. *And hurry.* Half an hour later, we gathered behind the city dumps. Gargoyles—brown leathery creatures with scaly wings—roamed the grounds, chewing up garbage into arable soil, and the air stank from their droppings. The smell made me queasy, but at least we didn't have to worry about spies.

Danzu snorted. "That's stupid."

"No," Yue said slowly. "Just impossible."

"Like I said—stupid."

I sighed and rubbed my aching head. Yue and Danzu were both right. The princess had asked for something stupidly impossible. No wonder Prince Tso-lin and Prince Fei-hsien had stalked out like that.

"So now what?" Jing-mei said. She had borrowed Gan's cards and was playing solitaire, snapping out cards one by one as I recounted what happened at the palace. She didn't look as enthusiastic as she had before. Come to think of it, neither did anyone else. I couldn't blame them. For once, I didn't have any idea what to do. But a posse leader can't admit that.

"We think," I said. "As hard as we can."

"Some plan," Danzu muttered.

"It's the only one we have," Yue said wearily.

"Right," I said. "So let's talk. What would a rich princess like this Lian want?"

"What would she *desire*," Gan said. "That makes a difference."

Danzu made a disgusted face. "She's a princess. She can buy anything she wants."

Jing-mei snapped out another card. Frowned. "Maybe she wants a present."

Gan and Danzu snickered, but Yue was nodding. "A gift. Yes. Something she cannot buy or demand. Kai, tell us again exactly what happened. Maybe we can discover some clues."

Though I didn't see the point, I repeated my story, this time including everything that happened from the moment Yue handed me the scroll to when Old Guard returned my certificate and escorted me out the palace. Yue listened with her eyes half closed. Every once in a while, she stopped me with questions or asked me to repeat a part of my story. When I told them about Skinny, her mouth gave a funny twitch. When I described the princess, Yue's face smoothed out and she went still. When I got to the part where the king and princess argued, her eyes flicked open, but she didn't say anything.

When I finished, everyone stared at me blankly.

"She sounds unhappy," Jing-mei said at last.

"She's cheating," Danzu muttered.

"Why would she cheat?" Gan said.

"Why not cheat?" Jing-mei said. "She's a princess."

"Just because you would doesn't mean everyone else does."

"I do *not* cheat!"

Jing-mei flung the cards at Gan. Before I knew it, she and Gan and Danzu were shouting insults at each other, loud enough that the gargoyles twisted their ugly heads around in our direction. I sighed and dropped my head into my hands, wishing I had one of Mā mǐ's headache potions.

"Let them shout a while," Yue said. "They'll get tired of it soon enough. Then we can talk."

"About what? Danzu's right—I have no plan, and we only have three days."

"Three whole days. Less time than when we convinced all the farmers in the Moon-and-Stars Market that we were the king's Secret Harvest Inspectors." She laughed, her teeth flashing against her brown skin. "Ai ya, my brother, my friend. We haven't eaten that well since."

"And my mother never beat me so hard," I said, laughing with her. But thinking of Mā mǐ and her last words to me stole the laughter from my chest. I sighed again and wished a couple of impossible things myself.

Yue touched my arm gently. "Did you talk to her yet?"

I shrugged. "Not yet. She told me she didn't want to see me again."

"Are you sure? That doesn't sound like your Mā mǐ."

"I'm sure. Sure enough." I plucked a broken straw from the ground and poked at the dirt, thinking that it hurt too much to remember exactly what Mā mǐ had said. "What about you and your friend? The one you owe lots of money to for that fancy certificate."

"I don't owe—" She blew out a breath. "I have a choice, Kai. Money or work."

"What kind of work?" I pressed her. "And how long do you have to work for this person?"

She regarded me steadily, her expression hard to read. "Call it an apprenticeship, if you like. I'll work hard, but I'll learn things, too. As for how long it lasts, that is my business, not yours." She glanced around at the others. "Ah, it looks as though the others are ready to call truce. Come, time for real talk."

We spun around a hundred different ideas, trying to figure out what Princess Lian meant by *heart's desire*. None of them made sense after the first minute. Finally, with the sun setting, I told everyone to meet me again the next day.

"Waterfront docks," I said. "Eight o'clock."

Everyone grumbled, but no one refused. We were all too tired. Yue disappeared first to meet up with her new friend, she said. The rest scattered for home. Since I didn't have a home, I bought a bowl of curry from a street vendor and trudged back to the stables, where I settled down for a lonely dinner—my last good one, because my pockets were empty. I'd get nothing except table scraps tomorrow unless we won our prize. Or Mā mī took me back.

If she took me back, I thought, stabbing at my curry with the cheap wooden chopsticks. For the first time, it came to me that I might have lost my home for good.

Don't think about that. Think about Princess Lian and what she wants. And what is the difference between want and desire?

The answer had to be a simple one. Take me, for example. I wanted money, lots of it. Nice clothes and maybe a haircut like that Prince Fei-hsien's. Oh, and a fancy new talk-phone with video. Money would take care of that too. What else?

Friends. Good times. A home . . .

Feh. No good to think about that anymore. I finished off my curry and lay back on my lumpy pile of blankets. A couple nags in the stalls next to me whuffed and shifted around, making the straw crackle. Above, I could see the night sky turning purple through the stable's uneven roof slats. Stars winked at me, and a cool whiff of air reminded me that autumn was approaching fast—another reminder that I no longer had a home.

Danzu was right. The princess was playing tricks on us. Why, I didn't know. Maybe Jing-mei was right, and she was just unhappy. I would be, stuck in that wretched palace with guards stuffed in every corner and video screens snooping in on whatever I did. In fact, if I were the princess—

Abruptly I sat up. *Chen!*

No answer.

Chen! Where are you?!

Chen popped into my brain with a grunt. *Stop shouting. I'm here. What do you want?*

I have to talk with Yue. Right now, I told him. *Help me get to her house without meeting any watch demons.*

And if I say you are one stupid boy?

Then this stupid boy goes by himself.

I was out the stables and running before I finished that thought. Half a city to cover, but I could do it. I could outrun the demons—

Chen materialized in my path, full-sized and bristling. He swung his head and knocked me off my feet. *You are mad,* he growled and thrust his bristly chin at me. *Go back. Wait until tomorrow.*

"Maybe I am mad," I said out loud. "But I need to talk to Yue. I have an idea. The sooner I talk to her, the sooner we can figure out a plan. And we don't have much time, Chen. You know that."

Chen grunted softly. *Yes, I know. Wait a moment.*

His eyes squinted to black dimples. He snorfled and grunted, paused, grunted again, as though talking to himself—or someone else I couldn't see. All around me, the night shadows swirled. Even this close to the stables, I was jumpy, thinking I saw watch demons lurking in the dark.

They are awake, he said at last. *Do not move . . .*

What are you—

The world vanished into inky blackness. A warm breeze washed over my skin, smelling of burnt ashes, hot metal, and the tang of lemons. There were voices murmuring inside my skull. I recognized Chen's, then another fluting birdlike voice. I sensed another presence inside me, next to me. A sharp inhalation that felt as though I were breathing it, but I wasn't.

You are mad, Kai.

Yue. My breath whooshed out in relief. But I still couldn't see anything. *Where are you?*

Home, but—

Ask and be done, said Chen. *We cannot hold the bond very long.*

I stopped the thousand questions clogging my throat. Yue was home. Chen and Qi had linked us somehow with their magic. Even now I could almost imagine myself standing in the two rooms Yue shared with her mother and an ancient aunt. Nearby I heard someone—probably the aunt—snoring softly. The burning scent had vanished. The air smelled of wool and soap.

It's about the princess, I told Yue. *Jing-mei was right—Lian hates the palace. She wants out. That's her heart's desire. That's the only thing that makes sense. We need to come up with a plan to get her out.*

Our bond rippled. I sensed a flood of sharp emotion, which was abruptly cut off.

I thought you didn't care about her, she said.

I don't! But we need to get her out to win the prize.

A pause. *What about her father, the king?*

What about him? If we fulfill all three impossible tasks, he has no choice but to give us the money.

Oh, I think he might, she murmured. *But maybe . . .*

I waited. My throat squeezed shut. Or was that Yue?

Her warm breath tickled my cheek, making my pulse dance up and down. *Let me think about it,* she said. *We'll talk tomorrow. All of us.*

Before I could say anything, the world blinked back into sight. Chen had vanished. I stood inside the stables, safe and alone.

At sunset the next day, Yue and I stood by that same useless-looking water fountain outside the palace gates. Gouts of water splashed noisily in the basin, sending a rainbow of mist over our heads. Most of the vendors had left the square. The rest were packing up their carts for the night. Off to one side, a crowd of raggedy students sang bawdy drinking songs.

Yue handed me a small ebony box. "You have your certificate, right?"

I nodded. Old Guard had returned it to me before I left the palace yesterday.

"What about the bracelets? And you remember the spells?"

"Yes, yes. Who do you think you are, my mother?"

"If I were your mother, I would feed you to the watch demons myself," Yue said. "Now, repeat the spells, leaving off the final consonant."

I did so, feeling more like a minion than a posse leader. But Yue was right, as usual. I was the one who flunked astrology and elementary spell-casting and all the other conjuration lessons Mā mī had tried to pound into my thick, miserable skull, whereas Yue could probably turn magician or even wizard if she once bothered with lessons.

When I finished, Yue nodded. "Good." Her cheeks dimpled briefly in a genuine smile. "And good luck, Kai-my-brother."

Then she was gone, running swiftly to join up with Jing-mei. They would both head immediately for the lower second kitchens, known for the generosity of its cooks, where they would beg for shelter and a meal. Gan and Danzu waited at opposite corners of the nearest lane, ready to create a distraction if necessary. And on the spirit plane, Chen, Qi, and the rest were running messages, keeping watch, and helping out.

Me, I just had to get an audience with Lian and persuade her to run away with me.

I swallowed and approached the gates.

"Halt," said the captain. It wasn't Old Guard, but he looked like he might be a second cousin.

I halted and, with the most respectful expression I could muster, held out my scroll. "I'm Kai, Prince of the Streets. I'd like an audience with Her Royal Highness, the Princess Lian. A personal one. Tell her it's about the contest."

The captain regarded me suspiciously, but maybe he had my name from Old Guard, because he flipped his talk-phone open and tapped out a number. He murmured something I couldn't hear, then listened. And listened. Meanwhile my hands sweated and my pulse danced faster. What if I was wrong? What if the princess called her guards to arrest me? What if—

You are making my head ache, Chen said rather shortly.

What are you doing here? I snapped back. *You and Qi—*

We are. We will. Qi says Yue says to stop worrying or you'll forget the spells.

I was about to snap back an insult when the guard flipped his talk-phone shut and nodded at me. "This way, Your Highness."

He ushered me through the gates and handed me off to a runner who herded me through a longer, different series of halls and corridors and gates. Our route took us up a wide stairway that curled up and around the inside of a tower, past more guards who demanded more passwords and special signals. Whatever doubts I had before vanished. If I were Lian, I would have run away years ago.

At last, I passed through a final set of doors and into a round sitting room decorated with silk tapestries and fine ivory figurines. And bookshelves, crammed with more kinds books than I had ever imagined—books about history and science and economics and politics. Books about mathematics and poetry. Books about magic that Mā mī would mortgage her shop and soul for.

"Did you come to stare or to talk, oh prince?"

Princess Lian appeared through another of those magical doorways with yet another book in her hand. Her pale gray trousers and tunic glinted with magic as she replaced the book on its shelf. She turned and regarded me with cool dark eyes. Eagle eyes. "So," she said. "Why did you request to see me alone?"

There were faint shadows under her eyes, as though she had slept badly. That made it easier to meet her gaze and say my piece. Sweeping into a bow, I said, "Because I have a gift that is for you alone. *Your* heart's desire, not your father's."

I offered the box. She reached toward it, plucked her hand away. Wary.

"Open it, please."

Just as Yue predicted. Muttering the key-spell under my breath, I tilted the box forward and pressed the latch on its side.

Immediately a pale white cloud poured out, enveloping us both. Whoever watched this room would see just a blurry blank spot on their video screens. We had less than a moment to escape. I shoved the box into my tunic and grabbed the two bracelets from my pocket. I snapped one onto my wrist and grabbed for Lian's.

Woof.

A body slammed into me, knocking me to the floor. Sharp teeth pressed into my neck, and an invisible weight made it hard for me to breathe. *Now?* said a ghostly voice. *Or do we wait for the guards?*

Oh damn. Her companion spirit. I caught a whiff of pines and rain water and the faintest trace of fox. Oh double damn.

"Wait a moment." Lian's voice floated high above me. "I want to ask some questions."

We only had a moment before someone noticed, I thought, giddy from terror.

It didn't help when Lian's face, cold and furious, loomed over me. "What," she said crisply, "did you think you were doing?"

"Um, rescuing you?" I said, finding it hard to speak. Claws pricked my shoulders. The fox spirit had not materialized completely, but that would not stop it from tearing out my throat.

Lian made an exasperated noise. "You idiot. What makes you think—"

She broke off. Her gaze went diffuse—listening to her companion spirit. Then she smiled in a way that made me shiver. "Ah, Jun has made a most interesting suggestion."

Still smiling, Lian took the bracelet from my limp hands. It was made from braided copper wire and looked like any bracelet you'd find in Lóng City's cheapest bazaars. According to Yue, her friend had imbedded magic in the wires, but cleverly so that no one could detect it until I spoke the key-spell.

"Tell me how it works," she said.

I explained about the key-spell, ending with, "It turns the wearer invisible. These are linked, so we could still see each other. But no one else could. That way no one would stop us while we escaped. If you had wanted to, that is. But I guess you don't. That is . . ."

I realized I was babbling, so I shut up. Lian ignored me, turning the bracelet over in her hands. Her gaze flicked toward me. Then she snapped the bracelet over her wrist. "Come on. Say the spell. We better hurry."

Before I could figure out what she meant, the weight vanished from my chest, and Lian dragged me to my feet. I managed to sputter out the spell without making a mistake. My ears popped with the sudden outpouring of magic flux, but to my eyes, nothing had changed. Just like Yue promised.

Lian's eyes widened, however, as though she could tell what had happened. "Where did you get— Never mind. We don't have any time. This way."

She grabbed my arm and hauled me through yet another magic doorway. The walls flickered open and closed, leaving us in darkness. Then lamps flickered on, showing a plain stone passageway. A servants' corridor, I guessed. "Where are your friends?" she whispered.

"Second kitchen," I said, not daring to ask how she knew about Yue and the rest.

Lian nodded. "I know a good, fast path."

She led me down the corridor to a small wooden door that opened onto a steep stairway. We hurried down to the next landing, along a walkway from one tower to the next, then down another three steep flights to a wide arched corridor. Far ahead, I heard the clamor of many voices, shouting in all the dialects of Lóng City. The second kitchen.

Lian and I waited for a brief lull, then darted through the kitchen doors. Yue and Jing-mei sat off in one corner. We skirted the room to their sides. "We are here," I whispered.

Yue blinked then touched Jing-mei's arm. Without a word, they both laid aside their bowls and headed toward the outer doors. Lian and I trailed close behind, using their presence to mask ours as we passed through the doors to the outer courtyard.

Outside the sun had set, the skies had darkened to the purple of late twilight. Gan gave the all-clear signal to Yue as we passed his post and rounded the corner. Just in time too, because I heard shouts from inside. We took off down the lane, me trying to recite the locking spell as I ran. My stomach gave a lurch as the magic flux vanished. Lian stumbled. Yue caught her before she fell.

Another left and right brought us to the entrance of a roofed passageway. Jing-mei stopped and shook out her hair. In less than a minute, she had turned her jacket inside out and rubbed rouge over her cheeks. She headed back toward the palace, ready to provide misdirection and delay. Yue, Lian, and I raced down the passageway, which I knew led to the nearest staircase. Down a couple levels, we could disappear into a maze of old tenements, where we were sure to find an unlocked basement to hide—

A keening echoed through the empty passageway. I scrambled to a halt. Yue fell over me, tripping Lian. We untangled ourselves, and I was helping Lian to her feet when Yue gave a muffled cry and tugged on my arm. "Kai," she whispered in a choked voice. "Look!"

I looked. My brain squeaked and went numb.

I had never seen one before, but I knew what I saw—a watch demon. It had no eyes, no mouth, just a huge blankness that wavered before our eyes, like a shadow flickering against the falling night. I found myself scrambling backward, holding tight to Yue and Lian. The watch demon keened again and surged closer.

With a ferocious roar, Chen burst into the streets between us and the demon, larger than I had even seen him before. His spines and tusks gleamed silver in the moonlight. He shook his head and stamped the ground. The next moment, Qi appeared—tall and sharp and quick—then Jun the fox spirit, Jing-mei's monkey spirit, Gan's ox, and even Danzu's scrawny goat with its horns lowered.

Run, Chen said. *We cannot fight this one for long.*

He charged and swung his tusks at the watch demon. It howled, so loud the air shook. I didn't wait to see more. We doubled back to the nearest intersection and rounded into a side passageway to the next plaza. Too late. I heard the noise of many boots from the avenue opposite. Guards had circled around and we were caught between them and the watch demon. There was only one place I knew that was safe from both.

I bent over the nearest metal plate. "Help me," I said to Yue as I hooked my fingers into one slot. She stared at me, uncomprehending, then realization flashed over her face. She grabbed the other opening, and together, we levered the sewer plate up and over to one side.

"Are you mad?" Lian said. "Do you know what's down there?"

"I know watch demons hate the sewers."

"Do you know why?"

"Who cares why? I know we don't have much—"

A roar sent us all clambering down the metal ladder into Lóng City's Hundred Sewers.

The dark was smothering, even before we maneuvered the cover back into place. Then, I sensed a buzzing of magic flux, and lamps winked into life, casting a dim light over us.

Tunnels branched off in all directions. Some, I knew, snaked around the mountains. Some dropped in steps to the next terrace, and some shot downward in precipitous falls toward the lower districts, or even, according to rumors, over the cliffs and into the valley below. The old kings had built the sewers centuries ago for when the city-kingdoms went to war and the rulers needed to escape to the mountainside beyond. Other creatures haunted these sewers, so I went underground only when I had to, but I knew a route that would take us to our warehouse hideout. Once there, we could make more plans.

We took out our knives and set off, single file, with me in the lead, and Yue guarding the rear. The air smelled dank, and we had to watch our footing in the ankle-deep muck. Princess Lian had not turned squeamish, I noticed with relief. If we didn't tire, we could reach the warehouse in an hour or two. Not quite the rescue I had imagined, but for the first time, I believed we could succeed.

One thing bothered me, however, so I slowed down to walk by Lian's side. "What changed your mind?" I asked.

She gave me a curious look. "About what?"

"About leaving the palace. You weren't going to at first."

Another swift, assessing glance, as though she were weighing how much to tell me. "True. But then Jun convinced me you could give me my heart's desire after all."

I grinned. "So you did hate the palace."

She gave a quick laugh, just as quickly smothered. "Oh

no, I love the palace and everything about it. But I wanted to travel, to study abroad. To learn about kingship and law and justice and magic." Lamplight caught a new expression on her face. No longer angry or closed, or even arrogant. She looked . . . beautiful and passionate. Like a queen, I thought. One who cares.

"And your father refused to let you go," Yue said, who had come up beside me.

"Yes. He told me I should hire teachers at home. Then he insisted on that ridiculous contest." Lian hesitated a moment. "You must not think I will abandon you to my father's anger. Once I reach the Phoenix Empire, I will write my father and explain that you are not to blame."

"Many thanks," Yue said dryly. "By then, it might be too late—" She stopped. Her eyes went wide and she put a hand on my arm. "What was that?"

It was a whispery sound, like a faraway tea kettle just starting to boil. Uncertain, I shifted my knife in my hand. The hiss grew louder, echoing from the ceiling and walls. I couldn't tell which direction it came from. Ahead? Behind? When I glanced over my shoulder, I glimpsed a rippling in the darkness. Then came a grating noise, like scales sliding over stone. I jerked my attention the other way. A strong burning smell filled the air, as though someone had released a flood of magic flux. . . .

An enormous ghostly head materialized in front of us. A ghost dragon—the largest I had ever seen—stared directly at me. Its eyes were large and luminous, its whiskers thicker than my arms, and curled around its bony face. Eddies of magic flux swirled around its translucent body, which coiled over and around and through the walls to trap us completely.

The dragon's lips pulled back to show a triple row of teeth like swords. *Who are you?*

Its voice thrummed inside my skull. My legs turned to water; my brain chittered in terror. Dimly, I realized that Yue was gripping my shoulder, and Lian had fallen to her knees.

I managed to unlock my jaw. "We are . . . We are—"

Thieves, it declared. *Trespassers.*

"No."

Lian drew a deep breath and lurched to her feet. "We are not thieves, Your Majesty."

The ghost dragon paused. Its whiskers pricked forward, nearly brushing Lian, who flinched. "We are not trespassers," she said. "No more than do your children trespass in the human kingdom above. Remember, Your Majesty, these tunnels were built by my ancestors and yours together. We both have right of passage. Or have you forgotten, Your Majesty?"

The ghost dragon's eyes flickered. *Who are you that speaks of rights and promises? Are you the king of Lóng City?*

Lian met his gaze directly, though I could see the pulse at her throat beating fast. "No king," she said. "But I am the king's daughter."

The princesssss. It sniffed, like a dog taking a scent, and I held my breath. *Yes, I remember you now. But—* Its great head swung around toward me and Yue, stirring the clouds of magic flux. *Those two were taking you away from the city and your father. I heard you speak of it.*

"If you listened, you know why, Your Majesty."

Why should I remember why? What are you to me, once you abandon your duty?

"I am not—" Lian broke off and drew a deep breath. "I am not leaving forever, Your Majesty. But for *my* duty, I must learn all that I can before *duty* calls me to the throne. Even you must admit that, if my father does not."

I must? The dragon's eyes brightened with some unimaginable emotion. *Hah. You are a stubborn creature. You would have me admit things I never denied.*

It slowly uncoiled more of its vast length so that its scales glittered in the dim torchlight. Yue and I glanced back nervously. I could think of no reason why this king would not crush us beneath its ghostly weight, or poison us with its breath. But Lian never budged. She continued to meet its gaze directly.

Sooooo, it said at last. *You wish to study magic and kingship. Why not learn from your father, princess? Why not learn from me?*

Lian hesitated just a moment before she bowed deeply. "Because I am a stubborn daughter of the throne. I must learn on my own before I dare to learn from such a teacher as you."

The ghost dragon hissed, an awful sound that I realized was its laughter. *Flattery,* it said, still hissing with amusement. *You remind me of your great-grandfather. Go, then, my child. Go in prosperity. We shall talk again.*

He waved a ghostly claw as though to dismiss us, then vanished into the walls.

The bells were ringing ten o'clock when we finally reached the exit near our hideout. Lian collapsed against the tunnel wall. Yue and I dragged ourselves up the ladder and levered the metal plate to one side. Light from a full, fat moon poured into the tunnel. Our hideout lay two streets over.

"I'll go first," I said, "and check for all clear."

And it was all clear, at least for one moment, while I

clambered out and onto the plaza. Then a horde of guards poured from out of nowhere and seized me. I only had time to shout, "Yue!" before someone shoved a cloth into my mouth. Inside of a moment, they had me trussed up and tossed to one side. Yue too. Guards swarmed everywhere, their helmets and scimitars flashing in the moonlight, their boots ringing off the stones. I heard the crackle of many talk-phones and dimly wondered why it took so many to capture two miserable street rats.

Magic sparked and burned in the air as someone lit an electric torch. By its harsh glare, I glimpsed Lian climbing from the sewers, shouting at the guards to release us. "They are not to blame. Do you hear me? Are you listening to me?"

"They are listening to me, not you, my daughter, my heart."

Like a ribbon unbraiding, the guards parted. His Royal Highness, Wencheng Li, dismounted from his horse and approached his daughter, who glared at him. "You," she said, her voice gone flat.

"Yes, me," he said. "Who else should chase after his runaway daughter?"

Lian jerked her chin away. "I am not a runaway. You know why I left."

"I know. Your heart's desire." He said this, wincing, as though it pained him.

"If you know that, you know I must go abroad to study. But no, you thought I needed a companion. Someone you chose—" She broke off, panting hard, and I heard the edge of tears in her voice. "I am no child," she said after a moment. "And if I am, I am not fit to be queen. Not today, not ever. You taught me that."

"So I did." Her father sighed heavily. "And perhaps I was wrong. Perhaps you were too. Have you thought what might have happened with these two, had you left them behind? Or did you think you would bring them with you, without regard to their families or their friends?"

Lian flinched. Two spots of bright red flared on her cheeks. "You do not understand."

"I understand more than you believe, and not as much as I would like. Come, Lian. You cannot expect me to—"

Sssssssstop.

The stones beneath me shuddered. The sky turned wispy gray, and the air reeked with the burning scent of powerful magic. The guard holding me down pressed his knee harder into my back, then flinched back as a thick, luminous fog oozed between the cracks in the street.

The ghost dragon king materialized around and above the crowds of soldiers.

You are both stubborn creatures, it said in a voice that made my skin prickle. *You are worse than the worm children who share quarters with these human children, and who told me where to find your daughter. Talk,* it made a spitting sound, and the air crackled with magic. *Talk means nothing if you do not listen. I did not bring you here for that.*

Wencheng Li opened and shut his mouth. Glanced to his daughter and back. "Very well," he said with obvious reluctance. "What do you say, my daughter, my heart? Shall we talk? And listen?"

"What about my friends?" Lian demanded.

"We take them into safekeeping. For their own sakes. Or would you give them over to the watch demons?"

She swallowed and sent me an anxious glance. "Very well."

Her father nodded to the guards, who hauled me and

Yue to our feet. A signal passed between them. I caught one last glimpse of Lian's father leading her away before they blindfolded us.

Our posse uses code words to disguise our talk from wizards and spies. So, too, the kings of Lóng City spoke in words and phrases nothing like what they meant. *Safekeeping* meant the guards ushered me into a small room with barred windows overlooking a tiny walled-in fish pond. No matter how comfortable, it looked like a prison to me. My only consolation was a brief visit from Chen, telling me that the spirit companions were well, and the rest of my posse had escaped home.

I slept badly, dreaming about watch-demons who chased me through an endless dark maze as I searched for Yue.

Not long after sunrise, a runner shook me awake. Princess Lian had summoned me to an interview.

Servants brought me towels and soap and bowls of hot water. The runner, a young woman, waited while I scrubbed the sleep from my eyes, then led me through yet another maze of corridors to a small intimate sitting room in a different tower. Lian sat on the opposite side of a low table spread with dishes of steamed rice, pickled fish, and delicately spiced noodles. She indicated a seat, which I took, and the dishes, which I had no appetite for.

"Yue went home last hour," she said quietly.

I nodded, not sure how to answer that.

"You fulfilled all three tasks," she went on. "Even the one I thought most impossible of all."

"Does it matter?" My voice sounded frog-like from bad sleep.

"To me," she said hesitantly, "yes, it matters very much."

While I drank down cups of hot tea, she went on to

say that she would get her wish to study abroad. She and her father and the ghost dragon—a king of his own realm, it turned out—argued for hours. Only toward dawn did her father relent, saying that she might begin studies the next autumn, on the stipulation that she visited home thrice a year.

"And so you did give me my heart's desire," she said at last. "Even my father agrees that you have fulfilled every requirement of our contest."

"Money and a princess," I said, not certain how I felt right now.

Lian smiled pensively. "The money is yours, yes. But I'm not certain you'd want this princess, or this palace. You might run away."

"You mean, you'd run away from me. Never mind," I said quickly. "I understand. I'd make a rotten prince, I know. No matter what that certificate said."

We both laughed, a bit painfully. It made saying good-bye easier.

The sun shone bright over Lóng City as I threaded my way across Golden Market to the noodle shop where I first called Yue for this adventure. Tucked inside my tunic were five credit scrolls, made out to me and the others in my posse. I also had a new no-wire talk-phone coded with Lian's private number.

"Kai!" Jing-mei called out to me across the square. "Yue said to watch out for you! What happened? Did you get the money? Did you marry the princess?"

Before I could say anything, she dragged me into the noodle shop where everyone else waited around a big table. The same old waiter hurried around, setting out bowls of tea and wiping up the dust. "You," he said. "Ginger soda. Right?"

"Right," I said, feeling strange.

We ordered a feast of steamed rice and cabbage, boiled dumplings, and spicy dried shrimp imported from the coastal cities. The waiter panted as he hurried to bring more bowls of hot tea, a beer for Danzu, and extra ginger ice cream for Jing-mei. All around me, my posse chattered about how they would spend their fortune. Ten thousand yuan apiece. Enough to buy a shop. Or purchase the best weapons. Or simply live without worry of debt or hunger for years to come. So many dreams, so many shapes to those dreams. Me, I felt tired and pinched inside, and I wasn't sure why.

Yue slid into the empty space beside me. "What's wrong?"

I shrugged. "Dunno. Tired, I guess. And you?"

"Same-same. Happy we aren't dead. Or walled up in prison."

We drank our ginger sodas. I felt words bubbling inside me, but none of them felt right.

Then Yue asked, "Do you miss her already?"

That made me blink. "Who? Lian?"

"No, the ghost dragon's queen. Of course I meant Lian."

"Oh." I tilted my glass and studied the fizzing soda. "No. I mean, we're friends."

These weren't the right words at all, I could tell. Nor for me. Not for Yue, who was frowning at the tabletop. I tried something else. "What about *your* new friend? Won't he kick and yell when he finds out you aren't his slave? Excuse me, apprentice."

Yue stopped frowning. Her mouth tilted into a smile. "Maybe. Maybe I want to be an apprentice."

I nearly dropped my glass in surprise. "You do? Why? What about the money?"

"What about it? If I study hard, the money means I can start my own shop someday. Same but different." She stood and laid down coins for her share of the feast. "You should come with me, Kai. My teacher said you weren't as impossible as she thought, and she might give you another chance. But you'd have to finish those homework problems first."

"What homework? You mean—" I stood up fast to block Yue from going. "Stop. Talk to me. You mean my mother took you as her apprentice?"

She nodded, her eyes bright with mischief.

I sat down with a thump. "You," I breathed. "You tricked me. No, you trick us both—me and Mā mī. No matter what happened, you got what you wanted. If we lost, you'd work for my mother to pay back your debt. And if we won the prize, you got the money for the apprenticeship fee. Both ways you got to learn magic and mathematics." Then another clue clicked into place. "And Mā mī had a chance to help me in secret. Isn't that right?"

Yue laughed. Before I could say anything more, she was dancing around me and out the doorway. I stood and paid my bill, my thoughts in a jumble about Yue, and why she admitted her tricks, and if that meant she trusted me, and even if there were more secrets she had, and why I even cared. Somewhere, in the back of my brain, I could hear Chen snorfling in piggish amusement, but I ignored him and hurried out the door after Yue.

So maybe I don't know everything, I told myself, but maybe I could find out.

WHO ARE THESE WRITERS?

Beth Bernobich is a writer, a reader, a mother, a traveler, a lover of history, and a software geek—not necessarily in that order, and not necessarily one at a time. Her work has appeared in venues such as *Asimov's Science Fiction Magazine*, *Strange Horizons*, the anthology *Nine Muses* and *Fictitious Force*. She is currently preparing for her second-degree black belt.

Beth threatened to beat me up if I made too many edits to her story. Her son is a black belt as well. They're practically a family of ninjas. —*Editor*

Holly Black is the *New York Times* best-selling author of contemporary fantasy novels for teens and children. Born in New Jersey, Holly grew up in a decrepit Victorian house piled with books and oddments. These days Holly lives in a Tudor Revival house in Massachusetts with her husband, Theo, and an ever-expanding collection of books kept in a secret library. She spends a lot of her time in cafes, drinking endless cups of coffee and glaring at her laptop.

Holly has a fear of zombies. So when she threw a Pretty Princess party at a writing workshop with Kelly Link, I showed up as an undead drag queen. —*Editor*

Cecil Castellucci's first young adult novel, *Boy Proof*, was named a Book Sense 76 Children's Pick, Best Books for Young Adults 2006, and a Quick Picks for Reluctant Readers by the

American Library Association. In 2005 she was also named a Flying Start by *Publisher's Weekly*. Cecil, who is also a director, was a founding member of the Alpha 60 film club, dedicated to discovering narrative voices and encouraging creative endeavors in film. She has also been a field producer on MTV's *Big Urban Myth* show. She now writes for DC Comics' new Minx line of comics.

This was Cecil's first attempt at writing fantasy. I made her revise and revise to show that the greatest villains in stories are actually editors. Cue evil laugh. End scene. —Editor

Cassandra Clare was born to American parents in Iran and spent much of her childhood traveling the world with her family. Since her family moved around so much, she found familiarity in books and went everywhere with a one under her arm. Cassie has lived in Los Angeles and New York, where she worked at various entertainment magazines and even some rather suspect tabloids. She hates working at home because she gets distracted by reality TV shows and the antics of her two cats, so she usually writes at local coffee shops and restaurants. She is the author of the *New York Times* best-selling City of Bones, the first book in the Mortal Instruments series.

Interpol has a file on Cassie. She travels way too much. Different passports, different names. All very suspect. She must be smuggling something. My money is on Kopi Luwak. —Editor

J.D. Everyhope attends Sarah Lawrence College and works with children in the Bronx. She graduated Clarion 2006. She visits her hometown often, where her father and godmothers live near the old-growth Washington State rainforests. She still refuses to jump into an icy lake, no matter how often her little brother insists that it's cool.

Soon after I met Jemma, I realized she was one of those "scary smart" girls. I wasn't surprised to learn she's studying in Oxford but I wanted it to be Mississippi not the UK. —Editor

Eugie Foster calls home a mildly haunted, fey-infested house in metro Atlanta that she shares with her husband, Matthew, and her pet skunk, Hobkin. She has won the Phobos Award and is managing editor of *Tangent*. She also pens a monthly column, "Writing for Young Readers," for Writing-World.com. Her fiction has been translated into numerous languages and has been nominated for the British Fantasy, Southeastern Science Fiction, and Pushcart awards. Her stories can be found in such magazines as *Realms of Fantasy, The Third Alternative, Paradox, Cricket, Fantasy Magazine* and *Cicada,* among others. Visit her online at eugiefoster.com

Eugie's Hobkins is a damn cute pet skunk. I asked Mirrorstone to use him on the cover of this book. The art department said I need some rest. —Editor

Gregory Frost is the author of the dark fantasy novel *Fitcher's Brides* and the short fiction collection *Attack of the Jazz Giants & Other Stories.* He has been a finalist for nearly every award in the science fiction and fantasy genres. His latest short fiction is "Ill-Met in Ilium" in the anthology *Secret History.* He collaboratively directs the fiction-writing workshop at Swarthmore College and was the lead instructor of the 2007 Clarion Science Fiction & Fantasy Writing Workshop in

San Diego, California. His fantasy duology, *Shadowbridge*, will appear from Del Rey Books in the spring of 2008.

If you ever get a chance to hear Greg Frost read, ask for him to talk like Cary Grant. It makes the story sophisticated. Honest. —Editor

Craig Laurance Gidney has had stories published *in Spoonfed, Say . . . Have You Heard This One?, So Fey,* and *Riprap.* His reviews of ethereal-gothic-ambient music have appeared in numerous online venues. He resides in his native Washington, DC. He would like to thank Neile Graham, David Schwartz, and Josiah Armour for their guidance in sewing "Mauve's Quilt," and Mr. Berman for allowing it to be displayed.

I've been friends with Craig for years. I told him the only way he'd sell me a story for this book was by calling me Mr. Berman. Heh, heh. —Editor

Jim C. Hines has been writing for about twelve years now, which makes him feel old if he thinks about it too long. His goblin books are published by DAW Books, and include *Goblin Quest* and *Goblin Hero.* He is currently working on a third book in the series. Hines's short fiction has appeared in more than thirty published titles, including *Fantastic Companions, Sword and Sorceress XXI,* and many others. He lives in Holt, Michigan, with his family, and keeps a Web site at jimchines.com.

Despite rumors to the contrary, Jim does not breed goblins for show. — Editor

Nina Kiriki Hoffman writes wonderful stories and stories full of wonder. Also full of horror, and love, and humor and science and magic. She's published several more books and close to 200 stories over the past twenty years, including her most recent book and they just go on being strange and, fun, and beautiful.

Oh, I wouldn't dare tease an icon like Hoffman. She's sold too many stories to take lightly. Instead, I need to hack her PC and plagiarize like there's no tomorrow. —Editor

Sean Manseau spends his time in New York City. He happens to know how to tell a good story, how to mix a terrific cocktail, and how to track down classic cartoons on YouTube. He may or may not have been a former lounge singer, at least as far as Google knows.

Sean looks like he stepped out of one of those 1950s biker movies. A few tattoos, some muscles, and a lot of hair. —Editor

Lawrence M. Schoen spent far too much time as a college professor and works in the mental health field. He's one of the world's foremost authorities on the Klingon language. He lives in Philadelphia with his wife, Valerie, who is neither a psychologist nor a speaker of Klingon.
Yeah, you expected me to make a Klingon joke, right? Too easy. — Editor

E. Sedia lives in southern New Jersey with one spouse, two cats, and many fish. Her short stories appeared in *Analog, Dark Wisdom, Jim Baen's Universe, Fantasy Magazine,* and several anthologies. Her latest novel, *The Secret History of Moscow,* released in 2007 by Prime Books. Visit her Web site at ekaterinasedia.com.

Though I grew up in southern New Jersey, I've never heard of the town where E. addressed her manuscript. I think she's lying. —Editor

Tiffany Trent has been writing since she was nine. Her Hallowmere series of dark fantasy novels (featuring Father Joe from "Blackwater Baby") was penned some years later. She has three master's degrees and though she swore she would never go back to school, teaches English at Virginia Tech. To feed the muse, she has lived and worked in Hong Kong, mainland China, Oregon, Montana, and North Carolina. She currently lives in Virginia with her globe-trotting wildlife biologist husband and four charming felines. Find out more about Father Joe by reading *In the Serpent's Coils*, Hallowmere, Book I.

Three graduate degrees?! Sheesh, Tiffany must like homework a little too much for my liking. Maybe that's why she teaches. Masochist. —Editor

Ann Zeddies spent her first three summers on a mountaintop in Idaho, and wanted to be a cowboy until she realized that the frontier had moved off the planet. Her interest in biology began at an early age, when she collected a bucket of assorted amphibians and turned them loose in the tent where she was living with her parents and younger brother. Her brother became a professional biologist; Ann chose to deal with strange lifeforms by writing fiction.

Ann happens to spend far too much time reading newsgroups and defeating e-trolls. She should be writing. At least, writing about defeating e-trolls. —Editor

ACKNOWLEDGMENTS

NEEDLESS TO SAY, IT'S VERY BAD FORM TO NOT THANK people who helped an author or editor along the way to the book's eventual release. It's sort of like accepting an award without mentioning who designed your dress. Oh, wait, that's for the red carpet interviews. Anyway . . .

First and foremost, I need to thank every author who is in these pages. Their enthusiasm for the project buoyed my spirits and any success or acclaim that results is entirely due to them (but I will still accept any gilded awards).

I owe Nurse Schulman for my introduction to some strange books produced by a company called TSR, Inc. I remember fondly pretending to be sick in second grade so I might go to the nurse's office and read the pages of the *Monster Manual.* Thank you, Ms. Schulman, wherever you are!

Without Nina Hess, my kind and patient editor, none of this would have happened. She was truly a delight to work for and with. I also feel that if Ellen Datlow and Terri Windling had not taken a couple of my short stories, I'd never have earned the chops to work on this book, so thanks to them as well.

Finally, I have to thank my wonderful parents, who indulged my hogging the family computer a bit too often, all under the pretense of working on this book when I was actually playing games. Fantasy games, so that's OK, right?

ABOUT THE EDITOR

Steve Berman has always had a fondness for magic. He has yet to pull a rabbit from a hat, though. As a teenager, he won a lifetime membership to the Roleplaying Game Association and still keeps the plastic member's card in case he needs to break into a closed hobby store. He has sold more than eighty articles, essays, and short stories to such anthologies as *The Coyote Road*, *The Faerie Reel*, and *Love, Bourbon Street*. He edited the anthology *So Fey*, which features new stories of faeries. His debut novel, *Vintage: A Ghost Story*, offers a twist on that age-old romantic quandary of boy meets ghost. He currently resides in the wild suburbs of southern New Jersey with some cats and books and more cats and more books.